Dreams
of the
Cottage
by the
Sea

BOOKS BY REBECCA ALEXANDER

Rebecca Alexander

Dreams
of the
Cottage
by the
Sea

bookouture

Published by Bookouture in 2023

An imprint of Storyfire Ltd.
Carmelite House
50 Victoria Embankment
London EC4Y 0DZ

www.bookouture.com

ISBN: 978-1-83790-164-7
eBook ISBN: 978-1-83790-163-0

To my mother, Jillian Alexander, who is as feisty and resilient as one of my characters, and who introduced me to my favourite books.

PROLOGUE

Nicole had never had so many dreams. Perhaps it was the pain medication she was on. Tonight's was one she didn't want to wake from.

She had been standing in thigh-deep water, cool, swirling around her legs, turquoise and clear down to the sugary sand beneath her feet. *Funny*, she thought, as she slowly woke. *I can feel the grains between my toes.* Around her, off the beach at Seal Cove, was the Atlantic, deepening through emerald to blue reflecting the sky overhead. She could hear the swish of waves just stroking the sand behind her, the cry of some distant birds. She knew she was alone on the beach, and was perfectly content.

As she woke fully, the dragging ache started again, and the sounds of monitors and drips shattered the peace.

If I get over this, I'm going back to the island. Back to Morwen.

1

PRESENT DAY, 2 JUNE

As the boat approached the stone quay, Nicole remembered the rough crossings from her student days. The island came into view, the houses stacked along the cobbled seafront like old books on a shelf, some leaning into others, painted in faded colours. Behind the tiny houses, green fields stretched up to the sky. The island skies were different – extraordinary shades of pure blue, reflecting the Atlantic Ocean.

The pilot tied the boat up to the quay. Nicole managed to get a good footing and stood. By hooking her arm under her injured leg she could step off the ferry. She wobbled a bit on the slipway, but got her balance, and watched the boatman carry her bags off. Four of them, heavy, mostly clothes packed around books.

'Is there any kind of taxi?' she asked, tipping the ferryman and running her fingers through her cropped hair. At least it was long enough to cover the scars, but it had grown back with grey threaded through the dark chestnut.

'No, sorry. But I'll take your stuff over to the pub. Someone there will help. I'm tight on time to get to St Petroc's, and then back across to the big island.'

The memory of the locals' nickname of 'the big island' for St Brannock's made Nicole smile. There was also West Island, and the other islands named after saints: Piran and Petroc. She could see a couple of the others from the quay now, with low mounds of sandy beaches. This island, Morwen, was always the rocky isle, and she had loved exploring it as an eighteen-year-old, returning to do her PhD thesis a few years later. She filled her lungs with the tangy, salty air, closing her eyes for a moment.

I love it here. I can take a year to work out what I want to do.

'Thank you,' she said, shouldering her bag, feeling it unbalance her. Her jeans and favourite jacket weren't quite keeping the Atlantic chill out, and she had been too vain to entirely dump her boots in favour of something more practical. 'Where is Chapel Hill?'

'Straight up there, beside the church.' He pointed. 'You've taken one of the holiday cottages?'

'I've rented Schooner House for a year,' she replied, taking a few careful steps on the slippery cobbles, using the walker to help keep her balance. *Stand tall...* The physio's words came back to her. 'How far up the hill is it?'

'About halfway,' the ferryman said, pushing his cap back on his head.

Nicole looked up the steep, narrow, cobbled lane. She managed to navigate the uneven road as far as the pub, a freshly painted Georgian building that almost seemed to be sinking into the patio that overlooked the sea. A deep threshold, presumably to keep the water out if the tide flooded the quay, almost stalled her progress, but she made it inside.

The room was cool and shaded, a relief from the sunshine outside. She dropped her bag and walked to the desk, hitting a buzzer for attention. A woman slipped out from what looked like a kitchen. 'Hello?'

'I'm sorry. I've just arrived off the ferry, and I need somewhere to leave my bags. Is it all right if I ask around, see if I can find someone to help me?'

The woman smiled over at the ferryman, who had carried and dragged the other three bags in behind her. 'Hi, Tink.'

'Sadie,' he said, smiling, standing one of the bags upright. 'I was wondering if one of your staff could help this lady with her bags?'

Nicole could feel the heat rising from her neck onto her face. She was worried people would notice her limp.

'I can manage one bag at a time, but there are four of them,' she said, through tight lips.

'Sure. I'll get a lad from the kitchen.' Sadie turned around. 'Francesco!' A young man, who looked barely twenty, put his head through the doors. 'Can you help this lady carry her bags, please? To...?'

'Schooner House, please,' Nicole said. 'On Chapel Hill.'

'Easy,' the young man said, effortlessly grabbing two of the bags. He was tall and athletic, with a mop of black hair and deep brown eyes. 'Oof. You rob a bank?' he said with a grin. He had a marked accent, presumably Italian.

Nicole couldn't help smiling. 'There are quite a lot of books in there.' She put a hand out to pick up another bag but he waved it away.

'No, no, is fine. I come back in a minute. You lead the way.'

She did, thanking Sadie and opening the pub door for the young man. The road was narrow, a line of houses of different ages and sizes, some double-fronted Victorian with high windows, some narrow cottages with doors barely six feet high. They were all painted random colours from mustard yellow and clear turquoise, to shocking pink. On the other side was a wall made of rough stones piled up and filled with flowers and plants. As the road was climbing, there was a impressive view over the top, across graves and a church to the sea beyond. It really hadn't changed, she realised. A few gulls wheeled overhead. One, perched on the wall, threw his head back and screamed at the sky.

'This is Schooner House, *si?*' he said, stacking the cases beside the door. 'You have key?'

Nicole dragged it out of her pocket, and fitted it in the low lock. The door swung open.

Her first impression was that it smelled lovely, of lavender and geranium and roses, and that everything was in miniature. The hall, which she had to step down into, was barely six feet high – not a problem for her, but the boy had to duck. The stairs halfway down the hall were as narrow as a ladder, and uncarpeted. They looked steep, and she could see that a bit more hall stretched beyond them. Compared to the warm sunshine outside, it was cool and shaded.

The first door led into a small living room. It was so small it just had a pair of overstuffed sofas, a coffee table and a few shelves each side of a fireplace. A tiny wood burner sat on the tiled hearth, but she couldn't imagine how hot the small room would get if she lit a roaring fire. She shrugged off her jacket and laid it on one of the chairs.

'Where you want the bags, *signora?*'

'I'm not sure.' Nicole looked up the stairs. 'I suppose I'll need that green case in the bedroom... Can you carry it up for me?'

'Easy,' he said, bumping it a little against the sides of the stairs. 'Front room?' he shouted down. 'Is bigger.'

'Thank you!' she called back. 'I'm Nicole, by the way.'

He appeared back in the hall, and waved at the front door with a smile. 'I get others.'

'Thank you.'

She walked further down the passage, balancing herself against the wall. The door at the end led into a bright dining room. Someone had combined it with a narrow kitchen and put a skylight over the sink. A table and four mismatched chairs, a wall of shelving and a Shaker-style kitchen led to a glazed back door. She was drawn to a tiny lobby beyond with a deep butler's sink. A last door led to a walled garden, equally small, about twelve feet square. Three sides had brick raised beds a foot high, stacked with climbers and plants falling over onto the slate slabs. A fruit tree was trained up one wall, and clematis and roses scrambled through it. She reached out to touch the leathery leaves of a fig.

Turning in the small space was difficult, and her leg was now so sore she couldn't wait to get the hated prosthetic off and sit down. Bathroom. She had been told there were facilities downstairs, and what she had thought was a shed turned out to be an outside loo, bare and old-fashioned, but clean.

'Nicole, where you want these two?' The young man was back, and she managed a smile for him as he burst out the back door. 'Oh, *bel giardino!*' he said, looking around the pretty patio. 'I put them in front room, is that OK?'

'That's brilliant. Thank you so much.' She reached into her pocket to find some money but he backed away, hands fending her off.

'No, no, I don't need paying. You come to pub for dinner this week, I cook lobster. You like lobster? You taste it and then...' He closed his eyes and kissed his fingers. 'You tip me. OK?'

She grinned back at him. 'OK, then. Lobster.'

Once alone, Nicole had to climb the stairs on her bottom, pushing with her one good leg and pulling herself up on her hands, the bare wooden edges painful. The bed was high off the ground but she managed to climb up the doorway and limp over to it. The landlady had made the bed and the smell of clean linen was heady. She sat on the edge and rolled onto her back. She swung her legs onto the mattress, trying to kick her shoes off. And failing, because her artificial foot couldn't feel her real one. Swearing a little, she sat up and pulled off the shoe and rolled off the sock.

At least she could lie back and look at the low ceiling, and through the lace curtains of the window facing the graveyard and sea. Sadness seeped into her, making her feel suddenly homeless and rootless. She had never been able to go back to the top floor of her house, the master suite, after her accident. It had been half emptied and tidied during the months she was in hospital. It had stopped being *hers*. Now she lay on a stranger's pillow on her rented bed, wondering if she was being stupid to lock herself away from family and friends, all of whom just wanted to help her.

She turned her head to look at the round bedside table, just big enough for the electric clock radio and a book. Curious, she lifted it, expecting it to be a Bible, but instead it was a guide book with a Post-it on the front, which read 'Welcome to Morwen.'

The book was filled with sketches and photographs, poems and anecdotes, and there were even a few pictures from the time when she had stayed on the island as a student. Open boats driven by grizzled old seafarers or their grandchildren, as comfortable on the sea as on land. The old pub where she'd been this morning, now spruced and renovated, was still called the Island Queen. There was the grand old hotel, so spruced up she almost didn't recognise it from her visit as a student. The old pictures depicted a café along the quay with a few tables outside, a couple of shops, some children dressed in seventies flares on the slipway down to the beach. There were pictures of Victorian bathing belles in sepia. A row of ancient sailing trawlers tied up to the stone quay, alongside pictures of seals, dolphins and birds. She remembered lying in a tent on the neighbouring St Petroc's island at dawn, listening to the overlapping voices of skylarks, each controlling a column of vibrating air as its territory.

Now she could hear the birds, the high-pitched black-headed gulls squabbling, the braying herring gulls and the rough screeches of black-backed gulls, the largest of them. Underneath, she could detect the sounds of blackbirds and robins. Nick, the boy she had shared a tent with as a twenty-something student, had loved birds and would lie awake listening to the late swallows as they stopped screaming and the bats took over. They had been besotted with each other for a couple of years. He was a geologist now, she had found him on social media a few months before, when she had been looking for former lovers who had known her when she was whole and happy.

She had so many happy memories of the islands. Snorkelling in the shockingly cold but clear waters, boat trips out to the other islands, and the brown-skinned teenaged fishermen everywhere, piloting boats, taking them out to see the lobster catches. She remembered one lanky boy in particular. She recalled he was too shy to speak, but used to free-dive for scallops effortlessly off the boat, coming up with bag after bag of the giant molluscs. She remembered eating them, seared on the barbecue, and drinking beers with him and her friends on the beach, in love with life, and the island.

2

MAY 1941

Lily Granville looked up at the front door before her, familiar from childhood visits to her mother's cousins, Bernice and Cissie. The long ferry to St Brannock's Island had been uncomfortable, the ship filled with supplies and air force recruits. The islands, floating in the green-grey sea, looked as otherworldly as ever, untouched by the bombs and fires of London.

The entrance to the flat was squashed between a dusty haberdashery – a few scraps of cloth, a couple of dozen reels of ribbon, and jars of buttons in the window, all that was now available with rationing – and a hardware shop, with stacks of useful things like metal buckets and garden implements. The stone building looked over St Brannock's quayside with the ferry still tied up alongside brightly painted trawlers and smaller boats. She banged on the door again, a little harder this time, and it opened.

Cousin Bernice stood in the tiny hall, stairs stretching behind her to the same flat she had lived in since Lily had visited years before.

'My dear Lily,' she said, and opened her arms. 'My poor girl.'

Something in Lily wanted to flinch back. She managed to freeze as the large woman grabbed her in her fleshy arms, hugging her into softness until she relaxed a little.

'Cousin Bernice—'

'Oh, I think it would be better if you called me Bernie, don't you?' her cousin replied with a smile. 'Now, let me take one of those bags, we'll get you upstairs...'

'Thank you,' was all that Lily could say, her voice thin.

Bernie grabbed one of the leather suitcases Lily had brought on the ferry. She managed to lift it with both hands. 'Goodness, what's in here?'

'It's my bookbinding tools,' Lily explained. 'Let me help you...'

Between them they managed to get all the bags into the hall and the door shut behind them. A small pane of glass at the top let in a little light. Bernie was half a head taller than Lily, and heavily built, her dyed chestnut hair in rolling curls, an old-fashioned dress straining over her tummy. She looked ample, abundant, a picture of vitality. Lily felt pale and fragile beside her.

'I was so sorry to hear,' Bernie said, after scanning her face for a long moment in the tiny space, 'about Grace.'

Lily nodded once, it was all she had left to give. 'Straight upstairs?' she managed to stammer, grabbing the biggest bag.

Bernie grabbed the other end and together they half marched, half dragged, the bag up to another door. 'I suppose your clothes are in the other ones?'

Lily swept her fair hair off her brow. 'The few that are left. After the bomb...' Her breath stalled. The memory of Mrs Underhill intruded, trying to walk across the rubble in heels and a fur coat, calling for her cat Mortimer, beside herself with grief when she found him. It hurt like a thump to her chest. 'I rescued what I could.'

'Oh, you poor darling,' Bernie said, and pushed open the

door. 'It was such a shame you couldn't get out of London before.'

Lily took a breath, then a deeper one, tears blurring her vision. 'We had to stay near the hospital, for Grace.'

Her daughter, Grace, had died between air raids, in her parents' bed, as peaceful as a bird fluttering out of a window. The bomb had landed three weeks later, while Lily and James were in the shelter in the street next to their own.

Bernie nodded briskly when Lily looked up. 'Well, you won't get bombed out here. And you'll be able to work at the library. Mr Prendergast has set aside a room for you in the basement.'

She disappeared downstairs and came back with the last bags as Lily dragged the heavy one into a small, colourful living room. Bernie showed her around. The main room gave onto a small kitchen through an arch, and beside it, a tiny bathroom squeezed in a room hardly bigger than a cupboard, the sink projecting over the end of the bath. On the other side of the living room, over the haberdashery, were two rooms. Both had small beds: Bernie's looked over the harbour between the two pubs, and the back one looked up the hill at granite houses and slate roofs. It was painted blue, with wooden boats lined up along the windowsill.

'I thought it would be quieter in here. This was Oliver's room,' Bernie said slowly, as if choosing her words. 'I always thought of him as more of a son than a nephew, really, especially after his mother became ill.'

'I'm so sorry,' Lily said. For a moment they stared at each other, two women who had lost their children. Cousin Oliver, rear gunner in a Lancaster bomber, had been shot down over the Channel in March.

Bernie shook herself, and forced a smile onto her lips. '"Missing, *presumed...*" they said.' She pressed a hand to her apron pocket, a paper rustled. 'Who knows? He might have been captured. Maybe he lost his memory. The air ministry chaps don't always get it right…'

'Maybe there's hope,' Lily said. 'But are you sure you want me in here, in his room?'

Bernie leaned over and swept the blankets off the bed. 'It's just empty, now. And I've got some nice aired sheets for you, and my old coverlet from when I was a girl. Your mother used to use them when she stayed.' She dumped the linens outside the door. 'How is she?'

Crushed beyond recognition since Grace died, wandering around repeating herself like an old lady. 'Um, she's getting better from her heart problems. She's moved to a nursing home in Cheltenham.'

'These are terrible times,' Bernie said, beckoning to Lily to follow her. 'Let's make some tea, I've got a bit of milk.' The kitchen was painted yellow, the cupboard doors were white. Two chairs and a table barely bigger than a tea tray sat behind the door. 'Have you eaten?'

'On the train,' Lily said, sitting on one of the spindle-backed chairs. 'I'll be able to get back to work straight away.'

'Mr Prendergast isn't expecting you until Wednesday. So you can look around, remind yourself of Hightown, maybe catch a boat to see some of the other islands.'

Lily wasn't sure she wanted time to think. She had a couple of half-dried books that needed immediate work, rescued from a burning, bombed-out church by firefighters.

'I'll pop in and see him anyway. I need to leave some books out to dry.'

'What are these books?' Bernie balanced a chipped blue teapot on a tray with mismatched china. A bottle with an inch of milk was added to the tray and put on the table. Despite the shabbiness, it looked so homely that Lily almost cried.

'One's a psalter, a prayer book. It was in a box under the altar when the roof collapsed and St Boniface's church caught fire. The other is a Bible from before the King James version, from about 1583. The Bible just got soaked but the psalter was scorched by falling wood in a bombed storeroom.'

'It's surprising they survived,' Bernie said, pouring out the weak tea. 'Paper in a burning church...'

'Oh, they aren't just paper,' Lily explained. 'Thank you, just a little splash of milk. They have leather and wooden boards, and the psalter is made of vellum.'

'So, you can save them? Won't the ink have run?'

Lily smiled as she breathed in the fragrant steam, took a sip. 'It might have faded a bit, but we will probably be able to see what the words were. A restorer can ink over if necessary.'

'So, what do you do?'

Lily put the cup back in its saucer with a soft clink. They might be mismatched but they were pretty cups, bone china. Her mother always said they would be the last to get broken. 'First, we dry them out so they don't get mouldy or attract insects. I have to tease all the pages apart so they don't stick. Then we decide what needs restoring and what can still be read.'

Bernie looked over her cup as she sipped. 'And I suppose these books are very valuable?'

Lily shrugged and wrapped her hands around her cup, letting the warmth seep through into her fingers. She was never warm now; since Grace's death she had struggled to eat, and had lost weight. Even her shoes felt a little loose. 'They are old and historically important, so it's hard to put a price on them.'

From her chair, Bernie reached into one of the cupboards and brought out an old biscuit tin, commemorating the coronation of the old king George V. 'I made some saffron buns,' she said. 'Don't tell anyone, but I had a few sultanas from before the war. Nice for a treat.'

The buns, halfway between a bread roll and a scone, were

delicious, but Lily struggled to swallow the small bites. 'Lovely, thank you,' she said, washing the crumbs down with a sip of tea.

Bernie topped up her cup. 'Drink up. You look so pale, Lily. Even your hair is almost white.'

'It's always been fair. It needs a cut,' Lily said, brushing her flyaway hair from her face.

'Will James be visiting? Can he get away from his work?'

Lily put the sweetmeat down on her plate. 'I don't think he can,' she said, the words coming out wooden. 'And we won't have room, anyway.'

'You could stay at a hotel together. What does he do, anyway?'

'He's a cartographer.' Tears sprang into Lily's eyes for no reason, as they often did. 'He makes maps from photographs for the War Office. Very hush-hush.'

'How exciting,' Bernie said, narrowing her eyes as Lily looked at her. 'How is he coping with everything?'

Lily managed the smile she'd been rehearsing for months, since Grace died. 'He's coping, as well as anyone would expect.'

And that was the end of that conversation. Between praising the tea, attempting another bite of the buns and announcing she must unpack, Lily was able to cut off the questions. But as she crouched by the chest of drawers, removing a few of Oliver's pyjamas and socks and putting her own things away, the tears squeezed past her defences.

3

PRESENT DAY, 3 JUNE

For a moment, Nicole didn't remember where she was. Light filtered through net curtains, casting floral shadows on the ceiling. An unearthly wail sounded, followed by a lot of pattering feet, making her sit up in bed. Then something shrieked, a mocking laugh-like call, echoing around a small fireplace. A little soot rattled into the grate.

I must have flaked out when I came up here. What time is it?

Her watch said five fifteen, which would suggest she'd been asleep for several hours, but something about that light – and her dry throat – said she'd been out for fourteen or more hours. At some point she'd crawled under the covers. She couldn't remember sleeping for more than a few hours at a time since the accident.

She hopped from the bed to the doorframe, luckily just a few paces away, then looked around the corner into an old-fashioned but lovely bathroom. There were enough handholds to get in to relieve her aching bladder, and she found a stack of fragrant towels waiting for her. The hip bath was small, too complicated to get in, but the shower was big and – thank goodness for Mrs Tresillian – had a large shower seat in it.

She found enough toiletries to manage a long shower, wrapped herself in a towel and moved back to the bed to stare in the dressing table mirror. The accident had melted weight off her; her cheekbones and blue eyes seemed larger, more prominent. The pain had added lines, though, and she looked older in a way she hadn't before. Her hair had been shaved off after the accident, in the twilight of a post-coma time she hardly remembered.

Francesco had put the green bag, with most of her clothes and phone charger, under the window. A make-up bag and brushes went on the dressing table, on an old-fashioned lace doily. She pulled a brush through her short hair, silver threads through the dark reddish curls.

It was strange not to be thinking about work. After the accident, people kept questioning when she would return to her job. Would she work from her hospital bed, just take a few calls? She had decided to make a clean break, but now the future was dark and nebulous; she had no idea how to not be a government scientist and lobbyist.

Dragging herself downstairs, she was confronted by the other bags in the living room. She shoved them under the window, which she opened for some fresh air, and went back to look in the fridge.

Mrs Tresillian had stocked it with a few basics, at least by island standards. Scones, jam and cream, and a bottle of milk. There were teabags and coffee in painted tins on a shelf above the kettle, which she flicked into life.

'Scones for breakfast,' she murmured to herself, then she saw the time on the gas cooker, with an old-fashioned, eye-level grill. Six twenty. It was too early to shop, so it really was scones for breakfast.

Folded up alongside the garden wall was a table and two tiny chairs in powder-blue metal. Carrying anything was difficult, but by unfolding the table just under the window she could arrange cups and plates on the work surface and pass them outside. *It's absurd to be made so happy by something so ordinary.*

The tea was good, the milk was fresh, and the scones were delicious. She couldn't remember whether it was cream or jam first on the islands, so did one of each. Hopefully the array of birds who came to watch wouldn't judge her, and they certainly enjoyed picking at the crumbs. She sat in the shade of the garden, sipping the tea, listening to the constant sound of the sea lapping the sand and hitting the quay.

Reality started to creep in. What if she fell here? Would anyone think to check on her? Her phone was upstairs charging – would anyone come if she shouted, or were the neighbouring houses all holiday lets? She felt cold at the thought.

'I could be lying here. Dead,' she told the birds matter-of-factly.

'Um, hello?' someone said, and Nicole jumped.

She looked around suspiciously. 'Who's there?'

'I'm Jade, from next door.' A young face appeared at the top of the wall, a mop of improbably magenta curls sticking out around her head. 'I just came out for a quick smoke before my mum catches me.'

'Oh, hi. I'm Nicole. I'm renting the cottage.'

'Yeah, Mum said. We're your landladies. It's nice to have someone staying long-term rather than someone new each week. How're you finding it?'

'It's good, lovely really. How do I get some shopping delivered?' She swallowed hard. 'I've got a problem with... with my leg.'

Jade peered over the top of the wall. As the houses were stepped up the hill, Nicole imagined she could easily see her from her raised garden. 'Mum told me. Are you coping with the stairs OK?'

'They're fine. I just don't fancy hopping all the way down on those cobbles and along to the shop.'

The girl dragged in the last of her cigarette, and blew the smoke away from Nicole's garden. 'Give me a list. I'll get your shopping. The shop opens at seven thirty in the summer.'

'That's very kind, but...'

The girl disappeared and a door banged somewhere.

Nicole finished the tea and passed the crockery through to the sink. She was just trying to think where she would find a pen to write a list, when someone tapped on the front door, before promptly walking into the kitchen.

Nicole was shocked. She clearly hadn't locked the door; she couldn't imagine doing that back in Richmond.

Jade didn't seem to think it was unusual. 'Mum's asking if you need anything now? Like, bread, butter, a bit of fruit, or cereal for breakfast?'

The woman was older than Nicole had initially thought: early twenties, dressed in stripy tights and a denim skirt that barely covered her slim bottom. Her T-shirt had two dinosaurs kissing on the front.

'No, that's very kind, though. I ate the scones your mum left in the fridge.'

'Oh, Mum's like that, she'll probably give you more scones every Saturday, like she does for changeover days.' She must have seen something in Nicole's expression. 'Is it OK to just walk in, by the way? We don't stand on ceremony on the islands.'

Nicole smiled. 'I remember. I came here when I was about your age, to study the marine life. Everyone was so helpful and kind.'

'Yeah, and *nosy*,' Jade said. 'Like, "Where are you from" and "What are you doing now". I forgot what it was like when I was away at college.' She rolled her eyes. 'I've just come home to work for the summer up at the pub.'

Nicole found her handbag and a pen at the bottom. 'I don't know what the shop has...'

'Most basic stuff, and a few deli items for the tourists. Fancy gins and olives, homemade cakes and pasties. We have our own island recipes, but I prefer the basic Cornish pasty myself.'

Nicole didn't know where to start. Looking around, she could see she would need bread and spread, and jotted down a few basics on a bit of junk mail. Ham, cheese, salad, rolls... Jade peered over her shoulder and suggested a few things.

'The bakery brings over these great sourdough cobs – we get those, but they might be in a bit late for you. They do locally made ready meals for the freezer, too, and you have got a microwave.'

Nicole wrote down some of Jade's suggestions and added a few of her own. 'This is incredibly kind of you.' She picked up her purse, which only had a few coins in it. 'Would you be OK using my card? I don't know how to get cash out here.'

'I don't mind, and I'll bring the receipt back. If you're OK with that.'

As Jade disappeared with her credit card, Nicole realised she had just allowed a total stranger to help her without feeling enraged or dependent.

There's something kind and engaging about Jade. If she robs me blind but brings shopping, I don't care.

Of course, Jade brought the shopping back and even put it all away while Nicole was sitting on the floor, sorting through one of her bags.

To make them lighter for travelling, she'd mixed books and papers with clothes and practical items like her hairdryer and laptop. Some of the folders were more than twenty years old, filled with different research projects she had worked on, first just gathering data as a research assistant, and later heading up projects. The cuttlefish project had been one of her favourites, but collecting seaweed samples from hundreds of locations in the Thames estuary had come a close second. But nothing matched her very first project, her PhD thesis, a study of a fish called a blenny. As she sorted through, she found a picture of the little fish, fanning his nest of eggs with his fins.

'I'll be off, then. Let us know if you need anything.' Jade looked at her more closely. 'What are you looking at?'

Nicole smiled up at her, opened the folder and showed her a black and white photograph of the animal. 'Would you believe it, I'm getting all teared up about a *fish*? A male blenny. I called him Sir Galahad. He would risk drying out to save his babies. I got quite attached.'

'So, you're a *fish* scientist?'

Nicole half laughed. 'I used to be a proper marine biologist. The last few years I've just been to a lot of meetings and read reports.'

Jade nodded. 'Bang on the door if you want anything. Nice to meet you – no, don't get up. You look very cosy making forts out of all your books.'

4

MAY 1941

Lily woke to the sound of a screaming of a gull and sunlight falling across the ceiling. It felt different. Every day of the last five months, she had woken to the shock that Grace was dead. The loss of the house had hardly registered, except for the agony of her neighbour, searching for her cat.

Days and night had blended into each other. James was cold and distant and she couldn't bear it when his grief culminated in a terrible argument. It had been a relief to take up her mother's suggestion that she ask to stay with Cousin Bernice on the island.

This morning, the grey shroud of pain had lifted, and she explored the blankness like a missing tooth in childhood. She was curious about what had disturbed her, and when she pulled back the curtains she found a pair of gulls on the roof opposite, sitting on a nest of a few strands of dried seaweed and a handful of stones. Both birds called at the sky, and one of them sounded like it was laughing at her.

She named them in an instant, because Grace would have. Ludovic, she decided, and Harriet, after a romance novel she had read at school. She looked around the tiny room, wincing at the memory of a gangly young Oliver for a moment, before walking to the bathroom to get washed. It was early, the clock on the mantelpiece said six fifteen, and by the time she pulled out creased clothes from the chest of drawers, she was ready for the day.

'Good morning,' Bernie said, putting her head around the door, her hair in rags under a cap.

'I'm sorry if I woke you,' Lily said.

'It was those blasted birds,' Bernie said. 'Every year they rear a couple of chicks, and every year one of them falls into the back yard and has to be rescued. Put the kettle on, we'll have some tea.'

Bernie disappeared again, and appeared soon after at the table and the prepared tea tray, dressed in a navy overall. 'I work three days a week, down at Mr Painswick's hardware shop,' she explained, as she sat down. Her curls were as stiff and shiny as if they were made of copper wire. 'Do you smoke, dear?'

'I don't, but please don't let that stop you,' Lily said.

Bernie pushed open the kitchen window and lit one. 'I just have three or four a day. I'm trying to give up – they're almost impossible to come by on the islands,' she said, blowing blue smoke towards the window. Lily didn't mind; it reminded her of her father. Player's Navy Cut with a sailor on the front of the box.

'I thought I would go down to the library and introduce myself this morning,' Lily said as Bernie lit the grill at the top of the cooker with a match.

'I don't want you to get your hopes up about the library,' her cousin said, putting her cigarette down to cut slices of bread. 'It's just a room off the town hall, and a bit of storage behind for the school books. How do you like your toast, maid?'

'Oh, I'm not hungry—' Lily started to say, but Bernie picked up her cigarette and pointed it at the toast, waving it for emphasis.

'Now, your mam wouldn't want me to let you go hungry, because anyone can see you've lost a lot of weight.'

'I was always slim...' Lily looked down at the table. 'But I haven't been eating much. I just feel sick.'

'Well, I saved up a bit of butter and I've got proper blackberry and apple jelly. Don't ask where I got the sugar – I had to swap half a bottle of sherry for it.' She put the thick slab of bread on a plate. 'I could see you were out of the habit of eating. But we'll get you back to health. You don't want to be fainting all over your precious books, do you?'

Lily couldn't help but smile. Bernie scraped a little butter on the toast for her, and put on a layer of the glowing, ruby jelly. 'There you go, my lovely,' she said, before attending to her own toast. The cigarette was half burnt so she put it out and returned it to the packet. 'I'll have that on my break,' she added, then took a large bite.

Lily took a nibble, and the flavours of autumn burst on her tongue. It had been a long time since food had tasted of anything much, and it brought back memories of making soldiers out of toast for Grace, before the war, when she was sitting in her wooden highchair. It had been the one Grace's father, James, had used as a baby. Jam had been smeared over Grace's fat cheeks. Strawberry, made from fruit Lily had raised in pots in the garden, blackcurrants that had grown under the kitchen window – plants that had been covered in rubble. She had been dark-eyed and dark-haired like James, none of the pale slimness of her mother. She had such a sense of humour, giggling at everything, calling her name to show her things. 'Mummy, Mummy, look!'

Tears filled her eyes, but she kept chewing. Toddler Grace laughing, her greasy, sticky fingers grabbing at Lily's hair as she lifted her out of the chair before she got ill. It was somewhere between delight and agony to remember, but that feeling was new to Lily. All she had been able to recall for months was the final days of her life, and the first few days after her death.

'Oh, that's good,' Bernie mumbled through a bite of crust. 'I was saving the jam for Oliver, and then for you. We'll pick some more berries come autumn, up along the aerodrome road. There's crab apples up there, too. I was just wondering if you might do me a favour, when you're free?'

'If I can,' Lily said, taking another nibble of the toast.

'It's on one of the other islands. Morwen. Do you remember it?'

'I think I do. Isn't it the rocky one? I remember seeing dolphins swimming beside the boat. You could almost touch them.'

Bernie finished her toast before she answered. 'You might have gone to see my other cousin, Edwin Chancel, there. He was a dean in the church, before he retired. Your mother knew him well.'

Lily waited for Bernie to carry on. She seemed to be having difficulty saying the words.

'They were always above us, if you know what I mean. They had a lot of money. The dean was the son of old Captain Chancel, born some fifteen years before your mother was.'

It appeared as if this should mean something to Lily. 'Captain Chancel?' she said blankly.

'The old sea captain, your mother's pa. He built a house right on the northernmost corner of Morwen Island, lived there and caused all sorts of upsets and scandal. Edwin was his younger son by his first wife, so he was my cousin. Or was it second cousin? I forget. Anyway, they had all the money.'

'How can I help?'

'Well, now that Edwin is dead, these last four years, his daughter still lives there. Emma Chancel, she's a bit of strange one. She had an accident when she was young, and she struggles with things. Her parents used to run Chancel Hall as a hotel. The war has stopped all that, and I don't think poor Emma gets any visitors now.'

Lily was confused. 'But what can I do?'

'Me and Emma's parents, we didn't talk. They didn't like to acknowledge the relationship, what with me and Cissie being born on the wrong side of the blanket, as they say. But now the council has asked me to look into whether Emma would sell to a builder. There is some concern the whole blessed place will fall down around her.'

'But if she struggles with things...'

'She could sell up, that's what the place needs. The council could buy it and put ministry offices there, and quarter some of their people. It's all very secret, something to do with the base on St Piran's. But Emma won't even see me, and I've written several times. Maybe you could persuade her – there's those on the island that say the house is in danger, that it will end up in the sea.' Lily had eaten all her toast, and Bernie topped up her cup again. 'There, just what you need,' she said, looking at Lily approvingly. 'There's more if you want it.'

'I'm fine, thank you. Would Emma even want to see me?'

Bernie shrugged, picked up the plates to put them in the sink. 'It's worth a try. I'm worried they will do one of those... compulsory purchases. She hasn't replied, so they approached me. But she won't let them in the house.' She turned back to Lily. 'Now, May Tolliver comes over for church once a month, you could chat to her after. She's been the Chancels' cleaner since she was a girl – she might be able to get you in.'

'I'll speak to her, if it would help you.' Lily put the cups in the sink over Bernie's objections. 'If I'm staying here, I must do my fair share,' she said, smiling, feeling the unfamiliarity of the expression pulling at her lips.

How long has it been since I smiled at anyone?

'Fair enough, maid. Now, I'd better get ready for work. That lipstick isn't going to apply itself. Think about going over to Morwen. She's as much your cousin as mine, you know, and she might speak to you.'

The flat seemed very quiet when Bernie left; even the dust was left hanging in the air as if unsure of which way to fall. Lily pressed her hand to her chest as the familiar ache started.

She was torn between two impulses: to cry and to pray.

5

PRESENT DAY, 3 JUNE

When she went to make another coffee, Nicole found a receipt and a piece of headed notepaper on the kitchen worksurface. *Morwen Delicatessen and Stores.* And a simple scribbled message in green ink.

> *We have a gin tasting evening on tonight at the Island Queen pub. You'd be very welcome, and it might be a nice way to meet some of your neighbours. Nibbles included, £25. Roz, Jean and Linda.*

Nicole scanned it and almost threw it away in the bin – *ah, forgot bin liners* – and looked at it again. She hadn't socialised in so many months, she hardly knew how to start.

But after crawling around separating files from clothes, stacking papers on shelves by the fireplace, and putting books away on the bookcase, she was dusty, tired and her knees ached. She replaced the clothes in the bag and dragged it to the bottom of the stairs, heaving it up behind her.

She put the clothes in a mahogany chest of drawers that looked like it belonged in a Victorian vicarage. It took up a quarter of the floor space but swallowed most of her items. For a moment she grieved for her lovely clothes, collected from around the world, now in storage. Most of her new outfits were easy to put on, and many concealed her damaged limb.

She carefully put on the leg, fitting the liner, sliding into the prosthetic and securing it with a long sleeve. It would do to stumble next door and chat to the neighbour, anyway. Putting on jeans and a jumper, she pulled a brush through her hair and looked in the dressing table mirror.

When she thought back to her accident, she remembered her favourite visitor had been her niece, Millie. She had woken up to find the eighteen-year-old curled in the hospital chair reading aloud – everything from crime thrillers to romantic comedy. Millie had been a vibrant, unbothered and unembarrassed part of her recovery. But recently, the teenager had been finishing her exams before university, and had retreated into her bedroom, at least according to Nicole's sister, Claire.

Shaking the memories from her mind, she made her way down the stairs and banged on the neighbouring door, to have it immediately swing open. It seemed no one locked their doors on the island.

'Hi, Nicole!' Jade opened the door wider. 'Do you want to come in?'

'No, I just wanted a word.' Nicole balanced against the doorframe. 'The people in the shop very kindly invited me to an event tonight. I need to politely refuse. I wondered if you could run a note down for me? I'll pay you, of course.'

'But you'd be very welcome to the gin tasting. I think I might go, it's always a great night out. There's always a new flavour that gets the locals arguing.'

Nicole smiled weakly. 'I'm just not sure...'

'Because you've got a problem with your leg?'

Nicole felt a spark of anger. *People here really don't have any filters.*

'I'm just tired, I travelled all day yesterday to get here. But I do want to thank them for the invitation.'

Jade looked at her calmly. 'Of course, if you want. I do have a plan if you change your mind, though – to get you there without hurting yourself.'

'Thanks. I'm sorry if I seem... well, you've all been very kind.'

Jade smiled more broadly. 'Maybe next time. I'll run that note down before they shut. No payment, it's five minutes away.'

'I'll go and write it, then. Thank you, Jade.'

Jade came in ten minutes later, just as Nicole finished the third draft.

'I can't believe you're going to miss it. Francesco's doing lobster bites just for you.'

Nicole managed a crooked smile. 'You're as bad as my niece! Now I feel guilty.'

'Last time they had cranberry and orange gin, it was amazing.' She rolled her eyes. 'And Francesco's going to be there, and he is the best thing that's happened to the island since I got back.'

Nicole could feel herself weakening. 'I just don't think I could get down to the pub.'

'Let me worry about that. Will you come? I'll make sure you get back, even if you have too much gin.'

Nicole laughed, gallows humour kicking in. 'Legless, you mean?'

Jade smiled, but went pink. She put her chin up. 'And if *I* get legless, you can give *me* a lift back.' She refused to elaborate, and just said, 'Be ready for seven, then we've got time to get you down there. Are you going to do something with your hair? It's nice and thick.'

Nicole ran her hand through the scruffy mop, all the same length since it grew back in hospital after being shaved. 'I don't think I can do much with it,' she said, grimacing.

'I can!' Jade said brightly. 'I studied hairdressing at college. Let me have a go, it might be fun. I'll just go and get my scissors.'

By the time Jade went down to the shop, to accept the invite, Nicole had had a bit of a trim around the sides, where her hair had been sticking out over her ears, and had been blow dried. She looked fine, she realised, after months of not being able to bear seeing herself in the mirror. Jade must have seen the scars of the surgery that had saved her life, but she didn't say a word about them. She simply worked, brushing and snipping and asking a barrage of questions.

Nicole found herself talking about the islands back in the nineties, describing the people she had known on her first visit. Jade seemed to enjoy working out who they all were, as most of them had never left. The gin tasting was in the pub Nicole had drunk in as a student.

Nicole had questions about the present-day islands. The old youth hostel had gone but the campsite was still there. The population had shifted as young people moved away, but there were still families, new babies, new businesses.

'There's Bran's pottery up the lane,' Jade said, snipping at the last loose hairs on the top. 'The haunted house has been done up as a fantastic hotel right along the shore.'

'I stayed there as a student. Creepy old place, but with wonderful views...'

'The art collective teaches painting up at the school during the holidays. There's even a farm now. The island's coming on, even if the fishing has mostly gone.'

'It had mostly gone when I was here before,' Nicole said.

'There's still one trawler and a few open boats. They take tourists out on fishing holidays now.' She looked critically at

Nicole's hair in the mirror she had propped up in the kitchen. 'I'd love to get some colour in there.'

'I used to keep it subtle. Dark, like I am naturally. Well, was, before—'

The breath got sucked out of her chest as it always did. She realised she still couldn't talk about the accident.

'Well, you could go for something a bit different. I could bring some colour charts around; we could do a patch test. Or you could go to Steph on the big island – she's very good.'

Nicole turned her head from side to side. 'You know, I've changed. My life has changed. Maybe it is time for a new look.'

'It's thick and curly, it's a lovely dark reddish colour. There's a lot of good things to work with. And we can cover up those few grey hairs easily.'

Nicole sat back and looked at herself. She wasn't as much of a stranger as she had thought. There was the slight smile that was on her graduation photograph, the serious look that had attracted the men in her life. 'Maybe it's the stress that's making the grey grow in,' she said softly. 'Coming close to death.'

'Well, you look great. Ready for a night out with the girls.'

'How much do I owe you?'

For being so accepting that I could reveal myself to you; for being so positive and inviting.

Jade looked like she was going to refuse, but then said, 'You can pay my ticket to the gin evening, if you like. And come with me.'

'You're so determined to get me there. Why?'

Jade gathered up her brushes and scissors. 'You know, sometimes, you really just *like* someone?'

Nicole laughed then. 'I do! Even if they are twenty years younger, and you've known them for about five minutes.'

Jade grinned at her in the mirror. 'And, added bonus, I think you would be dead funny full of gin.'

6

MAY 1941

Church had become Lily's solace. She hadn't been religious before but now, instead of prayers, she talked in her mind directly not to God, but Grace.

How are you up there, Grace? It's a bit rainy down here. There are some good puddles down by the shop. I almost jumped in one for you. I hope there are lots of puddles up there, and a stout pair of galoshes.

She pressed her hands against her eyes to block out the sights inside the church. Grace had loved stained-glass windows. Although small, unlike the soaring medieval master-pieces in London, these featured people in their everyday lives, with farm animals. There was a dove locked into blue glass that had enchanted her when she first visited. *Grace would love this.* The thought brought her crashing down. She had been four when they first noticed she was having difficulty seeing out of one eye, putting her head on the side to feed the ducks, starting to trip and stumble in her new shoes.

I miss you every day... Tears ran through Lily's fingers, and she stifled sobs. *You would like the silly gulls nesting on the roof opposite. I have given them names I know you would have approved of, because you called your doll Harriet, and you loved Great Uncle Ludovic's funny name.*

She slowly became aware of a hand patting her shoulder. A strange woman about Bernie's age held out a pressed, folded handkerchief. 'There you go, my dear,' she said.

Lily pulled her emotions back under control, wiped her eyes, blew her nose and looked up in time to stand, and sing the next hymn. When the congregation sat down, she asked the kind woman, 'Where can I return the hankie?'

'Bernie knows me,' the woman whispered. 'Thelma Goodings. I know about your loss, I quite understand. I used to go to school with your mother.'

Lily tried to concentrate on the vicar, but the thought ran around her head. Did everyone know about Grace? Had Bernie told all the islanders? She had preferred to be locked into her private grief; she didn't want to talk about Grace to anyone. Grace was *hers*.

At the end of the service, Lily stood up and Thelma stopped her. 'I'm so sorry for your loss. I hope you don't mind me mentioning it.'

'Not at all,' she said, the words sounding prim and flat.

'How's Bernie doing? She lost her nephew. He was more like her son, you know. We all loved Ollie.'

'She's coping.' Lily was uncomfortable in this circle of gossip. 'May I ask you a question? I was hoping to meet a Mrs May Tolliver. I believe she attends church here.'

'May? Of course she does, she comes over to see her daughter. She's... over there, in the purple hat. She got that in Scotland you know, on a railway excursion holiday with her husband.'

'Thank you,' Lily said, sidling out of the pew ahead of the gossipy woman. 'Excuse me, I need to have a word.'

She managed to reach Mrs Tolliver as she emerged into the sunshine of the churchyard and walked between the graves to stand before a new one, presumably her husband's. Lily waited respectfully for a few minutes, by which time the crowd had thinned out.

'Mrs Tolliver? My name is Lily Granville.'

The old woman's eyes were red, but she was standing tall. 'I wondered if you would come to say hello,' she said. 'I know who you are. I knew your mother when she was just a girl. How is she?'

'Not well,' Lily said, a lightning bolt of guilt stabbing through her. 'She's just removed to a nursing home. She had a heart attack recently.'

'I'm sorry to hear that,' May said. 'What can I do for you?'

'My cousin, Bernice, told me that Miss Emma Chancel is refusing to talk to anyone about Chancel Hall.'

'Well, it's her house.' Mrs Tolliver bristled. 'She can do what she likes with it.'

Lily leaned back from the hostility. 'I'm sorry if I spoke out of turn. Bernie has had letters, that's all, from the council.'

The older woman sagged, walked to a bench and patted the seat beside her. 'I'm sorry. I'm worried, maid. Emma won't let anyone in except me. My husband used to do the grounds, and she's been so sad since he died. And I'm no spring chicken – what will happen to her when I go? I can barely make it along the lane as it is. I should move to my daughter's house, really.' She looked at Lily, narrowed her eyes, stared up and down. 'You're a pretty maid, just like your mother. Fair as she was, too.'

'I just want to help Bernie. She's worried about Emma.'

'It's natural, I suppose, them being cousins – properly speaking. Although they've hardly ever met. Emma's dad, Mr Edwin, married late, he was religious. He was a dean of a cathedral somewhere near London. He retired here when he inherited the old house, tried to run it as a bed and breakfast. But it got too much for him, what with caring for his poorly wife and Emma as well.'

'But they didn't accept their... natural cousins?'

'That's a nice way of calling it, but their father's *irregular* – if you know what I mean – was right there living on the islands, a kept woman. They didn't speak. Well, the captain was a difficult man. Most families wouldn't let their daughters work up there. Emma and Charlotte were born in London, grew up there until they left school. Identical twins.'

'And then they moved back?'

'After the captain died.' May pointed through the graveyard. 'That's the old man's mausoleum over there. He's well weighed down, I will say that.'

'Do you think it's worth me meeting Emma? To explain the council's concerns? She doesn't have to do it, I'm sure, but if she doesn't reply it will make it harder.'

May stared a little longer then stood up abruptly, leaning on the arm of the seat. 'Do you know, Emma needs friends, family who are young enough to help her when I'm gone. I'm not saying she needs a guardian; she does all right despite her being a bit forgetful, a bit slow sometimes. But she could do with advice from someone who wants to help. I'll send you a note when I've persuaded her.'

'Persuaded?' Lily smiled at the thought. 'Will she be very reluctant?'

'She's a creature of habit,' May said, leaning on a walking stick. 'But you seem like a gentle sort; she might let you in, maybe listen to you. She's been that lonely since her dad died, like a rudderless ship.'

'Thank you,' Lily said, although she wondered what for. For visiting a stranger who didn't want to meet her, intruding on her home? But her heart went out to the woman – it resonated with her own emptiness.

The woman was right, Lily thought. Emma sounded like she might need some help.

7

PRESENT DAY, 3 JUNE

Jade's solution turned out to be a mobility scooter in shiny purple, courtesy of a resident in Chapel Hill who had bought it when recovering from an illness. The owner, Heike, was happy to lend it out as she was now back on two feet. She had given Nicole the instruction book and a charger.

After a few false starts, Nicole managed to bump the shiny vehicle down the cobbles. The pub had level side access and she was met there by a smiling Jade. 'I was just going to walk up to meet you!' She was rapidly introduced to a few other women and a couple of men, her neighbour Vanessa and the teacher from the school, a woman in her thirties called Charlotte.

'This is my first gin evening, too,' Charlotte confided, sitting next to Nicole, the scooter parked safely over by a coat stand.

'Are you not from Morwen?'

She shook her head, and took a few nuts from a bowl set out on the long table. 'My family are from here originally, but I'm quite new. I'm told you're just visiting?'

'I knew the islands about twenty-five years ago. I did my PhD here. I've rented a cottage for a year, while I contemplate new directions for my life.' When Charlotte raised an eyebrow,

Nicole continued. 'I'm a marine biologist – or I *was*. I loved being here so much when I was younger, I thought I would come back.' Her voice got tighter. 'I'm just getting over an accident.' There, the word that reached into her chest like dry tissue. She sipped a little water and was handed a glossy pamphlet and a pen.

'Well, be warned. I only came here for a few weeks to close down the local school and I ended up staying as the teacher, meeting my partner and adopting two young boys.' Charlotte smiled. 'If you're a marine biologist, you should meet Josh McKay. He's the wildlife warden for the marine reserve.'

'I'll look into contacting him.' Nicole took another sip. 'I could think of worse places to be stuck. People are so friendly here.'

'And nosy.' Charlotte laughed. 'Including me, apparently! We don't get many new people living here. Oh, here we go, we've started. Bright blue gin...'

There was a talk with each bottle, and a small shot and then a mixer with each. Francesco came out with trays of bread, olives and nuts, then a platter of seafood bites – with the promised lobster. The chatter got louder, and the gins were delicious and fruity, a few herbal ones reminding Nicole of cough medicine, and one that just smelled like lighter fluid. Everyone was asked to share the notes they had made with varying degrees of laughter or disagreement. The gin specialist was there from the brewery, and was very serious about taking notes. The fifteen gin tasters were less so, and grew more and more silly.

Part of Nicole was really enjoying herself, knowing she needed to just taste each glass. The other part of her knew she was a bit drunk, and could feel the loosening of the tightness in her neck and chest.

'So, what happened to your leg?' Jade asked. 'If you don't mind me asking.'

'I do mind you asking,' Nicole said reflexively, her voice coming out cool and crisp. The two women stared at each other for a moment and the room fell quiet, then both of them burst into laughter. Nicole could feel something inside her come untied. 'It was only a bloody car accident,' she said, unable to stop giggling. 'And now I'm *actually* legless.'

The laughter was more universal, and kind. 'We're recycling that joke from earlier,' Jade said, waving at someone further down the room. 'Cesco, more yummy snacks down here.'

'You ladies OK?' he asked, resting his hands on the back of their chairs.

Nicole held up her finger and thumb, an inch apart. 'A tiny bit drunk, I think, but fine.'

'I take you back when you finished,' he said, grinning at both of them.

'He's beautiful,' Jade said wistfully, clearly more drunk than Nicole had realised.

'And *engaged*,' he said, his eyes smiling through curly black lashes. 'To my lovely Maria.'

'Pff,' Jade said. 'What happens on Morwen stays on Morwen.' When he walked away to answer another query, Jade sighed at his retreating back. 'He's lovely. So charming. Why aren't English boys like that?'

Nicole looked at him. He was tall, well-built and well-tanned.

'I have no idea,' she said, toasting Jade with the dregs of the last watermelon-flavoured gin. At Jade's age she would have fallen for him, too. All the young men on the island seemed to have perfect tans and a physique from hard work, she remembered. 'It's probably not very politically correct to ogle him, though. Ob-ject-if-y him.' She had to sound the word out slowly and clearly. 'Oh, that gin is quite strong.'

There was time after the tasting to finish up the food, drink some sparking water and start to feel less spaced out. She hadn't drunk alcohol after the accident, worried that she would disappear into a bottle, but she felt confident she wasn't going to become hooked on watermelon- or lavender-flavoured gins. 'I should go home.'

'How's the cottage?' a woman in her late twenties asked. 'I'm Corinne, by the way. I think you met my partner, Tink, earlier. He drove the ferry when you came over?'

'I did. The house is lovely,' Nicole said. 'It's magical. Except for some gulls tap-dancing on the roof and singing down the chimney, anyway.'

Corinne grinned back. 'I think they charge extra for the resident wildlife.'

'They're so entertaining,' Jade said. 'Last year we had jackdaws. One of the babies fell down into the grate and terrified a couple of visitors. We had to get on the roof and put the baby back in its nest, but it survived.'

'Well, I won't need a wake-up call while I'm staying there,' Nicole said, feeling warm and relaxed and less dizzy. 'And so far, I'm loving it.'

Jade cleared the glasses onto a tray. 'Have you got any work to do while you're here, or anything you'd like to do?'

There was a general shushing as people waited to see what she had to say.

'I have no idea,' she said to the whole room, smiling.

8

JUNE 1941

Mr Prendergast was a man in his fifties, and his staff were both women. Lily had grown used to her world being run by older men now, the younger ones either off fighting or engaged in other essential war work, like her husband. Even the thought of James made her feel cold. When she had needed him most, he had been distant. He had taken to sleeping at work on a camp bed several times a week, and had only just made it home for Grace's final hours. Work, for him, had become all-consuming.

The latest letter from him was getting creased in Lily's pocket, and she was still not sure how she felt about it. He had found out she was working for the island's library, because her wages went straight into their shared bank account. Perhaps she should enquire about a bank account in her own name.

'So you're on your own here?' Mr Prendergast asked, in a chatty Welsh accent. 'And staying in the town?'

'I'm staying with a relative,' she said, not sure how to describe Bernie. 'My mother's cousin.'

'Where's that, then? I'd better make a note, if you're working here.'

She told him the address, and he smiled immediately.

'Bernie Pederick? We all know her, of course! She's been a regular in the library. Her and Percy.'

'Percy?' The name was out before she could stop it.

'Her companion. Friend, really. An older gentleman who used to lodge with her when her nephew wasn't there.'

'Oh, I didn't know.' She felt like there was a whole story running under and around her that she was not part of, locked into her bubble of pain and Grace.

'He died, I don't know... Elsie? When did Percy pass over?'

The taller lady looked over through wire-rimmed spectacles. 'The beginning of the war, Mr Prendergast. Hello, Mrs Granville. I'm Elsie. We're very pleased to have you.'

'Please call me Lily.' The two women shook hands, and Elsie introduced Margery, shorter and with darker hair. Both looked as if they were in their fifties, like Mr Prendergast.

'We cleared a space downstairs, in storage. It does have a bit of natural light and a good, strong electric bulb, too,' Margery said with a smile. 'We were told you have some very important books.'

'We'll be getting more,' Lily said. 'Some of them will just need a detailed inspection, a bit of conservation maybe, then proper storage. They will be much safer out of London. Like me.' Unbidden, the tumbled bricks and splintered windows of their London home came back to her.

'Well,' said Elsie. 'We're here to help you, if we can. We only open the library for part of each day so we're often available. I'd be happy to volunteer some hours to the cause.'

'Anything to thwart that awful Herr Hitler,' Margery said. 'And we are both trained in cataloguing and recording, too.'

Words of polite refusal crept into Lily's mouth, but she stopped them. Her instinct to avoid people, to hide away, had to stop. These willing, kind women could really help her.

'Everything I find has to be recorded,' she said. 'It takes up so much time, it would be very kind if you can help.'

'We live alone. Well,' Elsie said, glancing over at Margery, 'we share a cottage, for convenience and companionship. But neither of us has a husband or children to take up our time.'

Lily tried to smile, but was sure it came out lopsided. 'I could start today, if necessary? I have books drying out at Bernie's – Miss Pederick's – flat.'

'I wouldn't hear of it,' Mr Prendergast said, as he'd clearly been listening in the smaller room. 'You'll need to unpack and settle into your new quarters.'

'Well, tomorrow, then,' Lily said, with just a little pleading squeak in her voice. 'Nine o'clock?'

'That would be perfect,' Elsie said, beaming. 'Nine sharp, and we'll get you set up downstairs. Now, what tea do you prefer? We have a little Havergill's Special, but we have some Typhoo as well.'

Although they wouldn't let her start work, Elsie did let her get acquainted with the library. The children's section had a lot of textbooks, the librarian explaining that local grammar school students were often unable to get to school in Truro because of travel disruptions or the risk to the ferries to the mainland. Several students were studying from home with work sent by post. The local primary school visited, a group of children coming in to change their books, and Lily was asked to sit on a small chair in the corner and read aloud.

It came so naturally to read as she had to Grace, with all the actions and growly animal voices. It wasn't until she had finished that she made the connection between the storytelling and the aching feeling in her arms. Empty arms that were longing to hold Grace. The children were curious about her, as there were only a few hundred people living on the island and they didn't recognise her.

'Are you a teacher, Miss?' one child – six or seven, as dark haired as Grace, she realised with a lurch – asked her.

'No. I'm someone who mends broken books. A conservator. I work for the British Library in London.'

That caught another child's attention. 'How do books break, Miss?'

'Well, these books have been in a big city, in London, where a bomb went off.' The children didn't look surprised; they must have talked about the war, but apart from their gas mask cases, conflict seemed a long way away from island life.

'Is it true that people get blown up by bombs?' one little boy asked, looking scared. He slid his fingers into the curious girl's hand.

Lily crouched down so he could see into her face. 'Well, there are special shelters where people go to be safe from bombs,' she said. 'I know you have them here, too. The siren goes off so we can all hide away. And lots of children have moved away from the towns where the planes drop the bombs. They are safer in the countryside.'

'They have evacuees in Lowertown,' the girl said. 'One of them is in my brother's class. Her house in Bristol got burned up.'

The teacher, with a bag full of books, joined them. 'After the war, all the houses will get built up again,' she said. She made a face to Lily. 'It's so hard to explain the destruction to young children.'

Lily stood up. 'Honestly, it's hard to explain it to any of us,' she said. 'We just hope it will be over soon.'

'I understand you're working with ancient and valuable books. If you have time, it would be wonderful if you could talk about books and printing to the children. We don't get away to do educational trips on the mainland any more.'

Lily looked down at the children. 'That's a lovely idea,' she said. 'I'm being sent a lot of interesting books next month, suitable for the children to handle.'

'Well, that would be wonderful! Now, children, say thank you to Mrs Granville.'

The children thanked her, linked hands in pairs, and left Lily feeling between happy and hollow.

9

PRESENT DAY, 4 JUNE

Nicole walked down to the café in the morning after the gin tasting, on two crutches to ease the pressure on her leg. A large coffee helped clear her foggy head, and she recognised a couple of other gin tasters working behind the counter.

Lucy, who owned the café, and who she'd met last night, brought over a coffee and a slice of a lemon drizzle cake. 'I thought you might like this for breakfast?'

'Oh God, thank you,' Nicole said, tucking into the citrussy sweetness. 'Brilliant idea.'

Lucy gestured at the spare chair, and Nicole pointed with a fork for her to sit down.

'I hoped you made it home all right in Heike's scooter?'

'Francesco made sure I didn't drive off the quay or crash into anyone's house,' Nicole said, smiling at the memory. 'Nice boy.'

The bell on the door rang, as another of the gin tasters came in. Lucy waved to Ellie, Corinne's friend. 'Tough night with the baby?'

'After all that gin *she* slept like a log,' Ellie said, opening her eyes wider in the cool shade of the café.

Lucy looked at Ellie. 'Zillah's such a good baby. Your usual, Elowen?'

'Pure caffeine would be good,' Ellie said, over her shoulder. 'And a slice of that cake, too, please.'

Nicole was intrigued. 'Elowen? That's a lovely name.'

'It's an island name,' Ellie said. 'Like Branok – Bran. That's why we called the baby Zillah.'

'It's a lovely tradition,' Nicole said, sipping her coffee and closing her eyes in pleasure. 'I feel more alive here. Everything's more intense, even the coffee.'

'Maybe you're just woken up, away from all the distractions of a city. I found that at first.'

While Ellie got on with her breakfast, Nicole thought about her sincere words. 'Before I came here, I was in hospital,' she said, abruptly. 'Not just in a city, in a rehab unit trying to learn how to walk again.' She waited for the crushing horror and grief to hit her, but it didn't come. 'I've been finding it hard...' She shook her head. 'But it feels different here.'

'What are you going to do, now you're settled on the island?' Ellie blinked owlishly over the rim of her cup. 'Wow, that caffeine is kicking in.'

'When I was a kid, I always thought I would be this kick-ass scientist, saving whales and birds and fish.'

'So, what happened?' Ellie put the cup down, indicating she was really listening. That was an island thing, Nicole realised; everyone asked a lot of questions because they were genuinely interested in the answers.

'Success. I was very good at getting research grants, for other people to do the actual work on the ground. The higher up you go, the more offices you end up in, the more conferences and panels you spend time on. I hadn't seen the sea for four years – can you believe that? Except on holiday, that is.'

She remembered the last big promotion, monitoring fish quotas across the North Sea.

'Well, it doesn't sound like it makes your heart sing,' Ellie said. 'I used to be a forensic accountant, looking at bank fraud.'

'Sounds interesting.'

'*Really* not.' Ellie half smiled. 'Now I look into individual crimes against real people, little companies that get scammed or pensioners that get ripped off. I love it; I'm working for the police, and I know I'm helping people.'

'I guess you can do that around the baby?'

Ellie managed a hollow laugh. 'I wish. Bran takes her when I'm working. He fits in his sculpture and painting around her. She's always covered in clay and sometimes spattered with paints. Bran reckons she's a natural artist.' She drained her coffee. 'I'd better get back. Nice to see you made it home.'

Nicole smiled at that. 'If not, I think Francesco would have carried me, he's so keen to help. Bit of a mother hen, really.'

Ellie rolled her eyes at the door. 'But *so* good-looking,' she said, grinning, as she left.

Nicole's leg was uncomfortable but not hurting, so she followed the physio's advice and walked to the end of the quay and sat on a bench looking out over the sea at the neighbouring island. Strangers strolled past on their way to the shop, each one smiling and saying 'good morning'. It was a bit overwhelming at first, but when a white-haired woman stopped and squinted at her, she looked familiar to Nicole.

'I know you,' the lady said, sitting beside her. 'You were one of the students who stayed at the campsite from the university. You've got such a distinctive face; my husband took your picture and painted you. Lovely cheekbones.'

'Did he?' Nicole half remembered a local artist who had taken photographs of the whole rockpool project. 'Oh wait, yes, I remember – Peter, was it?'

'Pete.' The woman stopped for a moment, took a deep breath. 'I'm Maggi, his wife.'

To Nicole, her rich West Country accent was familiar. 'I do remember you. How are you?'

'I'm fine. Peter died, five years ago now.' She swallowed hard. 'It's not easy losing the love of your life. But the world goes on, and so do I. What about you? I seem to recall you were dating a very handsome young fellow.'

Nicole had a flashback to a laughing Nick, reaching out his hands to help her onto a boat, feeling so full of love for him. It was first love, powerful stuff. 'He's married now – he has three children. We communicate on social media occasionally.'

'No other loves?'

Nicole smiled then. 'Several loves, but none that I wanted to take home and keep.'

'And no children?'

The smile faded. 'No, I enjoyed my career and the freedom to travel. But I do have an amazing niece I love to bits.'

'Good for you,' Maggi said, standing up. 'I'm just off to finish my circuit then I'm joining the art group. I'm going to get them felting. Have you ever tried it?'

'I haven't,' Nicole said. 'But maybe I should, now I'm not working.'

'Well, you're a bit young to retire altogether,' Maggi said, smiling. 'Look at me, I'm still the postmistress in my seventies.' She rolled her eyes. 'They won't let you sit around on your butt here, you know. Everyone does something.'

The lifestyle on the island seemed to do wonders for Nicole's leg. After several more days of walking carefully, leaning on her walker around the village, she found that she wanted to go further, and she really wanted to visit the 'haunted house' holiday flats she had stayed in as a student.

Francesco had thoughtfully put her mobility vehicle on charge in the hall of the cottage, and the green lights which monitored the battery were all on. She managed to lean past it to open the front door then backed it slowly out of the narrow doorway.

It ran easily down the steep cobbles, and a couple of people smiled and said good morning. She drove it further, past the pub, along the slate gravel path between open ground and the low sea wall onto the beach. The whole place smelled of salt and the wind was less bracing sitting down. A gate crossed part of the path, but she could easily get around the end of it. Another path led to a series of tumbledown shacks that looked industrial. Then the path became better finished as she approached the northern end of the island.

As it came into view, the Victorian house was as imposing as ever, now renamed Chancel Hall Hotel, not the Sunshine Apartments, as she vaguely remembered them being called. Long windows reflected the sky, and a conservatory extended from one end.

As she grew closer, Nicole could see that the gravel path fanned out onto a stone terrace, protected from the sea by a low wall. Native shrubs like sea kale and thrift were just curling out of the sand as it ran towards the sea. The view was spectacular, the small waves tossing their heads out towards the current that made the island landings so hazardous. The Sound, that's what the locals called it. She noticed something smooth out at sea, echoing the waves, then another. Dolphins, several of them just breaching and playing in the relative shallows.

'Oh, wow,' a voice came from behind her. A man stood on the terrace, a steaming mug in his hand. 'The dolphins are back, we saw them a few days ago, too.' The man, in his thirties with cropped, russet hair stepped forward. 'Hi, sorry if I made you jump. I'm Justin. My husband and I run the hotel.'

'Oh, hello.'

Nicole looked up at the white-painted Victorian building with a modern, dark steel and glass extension.

'The *haunted* house?' The words popped out before she could stop them. 'Oh, I'm so sorry, I was here in the nineties as a student...'

He laughed. 'You have no idea how close we came to calling it that officially. It was called Chancel Hall when it was built, the name's over the door.'

'Well, it looks amazing now. How often do you see the dolphins?'

'We've been here six years, so I suppose a few times a year. You should ask the wildlife ranger if you're interested.'

'I will, I'm a marine biologist—' she started to say.

'We've heard all about you. I didn't know you had mobility problems, though. We have wheelchair access if you fancy a meal overlooking the sea. Let me get you the wildlife service brochure. We have all sorts of weird creatures here that I'm sure would interest you.'

He disappeared, and she drove the chair closer to the beach, the wheels beginning to sink into sand the colour of honey. The urge to explore was getting stronger. She swung her legs to the side to try and stand, but her feet couldn't find a solid footing.

Justin came back out, holding a brochure and a baby. 'Here you go, there's a contact number on there for the ranger. He records all the sightings of rare and unusual animals. We had a sunfish last year, and we get basking sharks every summer.'

Nicole backed her vehicle onto solid ground. 'And who is this little one?'

'Max. He's our youngest. I would put him down, but he only eats the sand and shells.'

The little boy stretched out as if to grab her and Nicole caught his hand. 'He's beautiful. The youngest?'

'Merryn is just six, she's at school at the moment.'

Nicole looked back over the sea, spotting the sleek metallic sides of the dolphins as they rounded the end of the beach. 'They must be after something,' she said. 'Sardines are making a comeback here, you know.'

'We do get a good range of local fish for the kitchen,' he confirmed. 'My husband Robert likes a challenge in the kitchen, but last year they caught a lot of octopus, and it was a hard sell after a while.'

Nicole laughed. 'I ought to get back. Thanks for the leaflet. I'll make contact and report the sighting.'

10

JUNE 1941

Lily walked up to the porch of Chancel Hall, facing the sea on the corner of the building. Mrs May Tolliver had written her a letter, inviting her to meet Emma Chancel. James had also written, quite opinionated about his suggestion – which sounded like an instruction – to leave Emma alone.

James had not, as he had planned, found a house for them in London. Instead, he had taken a couple of rooms near his office. There was a not very subtle suggestion that she would soon be joining him back on the mainland. She couldn't imagine going back to London, let alone to his cold grief, and his stilted politeness. She had hardly recognised him when she left.

Chancel Hall was made of stone but the old pointing had fallen out in places. The front had four ground-floor windows staring coldly out to sea, all of them seven or eight feet high. Lily wondered how tall the ceilings were as she stepped up onto the open portico, past stacks of dried logs and a couple of walking sticks. After her first reaction to the faded splendour, she saw knee-high weeds in the gravel outside, a terrace with cracked paving, peeling dark green paint on the door. She pulled a brass bell pull, and far away a bell jangled.

No one came. She walked outside and peered in the window, but it was dark inside, the curtains partially drawn, and the glass was covered in dust.

'Who are you?' The voice came from the other side of the building: a woman was leaning around the far corner of the house. 'I don't allow visitors.'

'My name is Lily Granville. I have an appointment with Miss Emma Chancel?' There was no change in the expression of the older woman, who looked about forty. 'May said you were expecting me,' she said, feebly, in the face of her unwavering stare.

'Oh, yes. May said you were coming but I couldn't remember the day.' She walked towards Lily, dressed in men's trousers and a shirt under a jumper with several holes. Her hair was short, and as ragged as if she'd cut it herself.

'Are *you* Miss Emma Chancel?' Lily asked. With a mop of dark hair she looked nothing like Lily. 'I'm your cousin Lily, your Aunt Elizabeth's daughter.'

'Yes, I'm Emma.' She didn't stop to shake hands, just walked past and pushed open the big door. 'I don't come in this way much,' she said over her shoulder. Then, grudgingly: 'You can come in, if you like.'

Lily followed, feeling awkward. When she got into a large square hall, Emma stopped at a door behind the grand staircase and gazed back at her. 'You have funny eyes,' she said. 'Very blue.'

'I do,' Lily said. There didn't seemed to be anything else to say.

'And you're pretty,' Emma said. 'But your hair is a funny colour. May said to put the kettle on for guests.' She pushed open the door into a sunny kitchen, the table scrubbed wood. Double doors led onto the garden at the back.

Lily's eyes finally adjusted to the gloom in the hall, and she looked around at the dark Victorian furniture.

The stairs were beautiful, the spindles turned and varnished, and the banister looked as if it was made out of a single piece of oak. Ragged carpet ran up the middle of each stair, the outsides painted black, chipped over some sort of previous green. A coat stand held a dozen coats, all covered in a sheen of dust. Most of the wall by the door was taken up with a huge mahogany sideboard covered with ornaments and glass domes filled with dead birds, all faded into the same beige. Stacks of post took up half the surface, with doors and drawers half open, contents spilling out.

'Come into the kitchen,' Emma reiterated, and it sounded much more like an order. 'Mother said we have to make tea for visitors.'

'Yes. Of course,' Lily said, twisting her gloved fingers together anxiously. 'Thank you.'

'Sit there,' Emma said, pointing at one of several chairs around the table. 'That's where May sits. She brought me some milk for your tea.'

'That is very kind.' Lily looked through the smudged kitchen windows onto a garden of grass and summer flowers spilling out of borders. Emma half filled a kettle and put it the top of an old-fashioned range. She tutted, opened the door and poked it about while smoke curled out into the room.

'It's not working,' she said. 'The chimney sweep needs to come.'

Lily took off her coat and hung it on the back of the chair before she sat down. She stuffed her gloves in a pocket. 'How do you contact him?'

Emma frowned, looking at an open book at the end of the table. 'I don't, he just comes every year.' She turned over a few pages. 'He should have come last month.'

'Can I help? I would be happy to contact him for you. Is he on the island?'

Emma shook her head. 'I don't know... I'll ask May.'

Lily had time to look around as Emma fussed over the slowly warming kettle. The whole side wall, behind the table, was taken up with a dresser. It had eight drawers, all of them with scuffed paint, and glass-fronted cupboards above. It was rammed with china, some very higgledy-piggledy, and some pieces looked chipped and broken. Under the top cupboards were hooks, many of them holding cups and jugs. Emma lifted a cup and took a saucer from the base of the dresser.

'This is my cup,' Emma said, not especially speaking to Lily. 'That one is Charlotte's. I'll give you Mother's cup, but you must be careful with it.'

'I will,' Lily said.

Before the kettle had fully boiled, Emma poured hot water on some leaves in a beautiful pot decorated with roses. 'This is special tea,' she said, without looking at Lily. 'It was my mother's favourite.'

'Thank you.' Lily looked around at the layer of dirt everywhere, concerned about the cleanliness of the china, but she could see the table was spotless, the sink and stove all clean, the floor swept. It was as if Emma only cleaned the part of the kitchen she used, or maybe that was May's doing. Behind Lily was another glass dome, and she peered in through a haze of cobwebs encrusted with grime.

'I don't like that one,' Emma said. 'That's why I don't dust it.'

It was a stuffed jay, its neck hanging at an odd angle as if it had been broken, blue glass eyes staring up at Lily. 'No, it's a bit the worse for wear,' Lily said, pressing her hand to her chest to calm her racing heart.

'Charlotte broke it,' Emma said, pouring the tea carefully. She passed Lily the cup – thankfully clean – and poured an inch of milk into a jug from a larder by the back door.

'Did she?' Lily looked around. 'Does Charlotte live here, too?'

Emma laughed, but as if she didn't find it funny. 'No, of course not.'

'Do you live here alone, then?'

'I have a cat,' Emma said, dripping a little milk into her cup. 'And May comes up here from time to time. We used to have guests, but now we don't. Not since Daddy died.' There was an air of sadness about Emma that Lily instantly recognised.

'I'm so sorry to hear that,' Lily said, choosing her words carefully before sipping the tea. The milk was a little stale, but the tea was good. 'How long ago did he pass away?'

'Four years,' Emma said, then added with a note of pride. 'They said I couldn't stay here by myself but he wrote everything in the diary. All I have to do is it follow it. I can read perfectly well, I just forget a few things.'

She patted the book, held open by a bookmark. Lily could see there was a day to each page, filled with writing. 'Does it say anything about the chimney sweep in there?' Lily asked, breathing in the fragrant steam from the tea. Emma's expression changed.

'You look,' she said, pushing it over. 'Eleventh of May. He never came.'

Lily soon worked out what she was looking at. Each page was a single day in a diary. It had dozens of instructions from when to take a bath to when to water the planters in the garden. Cleaning, sweeping, tidying, laundry, changing sheets, ordering shopping. It was ingenious. Every day Emma made a tiny mark in the corner of the page, so she knew that she was on the right date. Today's had four tiny crosses, the next page just had three. Emma explained, as if talking to a child, that the days were all wrong because there had been a leap year. The days of the week were kept on a little stand with wooden markers on, that she replaced each day. 'So I know it's Monday,' Emma crowed. 'I'm always right.'

For a moment, Lily could hear a proud note in Emma's

voice that reminded her of Grace when she completed a puzzle, or beat Daddy at a board game.

Emma's speech was unusual, and her manner more like a ten-year-old's than an adult in her forties, but she seemed sharp enough. Just impaired in decision making, May had said, and she had problems remembering things but could read and write and managed with lists. There was one on the dresser: a comprehensive shopping list, along with jars of money, presumably for different things. One was marked 'sweep,' and had a ten shilling note sticking out of the top.

'Do you have the sweep's phone number or address? I could ask him to call.' Lily sipped the last of the tea as Emma froze.

'It's at the back of the diary,' Emma eventually said, pressing her hand flat against today's page. 'But I don't like looking, in case I lose today's page.'

'We could put something in there, like this spoon,' Lily said, waving her unused teaspoon. 'And, anyway, we know the date today is the sixteenth of June, look. We'll find it again, I'll help.'

'All right,' Emma said slowly. 'But put the spoon in first.'

The sweep was on St Brannock's, so Lily promised she would walk around to his house and ask him to call.

'Your house is lovely,' she said, looking around, seeing strong bones in the details of the wide door, the high ceilings and the cornicing.

'May said I should give you a tour,' Emma said, although her voice sounded reluctant. 'But just downstairs because I don't want to upset my sister.'

Lily couldn't remember how many children the Chancels had. It was odd that May hadn't told her. In fact, she had given the impression that Emma was vulnerable because she lived alone.

'Come on,' Emma said, a little energy in her voice, as if she'd thrown off the sad flatness. 'I'll show you the dining room.'

There was another door at the back of the hall, almost under the stairs, beautifully carved with flowers and birds, all silvered with dust. Emma pushed against the blackened door plate, and it swung open.

The room was dominated by a large table with an oak top and what looked like more leaves tucked underneath. Five matching chairs were ranged along each side, and two carvers dominated the ends. More chairs sat in pairs either side of a mahogany sideboard with an ugly, dirty epergne – a cast centre-piece with arms that had spaces for serving dishes. Candelabras sat either side, all blackened and uncared for. Above, on the wall, were animal heads – a fox's mask and two deer with antlers – all staring blindly out over their heads. At one end of the table was a large picture of an old Victorian gentleman, with his hand on the charts in front of him.

'That's the captain,' Emma said, seeming to shiver. 'Our grandfather. I don't like that picture. That's his first wife.' She waved at the other end of the room, where a graceful Edwardian lady in her twenties or early thirties sat. If the paintings were done at the same time, they highlighted the forty-year age difference between them. 'And that's his second wife.'

'My grandmother,' Lily breathed. The woman had the same light hair, the same deep blue eyes as she had, although she looked taller and thinner. Her own mother had something of the captain's square chin and strong nose.

A successful seafarer, her grandfather had died before Lily was born. Her mother had always said he had no interest in his only daughter, born late in his life, only investing his energy in his sons by the earlier marriage.

'That's right,' Emma said.

The gloom was created by shutters, and when Emma folded them back the whole room came to life. Dark maroon walls, patterned carpet in the middle of a parquet floor, high windows overlooking the lawn at the back of the house. Lily walked over to it and peered out.

'The garden is lovely,' she murmured. 'Who does the lawn?'

'Mr May used to,' Emma replied, looking puzzled. 'Oh, I remember, he died after Christmas. Now the grass is getting too long. I'll have to get someone.'

It sounded like it had been learned by rote.

'We could probably do it,' Lily said, looking at Emma. 'Is there a lawnmower?'

'I could do it?' Emma looked confused for just a moment. 'I've seen him doing it. I used to help my dad. I suppose I could. If you show me?'

Lily smiled, looking around the room. 'It's so lovely in here, but I think we should look around the garden first, and see what we can do.'

Emma folded back the shutters. 'I don't come in here,' she admitted. 'I stay in the kitchen, mostly.'

'I would, too,' Lily said. She hesitated for a moment before adding: 'You know, I lost someone too. It's hard, isn't it?'

Emma's blank face started to move as she looked down. ''S hard,' she mumbled. She glanced up. 'Who did you lose?'

Tears immediately sprang into Lily's eyes, as they always did. 'My little girl, Grace.'

Emma bobbed her head, once, twice, as if coming to a conclusion. 'I'll show you the drawing room, then I could look for the lawnmower?'

Lily sniffed back the tears. 'Definitely.'

11

PRESENT DAY, 4 JUNE

There was a landline available in the pub, which was good as mobile signals were patchy, so Nicole walked down with her crutches in the evening. She was surprised how quickly her balance had improved, now she was walking more.

She ordered a local cider and left an answerphone message for Joshua McKay, explaining that she had seen five or six common dolphins, which she had identified from the size and markings. Reading the leaflet through, she was impressed by the information, telling visitors how to use their phone to capture images of washed-up creatures, including jellyfish (and which ones to avoid), fishing catches and general observations. The address was of an aquarium on St Brannock's island, only open by appointment.

Nicole walked back to the cottage then relaxed on the sofa without her prosthetic. Before she'd had time to get comfortable, someone banged on the door.

'Come in!' she shouted, but no one answered. The person pounded again. 'It's open!' she shouted. Someone pushed the door just as she leaned forward to see who it was.

'Auntie Nicole?' A mop of auburn curls and round blue

glasses appeared around the doorway, along with a big grin. 'Surprise!'

'Oh, Millie!' Nicole burst into tears, full of emotion. 'Why didn't you tell me you were coming?' She couldn't leap to her feet, but Millie threw herself down next to her and hugged her tightly.

'I did. You aren't answering your phone, though, so I just followed you down.'

Nicole laughed through the tears. 'I don't get any phone signal here. You should have emailed me or something.'

'Email?' Millie laughed back. 'Or I could just have posted you a letter written on vellum with a goose-feather pen. I'm here now – it was quicker just to travel.'

Nicole caught some inflection in Millie's voice. 'Have you finished all your exams?'

Millie shrugged and leaned back. 'Sort of. I wasn't going to pass maths anyway, so I left the last two papers. Honestly, I'm just saving someone giving me a fail.'

'Oh, Millie.' Lots of ideas crowded to her tongue, held back just in time. 'What do your mum and dad think?'

Millie stood up and started examining the tiny room. 'It's my life. I'm nearly eighteen.'

'But do they know you're here?'

Millie turned to glance at her, a little twist to her lips. 'I'm sure they'll work it out. Can I stay?'

Nicole thought about it. On the one hand, she'd love the company, but the last thing she needed was someone else to look after. Not to mention the fact that her sister would never forgive her for interfering.

'I don't know. Your mother might kill me if I say yes.'

'Just ask her. She can't wait to get me off to university and get rid of me.'

'Oh, Millie.' The girl had wandered out to the back room, and opened the squeaky back door.

'Oh, this is amazing! Have you been out here?'

'I have my breakfast there.' Nicole hopped through, realising as she got there that she had never let Millie see her without the prosthetic. Millie looked down, but didn't say anything. 'Look, I'll phone Claire and see what she says. OK?'

'Thanks, Auntie Nicole,' Millie said, subdued.

Nicole hopped to the doorway, then turned back. 'Can you drop the "auntie"? It makes me feel a hundred years old and we're both grown-ups.'

'Thank God,' Millie said, grinning and rolling her eyes. 'But I want to pay my way. Mum said this place was costing you a packet. I'll see if there are any jobs going.'

'I know they are advertising in the pub for waitresses and kitchen porters,' Nicole said. 'Let's go down there, and I'll call your parents. We'll see what they have to say.'

Claire was angry, mostly because she and Millie had had their first real screaming row, and the girl had packed up and fled in the night.

'She's an idiot, like all kids,' Nicole said, soothingly. 'We were just like that, too. Remember when we ran away just because Mum and Dad wouldn't let us go to Glastonbury Festival?'

'I do,' Claire said. 'How old were we – fourteen and sixteen?'

'About that.'

'We only got about five miles,' Claire reminisced, a bit of laughter creeping into the anger.

'Before we ran out of drinks and crisps,' Nicole said. 'At least Millie packed and travelled all this way by herself, and she has a plan to get a job to pay her rent.'

Claire sighed. 'Did she tell you she walked out of her exams?'

'She did.'

'She has three good offers to universities. She said she doesn't know what she wants to do. You always did, didn't you?'

It was hard to recall what she'd wanted to do before marine biology had caught her attention. 'Actually, I wanted to run a zoo and I was disappointed that zoology didn't lead straight to a job looking after tiger cubs.'

Claire laughed at that. 'If you don't mind having her, I think I could do with a bit of a break. But do let me know if it's too much for you, after all the...' She tailed off again. Claire hadn't been able to cope with the accident. Probably because Nicole hadn't been able to deal with it, either.

Nicole breathed in and tried to ride the wave of anxiety that came with the memory of the sound and pressure of the smash. She took another breath, aware of the silence stretching out on the phone.

'I'm doing fine,' she said carefully. 'I've even borrowed a mobility scooter. You know, the ones that run outside. It's like the oldest, least cool moped in the world but it works.'

'You said you were never going to use a wheelchair, ever.'

Nicole winced. 'I said some stupid things. Living here has really helped. It's made me realise I don't need sheltered housing in some little bungalow somewhere. It's just a leg.'

'Well, good. Just be careful not to overdo things, will you? It hasn't been that long.'

It occurred to Nicole that if she fell over and couldn't get up, now at least Millie would notice.

'I'm safe,' she said, smiling to herself.

It was a bit embarrassing to bump up the stairs on her backside, but Millie didn't say anything. The back bedroom was small with a single bed, just covered with a blanket. A door in the wall led to an airing cupboard, with sets of clean beddings and pillows.

'This will be lovely,' Millie said, sitting on the bed once they had made it up. 'Look, I'll be able to look out of the window at the garden.'

'It's nice,' Nicole said, leaning on the low window frame. A hoarse shriek made her laugh. 'But we have gull chicks on the roof. They are early risers.'

'You know me,' Millie said, pushing back her mop of reddish curls. 'I can sleep through anything.'

She looked pale and thin under her baggy top. Nicole remembered how worried Claire was, about how reclusive Millie had become.

'Are you really all right, Millie?' she asked.

She shrugged. 'You know. It felt like a roller coaster, applying for university, doing my mock exams, revising. There wasn't much me time, if you know what I mean.'

'I do,' Nicole said, looking at Millie. 'You were brilliant when I was in the hospital. You were the only person who didn't tell me what to do all the time.'

'Well, I'd had enough of it myself,' Millie said, half smiling. 'And I just thought you needed time. So coming here seemed like a great idea to me, whatever Mum says.'

'I love that you read *Winnie-the-Pooh* to me.' Nicole started to laugh. 'And did all the voices.'

'You used to do all the voices for *me*,' Millie said, in Eeyore's voice. 'Of course I did. That's how I hear them all now.' She hugged Nicole, without pushing her off balance. 'Now, come downstairs. How on earth do we order pizza on an island?'

12

JUNE 1941

Lily stretched her feet out on the small boat taking her back to St Brannock's. She had been charmed by Emma, by her straightforward honesty and practicality.

Once they had found the lawnmower, oiled and wrapped in sacking against damp and the winter cold, the two of them had worked out how to fill it up from a can of fuel, and start it. The blades had torn up some of the long grass but had chopped more, and the lawn looked a lot better. Emma knew enough to clean it afterwards, and Lily made sure it was turned off and wrapped back up in the shed.

There had been a few mishaps, and Emma had lost her temper when she tumbled over into a flower bed. Lily had been hit by some flying seedheads, filling her hair with sticky pods. But there had been some laughter, and Lily enjoyed the boat ride back. The driver, a young man, was smiling so much she asked him why.

'Well, maid, you've got oil on your face, and you must have wiped your muddy hands on your skirt.'

Lily stood up to look at the back of her dress. 'Oh, bother!' She laughed with him. 'I've been gardening.'

'So it seems,' he said, narrowing his eyes as he steered them around a stack of rocks. A flash of colour diving into the sea made her jump.

'What is that? Oh, look.'

He glanced over, raised his eyebrows. 'First kingfisher I seen this year. They's rare round here.'

She held onto her bag as they hit a rough patch around the end of the rocks. 'I've only seen them in rivers.' She leaned in as the boat leapt over one wave, then another. 'Do you know a chimney sweep? Maybe on St Brannock's?'

'Well, there's old Cornie Fisher, but he's retired now. His son was going to take over but he's in the navy. If you need one, I'd try Fred Elliott on St Piran's. You can send a message to him through the post office.'

'Thank you.' The water to the big island was calmer, and she loved the wind in her hair. She pulled off her hat and crammed it into her bag along with her discarded gloves. This didn't seem like a hats and gloves sort of place. Her mother would not approve.

'You visitin', then?'

'I'm staying with my cousin, Bernie Pederick.'

'Oh.' He looked away for a second. 'You lost your house in London, they says.'

'That's right.' She winced into the wind. 'I came here to get away from the bombing.'

'There been a few Jerry planes over,' he said, waving at another boat. 'They tried to bomb the radar station. Stands to reason. And the army got secret agents on the islands, too, going to France, regular. Your husband overseas? I saw the ring,' he explained.

'No, he's still in London. He's in a reserved occupation.' She wondered for how long. He'd been talking about enlisting in a front-line outfit, taking photographs behind the German lines or over occupied France. 'He works for the War Office.'

'Oh, that's good.' He slowed as he approached the main quay. 'I'm off next month. Navy, though, like my brother and my dad. I'm Davy Ellis, by the way.'

'Well, good luck to you.' A lump jumped into her throat at the thought of this young, vibrant man, not much more than a boy, being at war on the sea.

He smiled as he pulled alongside and held out a hand to her. As he passed her towards the stone quay, still grasping her fingers, she turned and kissed his cheek. 'Very good luck indeed, Davy.' She didn't understand why she had done it – she felt as confused as he looked – but then he grinned.

'Well I'll be lucky *now*,' he said, letting her go as he pushed the boat away.

Lily walked up from the quay, suddenly aching. She hadn't worked so hard physically for months, not since nursing Grace... Her mind cut off the thought, leaving her feeling hollow.

Bernie never locked the door, even overnight, so she was able to push it open and walk up the stairs. The boat driver was right; she needed a good wash. She could see a smear of oil in the mirror at the top of the stairs. Bernie called it the 'check' mirror, just to ensure she didn't have lipstick on her teeth or a curl out of place. Lily didn't worry any more – she had no reason to wear lipstick, and kept her hair tied up. Today, half of it had fallen down during the gardening, or had been blown by the wind on the crossing. As she tucked a strand behind her ear, she heard a sound. Standing still, she heard it again, a distinct sob, stifled deep in someone's chest, the way Lily had cried when she didn't want James to hear.

She pushed the door open, and Bernie swivelled in her chair away from Lily. The room was still light, although the evening was well advanced.

'Oh,' Bernice gulped. 'There you are. I wondered when you were coming home.' She blew her nose loudly. 'It's the pollen.'

'No, it isn't,' Lily said, walking into the room, feeling guilty now. She had acted as if only she had lost someone, as if she was the only one with sorrows. 'I stayed longer than I expected with Emma.'

That made Bernie turn around, tuck her handkerchief into her sleeve. 'Well, I'm glad she let you in.'

'It took her a little while to trust me,' Lily said, putting her bag down. 'Do you want to talk about it?'

Bernie flapped her hand. 'Oh, this? Just my nonsense. You know, Oliver. Anyway, I kept a sliver of ham and egg pie for you, and some salad. You must be famished.'

Lily could feel her stomach growling. 'I am tired. I mowed the lawn with Emma. It was quite a job, it had got so long.'

'Well, George died, you know, May's husband. She's struggled to go to the hotel as often, I've heard. She's a good woman but she must be nearly eighty. How is Emma?'

Lily sat at the tiny table, laid with a clean cloth over the top. Bernie whipped it off like a magician. The plate of tomato slices, radishes, lettuce and ham pie looked beautiful, a few pickles around the edge. A small bottle of salad cream was beside the salt, and a slice of bread and margarine on a side plate.

'This looks lovely,' Lily said, and Bernie managed a small smile.

'I had a letter from my sister,' she said, sitting opposite Lily. 'Go on, I've eaten mine. It was my own letter, it was returned. I don't know where she's got to.'

'Where would she go?' Lily could see Bernie was worried, her forehead uncharacteristically lined.

'She might be in hospital,' Bernie said slowly. 'She's been confined before. To an asylum, I mean.'

That made Lily jump, just the word asylum. 'Has she been taken ill in the past?'

'Well, Ollie disappearing made her worse, but yes, she's been in before. Melancholia of childbirth, they called it, the first time. And moral insanity, they said, because Ollie didn't have a father.' Bernie sighed. 'Oh, listen to me, of course he had a father, but she never said who it was. She was a bit free with her favours, if you know what I mean. It runs in the family, according to her doctor, as our mother wasn't properly wed.'

Lily didn't know how to answer that. She didn't want to sound like she was judging, but it was unusual, especially on the islands. 'I've not heard it called a disease before...'

'Well, she isn't the sharpest pencil in the box, but she's not stupid. She was like our mother, Bertha. *She* got pregnant with me, and the father put her up in her own cottage, down by the quay on Morwen Island. It was such a scandal; people weren't very kind at first, but they got used to her, especially when Cissie was born, and then it all stopped when he died. Then we moved here.'

'Who was he? Your father?'

Bernie looked at her as if she was stupid, then her frown cleared. 'Of course, no one would have told you. But your mother knows. My father was Captain Chancel, same as your mam's.'

Lily's heart skipped a beat. 'He was? I knew you and Mother were cousins, but I wasn't sure how. Did you know him at all?'

'He died when I was little, but he left my mother a bit of money. Enough to buy this flat, and the haberdashery shop below. They pay me a little rent.' Bernie stood up, filled the kettle. 'It's not easy being his natural child. People were sometimes harsh on Morwen but less so over here.'

'But it's not your fault. I can't see why anyone would blame the child.'

Bernie smiled down at her, her face twisted more with sadness than amusement. 'You're from a different generation, lovey. I couldn't get a job, no one would walk out with me unless they were hoping to get me in the bushes. People thought I was a lightskirt, like my mother, and like my sister.'

Lily watched her potter about the kitchen, warm the teapot, measure out the tea and the water so it wouldn't be too weak but wouldn't be wasted. 'Did you ever marry?'

'I got engaged once. In 1917, to a nice lad who worked in the Plymouth dock, an arc welder, he was. I was thought to have done very well for myself.'

'How did you meet him?'

Bernie sat down and swirled the tea around. 'Back then, there were a lot of girl welders, especially as most of the men were in France and beyond.' She poured the tea with a look of concentration. 'I was a good welder, although I got burned quite a bit. Vicious sparks.' She held out one hand, the back of which was covered with brown spots. 'He took a shine to me, and that was it. We spent many evenings together, went to a few concerts and dances, and he bought me a ring. We were just about to set a date when he was killed at sea.' She stared intensely into her cup, and Lily could feel her own throat grow tight. 'Back then, they took civilians along to continue repairs, even when sailing into combat. He was killed outright.'

'Oh, Bernie. I'm so sorry.'

'So then there weren't many men around. I came back to the island, started working to support my sister and her baby, and to help my mother out.'

Lily let the tears tickling her lashes fall. 'You must miss him terribly. What you could have had...'

'Well,' Bernie said, briskly, getting up and putting the dirty crockery on the draining board. 'Who knows if we would have been happy? I've had my friends, and I've thought about marrying again. And I'd have been grateful for a child...' She stalled and looked at Lily, stricken.

'It's fine,' Lily said, drying her cheeks. 'But you're right, your own child is the happiest thing, the greatest gift. Losing them doesn't take that away, does it? I'd rather have had Grace and lost her, than have never met her.'

Bernie nodded. 'That's how I feel about Oliver,' she said. 'I had him when Cissie was in hospital, from a tiny scrap, and for long periods afterwards; when she was ill they both stayed. And I'm so proud of him, giving everything for his country.' She shook her head as if to shake off the sadness. 'Now, Mr Toomey had some fresh pork in, so I got some sausages for tomorrow. We'll have toad in the hole.'

Lily stood up, put her arms out and hugged Bernie. 'Thank you,' she said.

Although she didn't really know why, she felt better.

13

PRESENT DAY, 5 JUNE

Nicole woke up after eight, which meant she must have got used to the raucous screams from the roof. Someone was banging on the door, and the idea of finding her dressing gown, putting on her sock and leg and stumbling downstairs was too much.

'Millie!' she called, but there was no answer from the back bedroom. 'Millie!' she bellowed, when the bang became more vigorous.

Muttering under her breath, she stuck her head out of the open window. A very tall man looked up, his hair and beard tawny brown and wavy, his skin tanned.

'I'm guessing you're *not* Millie?' He grinned then, and she realised she was wearing nothing more than a low-cut nightie and was showing too much cleavage. She comforted herself that the gulls got more of a view than he did.

'I am not. This is very early to be banging on a stranger's door, you know.'

'But we're not strangers.' There was something slightly familiar about him, but she couldn't place him. 'And you left a message on my answerphone just yesterday. Josh McKay. They told me where you were staying at the pub.'

'Oh! Josh.' She paused. 'I'll get dressed and come right down.'

'Why don't you invite me in and I'll make some tea? I have a questionnaire to complete. Some bureaucrat in London makes us fill in a form every time a bird craps on the quay.' His hand was already on the door.

I left it unlocked, again? Didn't Millie think to lock it last night, either?

'I suppose,' she grumbled. 'I like my tea strong. Milk's in the fridge.'

He opened the door and she hopped to the landing to find Millie's room in disarray, with half-open bags everywhere, but no Millie. A note on her pillow explained.

Insane birds woke me up, I have gone for a walk. See you later,
M xx

Nicole went back and put her prosthetic on, got dressed, dragged a brush through her hair and stood at the top of the stairs. She could walk down, holding on, but the motion would hurt her leg. She dropped down to scoot down on her bottom and, of course, he was standing where he could see her. He didn't comment.

'Where do you want your tea?' he asked, as she managed to stand up from the third step in one movement. His shoulders were so broad they almost touched each side of the doorframe. She smiled at the thought.

'How about the garden? It's a nice spot. Now, why did you bang on my door so early?'

He placed the cups on the table, set a chair for her then sat down. 'It was the only tide until this evening. I've only got an hour as it is.'

He was wearing cut-off shorts, which revealed very long, perfectly brown legs, and a T-shirt with tears in it. Shorts – more things she couldn't imagine wearing again. Some of her favourite dresses... Grief hit her in stinging little nips.

'Well, I'm up now. Ish. I assume you're from the wildlife rangers?'

'Ish.' He sipped the tea for a moment. 'My actual title is Head Ranger. I'm part of the team looking after the marine reserve, and I am the warden for Gannet Rock. It's an uninhabited islet, except for the birds, most of which are nesting right now.'

He had a local accent, and she remembered a silent young man, just as broodingly good-looking. A thin teenager, with bony, broad shoulders that he'd grown into. She had chided herself for staring at him while Nick was sat beside her, and because he was so much younger.

'Did you ever have a boat?'

'I've always had a boat. I used to drive some of the local boats for visitors when I was a teenager.'

'That's where I've seen you before!' It came to her then. 'I remembered your name as Joe.'

'Josh. Joshua to be precise. And you are Nicole. I remember you when you stayed on St Petroc's with your boyfriend. I remembered you, very glamorous.'

'I was doing my PhD thesis.'

'You did the fish research on blennies? It was in the papers. We had to stop visitors pulling them out of the cracks in the rockpools for years afterwards.'

'Sorry about that.' She sipped her tea. 'What do you need to talk about?'

He pulled out a messenger bag with a form and a notebook. 'You think you saw dolphins, and so I need to fill this in for the marine mammal conservancy council. Time and date, so I can work out the tide, weather, what you actually saw. Lots of people think they see dolphins but it's just wave formations, seals, a trick of the light.'

'I know dolphins when I see them.'

He smiled at the snarky tone in her voice. 'I suppose you do. Any impressions of numbers?'

'Five or six, maybe a juvenile but I only saw it once. Five the first view, six the second. Common dolphins for sure.'

He scribbled on the form, ticking boxes, writing notes. 'Where were they headed?'

'About north-west, from the corner of the island, in front of the hotel.'

'That's a perfect view. I know the hotel pretty well, used to see cetaceans all the time when I was a kid: porpoises, dolphins, even the occasional whale. Not so much now, though.'

Nicole carefully got to her feet and stumbled indoors for a packet of biscuits, returned and put them on the garden table. 'I'm having some of these for breakfast. Do you want one?'

'Thanks.' She watched him as he filled in the form some more, and bit down into a biscuit with strong, white teeth. They were a little crooked, his eyebrows were a little lopsided. He was pleasantly irregular, she decided. She remembered his very direct gaze back then, too.

'Are you studying me?' he asked, without looking up.

'Should I fill in a form?' she asked cheekily. 'I'm a scientist, I'm observant. I'm a bit surprised I didn't remember you, if you remembered me.'

'You were an unobtainable goddess,' he said, then finished the biscuit. 'You were what, early twenties? I was seventeen. I was mostly elbows and spots. I stared at you a lot.' He grinned up at her. 'You were beautiful, long red hair, flashing blue eyes. And you were all going to have brilliant careers and earn loads of money and come back to the island in your yachts.'

'No yachts,' she said, trying to keep her voice light. 'Just me trying to have a holiday on my own. And you grew out of the spots and your elbows seem in proportion.'

Am I flirting with him?

'Alone. Except for the mysterious Millie.'

'Except for my niece Millie, who has gone for a walk. She's run away from home for a few weeks.'

He looked around the garden, stood up, pointed out a sagging plant in the sunshine. 'Shall I...?' He picked up a watering can, half full, and sloshed some water over it.

'I forgot about the garden. I only had a small yard back home... I needed the parking.' For the two cars she could no longer drive, for manicured pots watered twice a week by the cleaner. 'Thank you. I'll keep an eye on it.'

Both gulls set up their donkey screeches from the roof. 'Oh, lucky!' he said, shielding his eyes and stepping to the back wall to try and catch a glimpse. 'They are black-backed gulls, not the herring gulls most people get.'

'I know that. Are they also louder?' She couldn't help a little acidity creeping into her voice. 'They start calling an hour before dawn. Sometimes they shout randomly in the middle of the night. And the back wall is covered with their droppings.'

'A few more weeks and the babies will fledge and there will be new black-backed gulls to stave off extinction. They're vulnerable already, forced out by habitat loss and competition from the herring gulls.'

'Well, I'm *so* glad to be doing my bit for an endangered species. I'll resist the urge to shoot them every dawn.'

He hesitated before taking another biscuit. 'Look, this might be a colossal dead end, but I've found something that may or may not be groundbreaking. My dad and I used to run the aquarium on the big island. It went bust over lockdown and he had already died, but about five years ago we were being brought creatures people found on the beach. One was a peculiar fish, probably a blenny. It was almost dead, but we managed to keep it alive for a few weeks before it keeled over.'

'OK...' Nicole said slowly, wondering what it had to do with her.

'Only, I've got it in the freezer, and I could do with an official ident.'

'Could you send me a picture?'

'I've tried that with the Natural History Museum, but it didn't photograph well.' He took a deep breath. 'The thing is, I think I've seen one before, when we were applying to become a Marine Conservation Zone.'

Nicole thought back to meetings about areas of restricted-fishing to increase biodiversity. The Atlantic Islands looked like they were going to lose their application for a full reserve.

'Describe the fish to me.' She didn't recognise it from the description. It was bigger than any British blenny she knew. 'Maybe it washed up from the Gulf Stream. You did say it was dying.'

'Yes, but I'm sure I've seen it before, when I was a kid, living at the hotel.' He leaned back in the chair.

'You lived at the hotel?'

'We lived in the cottage by the haunted house. Yes, that was my childhood home. My mother used to run it.' He smiled at her, deep creases around his eyes suggesting he smiled a lot. 'Look, I have to get back to my boat. Can I persuade you to come and have a look, see if it reminds you of anything? It might trigger my memory, too.'

She was overcome with something unfamiliar, shyness maybe. 'I don't get around much, my leg...'

'I can take you over on my boat, no problem. Any time, just let me know.'

'I'll talk it over with Millie...'

'Of course.' He stood and rummaged in his shorts pocket.

'My card. I check my mobile more often than the old aquarium number.'

'I'll see you out.'

He grinned as he walked down the hall ahead of her, while she limped behind him, concentrating on her steps. 'Making sure I've gone?'

Part of her didn't want him to go; it was nice to talk to someone new. 'You'll have to tell me about the haunted house when we meet again. I always thought it was abandoned.'

He stepped onto the cobbles outside. 'It was, for a while. Thanks for the sighting, it all adds to the application.'

Probably not. 'I'll be in touch.' She looked at the card. 'Mr McKay.'

'Seriously, Josh.' He smiled as he loped down the road, passing Millie on the other side, who smiled a hello then widened her eyes as she approached the door.

'Who's that? Bit of a fox, isn't he?'

'He's a wildlife warden,' Nicole said primly. 'Nice walk? I'll put the kettle on. Did anything happen?'

Millie fell against the hall wall, her hands clutched to her chest. 'Apart from me falling in love, you mean?'

'You've met Francesco, then.'

'I have a job interview at the pub,' she said, smiling at Nicole. 'And I talked to the most beautiful boy in the world.'

Nicole spent the afternoon distracting herself from speculating whether Josh was married by puzzling over his description of the fish. As a last resort, she opened up an old book on rockpools by a local author, Patience Ellis, kept in pride of place on the bookshelf. She had written about the usual suspects: blennies, butterfish and Cornish suckers, all small and diverse rockpool fish.

On the page devoted to blennies, one stood out as

completely alien to her. Having spent six months shadowing hundreds of small fish, it was odd to see something completely new. Based on the details Josh had given her and the sketch and measurements in Patience's book, she narrowed it down to two contenders. One was a Mediterranean fish that looked more like the description but would have been a long way from its home territory. The other was from the Bay of Biscay, not discovered as far north as the top of the Celtic Sea. Both would be ground-breaking, if only in the tiny world of rockpools. She checked her phone, but it had little reception, so she shouted upstairs to Millie.

'Do you fancy a meal up at the pub? I need a decent signal.'

'See Francesco again? Sure. And they have proper Wi-Fi.' The words drifted down. 'We need to get broadband here, or we'll go nuts.' Clattering on the stairs like rocks down a cliff, she appeared in the living room. 'I'm definitely up for dinner. But I'll pay. I've got a bit of money Mum sent me this afternoon, just until I get a job.'

Nicole smiled. 'She doesn't have much faith in your ability to get a job, does she?'

'I'll show her,' Millie said. 'Let's go out, then. What do you need to do so urgently?'

'I need to contact that ranger again. It's a marine biology question.'

'Right,' Millie said, folding her arms. 'It's a *science* question.'

'Purely professional.'

But Nicole's heart did race a bit at the thought.

14

JUNE 1941

Lily arranged to visit Emma again and to bring the chimney sweep with her. He had been reluctant at first.

'The place has a ghost in every chimney,' he had asserted. 'And that woman is known to be *strange*. She won't let anyone in.'

'She'll let me in,' Lily had reassured him, and promised him an extra few shillings for his visit.

She travelled over with him, with two slices of cake in a biscuit tin and some fresh milk. May had warned her the milk allowance didn't last very long without a refrigerator.

Emma did answer the door, but only after Lily shouted through the letter box. She ignored the sweep at first, but Lily introduced the two and led him to the kitchen.

'Ah,' he said, sniffing the air in the kitchen. 'You got a birds' nest in that chimney, I reckon. That will need getting out.'

'What about the baby birds?' Emma immediately said, looking at Lily with horror on her face.

'They's probably only jackdaws,' the man said, casually.

'Could you check first?' Lily said, not keen on harming a nest full of baby birds, even if they *were* jackdaws.

'You can get onto the roof from the attic,' Emma said.

He argued against it, scratched his head a few times as he looked at the roof from the garden, and finally agreed to at least have a look. Emma led the way to the attic, up the grand staircase, past painted doors, up a less grand straight staircase to the nurseries and servants' quarters, Lily guessed, and finally to a small door hidden away in the corner of a landing. It led to ladder-like steps.

'I don't go up to the attics,' Emma announced, leaving Lily and the sweep staring at each other.

'I ain't going up there on my own,' he said, shaking his head.

'Come on, Emma,' Lily said nervously. 'We'll all be together. What could happen?'

The attic steps led to a small landing with two doors. The smaller of them went through into a lumber room full of old furniture. Lily reached out a finger to touch a bed coverlet; it crumbled at her touch. A dormer window had three steps leading up to it, and Emma squeezed in close behind her. 'There,' she whispered.

'You'll have to watch me,' the sweep said, struggling to open the small window. It eventually shot up, and he leaned out to look up. 'You're right, maid,' he said. 'There's a flat roof here. You need to get it checked, though – the flashing looks rough.'

He slipped through and disappeared, Lily watching him. He stood on tiptoes and pulled out a handful of sticks. 'No birds, all gone,' he said cheerfully. 'You have a lovely view from up here, missus,' he said, turning slowly around. 'I'll get the worst of the nest out then pass a brush up. Did you know you got another, what, seven chimneys up here?'

Lily supposed there must be one for each main room. 'Come down safely, please, Mr Elliott.'

'It's Fred to you, missus,' he said.

He climbed back in and shut the window behind him.
'We'll have to check all the other rooms,' he said to Emma.

'No!' Emma started stammering. 'No. I-I just want the
kitchen one done.'

'Well, I came all this way. I'm going to charge you for the
whole house, we may as well do them all.'

Lily let him stomp back down the stairs and walked over to
Emma, lowering her voice. 'You don't have to. But are there any
rooms you might use, that you can let him do? Maybe that
lovely dining room? The fireplace there is magnificent.'

Emma nodded quickly. 'Yes, the dining room.'

Lily started guiding her towards the stairs. 'And you have
the front parlour at the front, you showed me that one. Does
that have a fireplace, too?'

Emma stepped down. 'Yes. Marble,' she said, out of breath.

'And what about the other door? The one on the corner?'

Emma shook her head. 'That's Daddy's study.'

Lily followed her all the way to the ground floor. Emma was
shaking so much, Lily sat her out of the way by the French
doors in the kitchen, and chatted to Fred. Once he had cleared
the obstruction and a sack of soot from the chimney, Emma
warily approached the stove. Once he moved on to the dining
room, she put a match to the paper scrunched up inside. It lit
quickly, a yellow glow lighting up her face as she smiled.

'You get the fire hot, and I'll check on the sweep,' Lily said,
making sure he had covered the old but beautiful rug in the
dining room and then directing him to the living room. She
pushed open the door and saw bookcases full of leather-bound
books. There were two sofas and chairs in several groups,
presumably laid out to entertain the hotel guests, already
protected by dust covers. In the front window embrasure was a
brass telescope, bolted to the wooden flooring and pointed out
to sea.

Lily returned to find Emma just putting a kettle on,

although it would be a few minutes before it heated up.

'Emma, I'm sure your father used to have his study chimney swept along with the others.'

Emma looked up and Lily could see emotions tracking across her face. 'I haven't been in there, not properly,' she admitted. 'Not since he died.'

Her words hurt Lily, like a blow to the chest. Grief, she could understand. 'You don't have to,' she said gently. 'Shall I get the tea tray ready?'

Emma didn't say yes or no, just stood as if frozen while Lily lifted down the tray and took down her usual cups.

'What cup will we use for Mr Elliott?' Lily asked.

Emma turned, and Lily could see the tear tracks down her face. 'Um. Grandma's cup,' she said, reaching for it and lifting it down. 'But it's a bit dusty.'

While Lily washed the cup and found a saucer, Emma watched her for a couple of minutes. Then she walked to the dresser and reached up for a small bunch of keys. 'Daddy *would* want his study done,' she announced.

Lily followed Emma back across the hall, Emma selected a key, and, with a lot of squeaking, the lock turned, and the door opened.

The room was small but charming. Being right on the corner of the building, it had one small window looking out the front and one to the side. Lily could see something at the edge of the garden, covered in ivy and other climbers but with a slate roof. A large desk took up a lot of room under the side window, and a small fireplace sat right in the corner.

The rest of the walls were lined with books – not the classic tomes of the parlour but popular books, children's books, atlases and bound periodicals. Mr Chancel had obviously had eclectic tastes, and he seemed to have shared the shelves with his wife's interests as well as his children's. A large armchair had at one time been upholstered in a tartan fabric, but it was now faded and worn. A small upright chair was beside it, and on the desk sat an old-fashioned wind-up gramophone, a selection of records stacked against it, and a desk lamp.

'I used to sit there,' Emma said, pointing at the floor in front of the armchair. 'We used to play music and Daddy would read to me. Sometimes, I read to him.'

Lily could tell no one had been in the room for ages. Beyond the charm and homeliness of the room, there were cobwebs everywhere, and layers of dirt.

'It's a lovely room,' she said with sincerity.

'I found him,' Emma said. She pointed at the armchair. 'He was there.'

The truth slowly dawned on Lily. 'Was he... taken ill in here?'

'He was dead,' Emma said. 'I thought he'd just fallen asleep; he used to have a nap in here in the afternoons, sometimes. Especially after Mother died.' She shuddered. 'I didn't know what to do. Daddy always said I shouldn't go out without telling him.'

'Of course.' Lily shivered at the thought of the frightened woman and her dead father. 'What did you do?'

'I waited,' Emma said. 'I didn't want to leave him, so I sat there, on the floor, where I always sat. May came in the morning, she helped me. It got dark, because Daddy always put the generator on if we needed the electric. He said never to do it without him.'

Lily shut her eyes at the thought of the lost, frightened Emma sitting beside her dead father all night. 'You poor dear,' was all she could say.

'Now I can sit in here again, if I want to,' Emma said, her voice gruff. 'When the sweep has finished. Maybe he's sweeping out the ghosts, like he said, from the chimneys.'

For a moment, Lily thought how wonderful it would be to be able to sweep the agony of grief away.

15

PRESENT DAY, 9 JUNE

A few days later, Nicole arranged to go and see the mystery fish with Josh. She had managed to do all her prescribed exercises after a long shower. She had unpacked the last bag and found clothes from the previous summer. There were shirts and cropped trousers, flowing skirts from a conference in Greece, summer dresses that she had collected from her holidays.

She was so self-conscious about her injuries that she had become resigned to living in layers from ankle to wrist. She broke her arm in the accident; it had needed surgery and the train tracks of stitches were still obvious. She sat on the edge of the bed, looking at the scar in the light. Her fear of it being visible was fading a little. She took some moisturiser off the dressing table and started rubbing it in down her hands, between her fingers, over both wrists. She could feel the raised nub where the healing bone had grown, a step where a metal plate held the bones together. Her collarbones were more prominent now, and it almost made her laugh. All that time counting diet points and exercising, when pain and fear had burned away any unwanted weight. She rather liked the new, sculptural shapes, even though her skin was pale. She continued rubbing the cream in, enjoying its familiar scent, quite different from the stuff she had used in hospital.

There had been months when she had accepted that no one was ever going to see her skin, ever again. But could she let anyone see her now?

You meet one attractive man and you're wondering about him seeing you naked? The idea made her smile, but also brought a lump of sadness to her throat. No, that part of her life was over. She looked at her wrist again. It was going to be a hot day, and with the long linen trousers she was wearing, she didn't want to be covered up completely. She looked through the tops, finding one with a straight neck – showing off those new collarbones and even a bit of cleavage – and decided to pair it with a cardigan until she was confident enough to show off her wonky arm. She laughed again at the thought that she was dressing for the ranger.

She was already too warm as she stood on the quay waiting for Josh, who was picking her up around eleven. The breeze along the quay was dying away as an open boat, scuffed and shabby, came alongside, the tanned ranger just as scruffy, just as attractive as he had been as a teenager. She looked at the drop from the sloping slipway and shook her head. The knee on her injured leg wobbled as she tensed her muscles, grasping the top of the railings.

'I can't,' she said, her voice coming out squeakily and involuntarily. 'You'll have to move the boat round.'

'It will be fine, trust me.'

She stared at his hands, held out to her. They were brown, long, the fingers knobbly and rough. They looked huge in her panicked state.

'I'm sorry, this is difficult—'

He waved his fingers again. 'I promise you won't fall.'

She let her hand drop into his, its warmth making her realise how the anxiety had made her shivery, even in the sun.

By the time she had clasped the other one, her weight was carrying her forward. The prosthetic made her feel like she was stepping into space, no solid surface. She shut her eyes and let momentum carry her down to the boat, feeling the resistance as he swung her around to a bench to sit down. She opened her eyes.

The boat smelled delightful. There was the faint odour of paint where the sun was beating down on it, under layers of old salt, crystalline and shimmering on every surface. The scent of fuel from the outboard behind her was familiar, and there were a few scales and the salty tang of fish, too.

He clambered in to take up a position behind her, and cast off the rope holding the boat to the slipway. It reversed out as she grasped the side for balance. It was wonderful. She'd forgotten the little dinghies they had taken over those summers when she was doing her research, the sensation of water parting either side of the bows, bubbling up, the texture of small waves under the keel. She took a deep breath, then another one.

'Better?'

'Thank you,' she said, smiling. 'I love boats.'

'I hope you don't mind, I have to pick up some samples from the hut on Gannet Rock.' The name was familiar; she remembered one of the neighbouring islands had an uninhabited islet, adjoined by a rough causeway.

'I thought no one lived there?'

'No one does, properly, but I stay on it during the breeding season. It would only take one idiot walking his dog over the causeway to disrupt hundreds of nests. I monitor and do bird counts as well.'

After she started her recovery, Nicole had dreamed about being on an isolated island. She craved a place where she could just be, and no one would see her, where she wouldn't have to be grateful or make an effort or care about anyone else.

When she'd come around from an induced coma, everyone

was so emotional. Parents, sister, friends, colleagues, all crying or sending her stuff or making well-meaning but useless suggestions. She was tired of being nice and smiling to make other people feel better. In the two weeks she'd been living at the cottage, all her smiles had been genuine, and she'd already laughed more than she had for months.

'It sounds lovely,' she said, but she already knew she wouldn't swap it for getting to know her new neighbours and friends better, spending time with a grown-up Millie.

'If you don't mind living off-grid with a composting toilet and the stink of bird poo every day, it would be. The tinned food gets a bit monotonous, though.'

'So, how can you be away at all?'

'High tide. The landing places are all fenced and locked, it's just the causeway that's a problem and that's only uncovered at low tides.'

'What about boats?'

'I had a couple of teenagers try to land an inflatable last month, and a few boats make an attempt. The pilots and harbourmaster usually give me a heads up if someone's likely to ignore the gazillion signs and warnings. It should be OK for a couple of hours.'

He pushed the engine more, the boat responding easily, pulling up at the bows as it surged towards the northernmost point of St Petroc's. She knew Gannet Rock well, and had often wondered about walking across the causeway. There had only been a safety warning then, no one took care of precious seabirds as they did now. She trailed one hand in the water, causing little ripples and whirlpools that were soon sucked away behind the boat. Even on the water, the sun had a lot of heat in it, she was too hot. It took a couple of minutes for her to take off her thin cardigan, tie it around her waist with one dry and one wet hand, the water a shock on her warm skin. She tucked her sunglasses more securely on her nose and leaned back a little, staring at the perfect sky. The blue was different over the islands – she remembered that from her twenties – reflected off the vast Atlantic Ocean, which barely paused at the island archipelago.

Josh started to turn the boat a little. She could see the gap between the island and its smaller twin, the water shadowed green over the causeway. He slowed, took the boat past the end of the rocky pathway – just a cleared way through the seabed, really – where a high fence and gate now stopped casual visitors. Beyond, just out of sight from Morwen, was a rocky landing platform and some bollards to tie up to. He threw Nicole a rope, and without question, she leaned forward and looped it over to secure it as he eased the boat into reverse. It pulled up perfectly, with hardly a nudge on its multicoloured fenders.

'You remembered,' he said, and when she glanced over her shoulder, he was laughing. 'I taught you to do that, when you were just a city kid.'

'You probably did,' she said, suddenly self-conscious about being alone with him. Just him and about a million seabirds. At her words, hundreds lifted off the cliffs, screaming and screeching in different tones.

He stepped onto the stone platform, put both hands out to support her, and boosted her up to shore. She was very close to him; his physical presence was powerful, partly from his height and broad shoulders, but there was something beyond that, too.

'How tall *are* you?' she asked, almost annoyed. Before, she'd always loved being one of the tallest people in a room, although some of that was down to the heels she used to wear.

'Tall enough,' he said. 'These steps are rough – do you want to wait or come up?'

'I want to see this luxury villa with sea views,' she said, grasping the safety railing someone had put up. It was rusted, and she just hoped she could wash her hands at the top.

Step – pull – lean onto the foot until you feel the balance – pull up the artificial foot. Repeat.

She looked up to see if he was watching her struggle up the steps, but he had gone ahead and was almost at the top.

'Coffee? Tea?' he called back to her as she followed slowly. *If I had known there were a hundred steps, I would have waited.*

'Tea!' she shouted back. At least the birds had mostly settled back onto their nests and were now grumbling and calling to each other.

As she walked up she smelled fish and guano. The shack – he hadn't been overselling it: it looked like it had been rescued from someone's allotment – was tucked against the cliff, half under a metal staircase. The middle door was open, a window each side pushed out, and a veranda shaded the whole thing. Josh walked out with a blanket, gave it a quick shake and put it back indoors. When she walked in, breathing hard from the effort, she saw he had draped it over a tired garden recliner, and had a stool pushed up to a narrow desk shelf under one of the windows. On it were notebooks, two pairs of binoculars and a loudhailer.

'Where do the steps go?' she asked, sitting in the chair with a sigh of relief. 'Overhead, I mean.'

'Up to what everyone calls the new lighthouse. The old one on Morwen fell down a hundred and fifty years ago – they used the stone to build the hotel. This one was manned up to seventy, eighty years ago, then automated.'

'Is the building still intact?'

'Sort of. The birds got in about thirty years ago. There is a pair of peregrine falcons nesting up there this year. We are hoping, of course, to eventually get sea eagles.'

'Do the falcons take a lot of the chicks?'

He shrugged. The camping stove he had lit was hissing under an old kettle. 'The ravens take more. It's a balance. We always have a percentage of chicks that are excess to requirement for that species, that become essential for others.' His legs were bare, and he had slipped his sandals off by the door. He had heavily muscled calves, and his feet were as big and bony as his hands. 'There you go. Fresh milk in the cooler.'

She put milk in both cups when he nodded. He sat on the tall chair, looking out of the door at the sea. The steps lifted the hut a long way above sea level but in winter storms...

'Does it flood up here?' She sat in the recliner, cradling the old mug.

'Sometimes. Not much. Most of the waves break on the corner, on the other side of the bluff. We have to do repair work when we come back each spring. It's amazing to be here in a storm, though.' He leaned forward and pointed back at the far northern corner of Morwen, over the sea. 'The hotel.'

'Where you used to live. How? I thought it was abandoned.'

'I grew up in the old cottage next to Chancel Hall, which had been divided into holiday flats – Mum and Dad used to work there. Dolphin Cottage was the original Chancel House. My grandmother inherited it. But the hall was built by the old captain. He was a bit of bluebeard character; he has a very imposing mausoleum in the churchyard.'

'I might look it up. I stayed in one of the flats, when I was studying here. My boyfriend at the time was convinced it was haunted.'

'We had the house to ourselves out of season, and I had loads of kids to play with in the summer.'

'What an amazing place to live.'

'Not to my dad. He left when I was about twelve. He inherited the aquarium from his grandmother, went over there to run it and gradually spent more time there. One day, he just said he wasn't coming home.'

Nicole stretched her legs out. She still hadn't worked out how to cross her ankles. 'That must have been hard.' Her own parents were so together they sometimes finished each other's sentences and bought colour-matched clothes. Or maybe that was just because her mother shopped for both of them.

'It was. Especially when the flats were condemned and closed up. Mum and I lived in the cottage with my grandmother, after Grandpa died. It was hard for a while, until I was old enough to help in the ice cream shack, work on the boats.'

'That's where I met you.' The moment she said it she felt awkward, like it was a romantic statement. 'Just a lanky kid hopping from island to island,' she said, keeping her voice light. 'What was it like, living next to the haunted house?'

'Where we first met,' he said, grinning at her. 'The big house always felt creepy. Mum had to go up when kids broke in to explore, but she usually had me to back her up. It was an old house with lots of stories.'

She finished her tea and stood up, bracing herself on the doorframe. The shack, although filled with sparkling windows and a terrace covered with wildflowers, still had a powerful, masculine presence. 'You were collecting something?'

'These,' he said, sweeping a package off the desk, ready for the post. 'I forgot it this morning. Samples from the puffins.'

'Do you sleep here?' she said, looking around. A single bunk with a cushion ran along the wall, squeezed behind the chair.

'I do.' He shut the door behind him and locked it.

'That's the first time I've seen someone lock a door since I came back to the islands.'

'Well, the equipment isn't mine.'

He started down the steps again. Walking down was slower for her, but he didn't seem to mind or comment on it, just waited for her about ten steps down.

'Where do you live, when you're not here?' she puffed, out of breath again.

'On St Brannock's, over the aquarium. I'll show you, if you like.'

16

JULY 1941

The envelope for Bernie came in the afternoon, the island post being reduced to once a day when the ferries were running. Lily propped it up against the salt pot and went back to making pastry for a bacon and egg flan that was the result of one of Bernie's friends having an excess of eggs from her hens. She wondered about Emma, sitting alone in the huge house, haunted by her past. She was trying not to worry too much about what was going on with her husband; she had attempted to telephone several times but he was never at home.

The work on the books was going very well; more books had arrived looking battered and sad, wrapped in layers of tissue then padded with newspapers. Lily brought the papers home to read – they were only a week old. She was just reading about the lawns at the Royal Hospital Chelsea producing boxes of fresh strawberries, when Bernie came in.

'Are those Freda's eggs?' she asked, hanging up her jacket. 'Oh, my feet are *killing* me. I was up and down the ladders all day at the hardware shop. Why does he put the most popular paints up high?' She sat and noticed the single letter. 'Oh. Another one from Cissie.'

She opened it, and Lily stopped rolling pastry as Bernie froze, making a choking sound.

'Bernie?'

Another choke, then a sob, and she held out the paper with a shaking hand. Lily took it. Inside a scribbled note was a folded telegram. Lily scanned it quickly.

PILOT OFFICER OLIVER PEDERICK REPORTED RECOVERED ALIVE BUT INJURED IN FRANCE STOP ADMITTED TO ST MARYS HOSPITAL, EAST-BOURNE, SUSSEX STOP LETTER TO FOLLOW STOP CHIEF MEDICAL OFFICER UNDER SECRE-TARY OF STATE STOP

'Ollie's alive? Oh, Bernie, I'm so happy for you.' She quickly read the accompanying letter. 'Your sister says he's on the burns unit, but is doing well. She's not able to visit...' She turned the paper over. 'But she wants you to telephone the hospital to see how he is. The matron on her ward spoke to his doctor and said he is likely to make a good recovery. Oh Bernie, that's the *best* news!'

She put the letter down and hugged Bernie, who was slumped down in her chair, hands clamped to her face. After another minute, Bernie leaned forward, took a proffered hand-kerchief from Lily and stood up, shaking.

'My poor boy,' Bernie said in a trembling voice. 'And look, this telegram is dated from four days ago. It should have been sent here... I've been more of a mother to that boy than anyone.'

'But the most important thing is that he's alive.' Lily put her hands on Bernie's shoulders and shook her a little. 'We'll send a message to him straight away, then we'll go and see him tomorrow.'

'We're both working tomorrow,' Bernie said, looking dazed.

'We'll try Saturday. I'm going to lie down while you make tea. I'm sorry, I feel a bit...'

Lily guided her to her bedroom and watched as Bernie shut the door. As she returned to lining the flan tin, she could hear the sound of her cousin's sobbing. Glancing at her own open bedroom door, she remembered that it was once Oliver's room. *And it will be again, one day.* Pushing aside thoughts of where she was going to stay, she trimmed the top off the pastry with a knife.

17

PRESENT DAY, 9 JUNE

After the twenty-minute boat ride to St Brannock's, Nicole and Josh arrived at the aquarium. The building looked like a Victorian warehouse, with several doors filled in with obscure glass. The windows were all decorated with decals of the animals within: rays, eels, jellyfish and an octopus. They looked shabby and some were starting to peel off.

Josh unlocked the door and held it for her to limp past with her stick. Inside, the floor was unexpectedly tiled with old mosaics, depicting all kinds of sea creatures and waving weeds. She could identify a few at a glance.

'This is amazing,' she whispered.

'The floor was laid by the first owner, Dorothea Fremantle. She did it herself. This is one of the earliest Victorian aquaria, quite amazing. She used to go down to the quay when the fishing boats came in, to buy specimens. She was quite a famous illustrator; her father wrote natural history books.'

On the wall were laminated information boards, the first one with a picture of a heavyset young woman in her thirties, frozen in an old sepia photograph. Beside it were drawings of strange, microscopic organisms, some of which she recognised. 'That's wonderful. Is she an ancestor of yours?'

'Sort of,' he said. 'She never married, but her partner left it to a nephew, and it came down to my dad. That was her partner, Ursula. She was a character, too.' A smaller picture was at the other end of the display, of a woman in a fisherman's smock, wearing round glasses. 'She was a proper islander.' He grinned at her. 'Dorothea had grown up in the real world. The locals were pretty bigoted at first, two ladies living together. Ursula used to wear trousers a lot, except for church.'

'That was life in Victorian England,' Nicole said, squinting at the information in the low light. 'Do you still have any display tanks?'

'They're through here,' he said, pushing a one-way gate the wrong way. 'We have a few exhibit animals. They're too old to go back to nature and I'm hoping other aquaria will take them. But they already have really old, grandpa lobsters. This is ours, the Major.' The animal had a bristling moustache, and scuttled forward when it saw them. 'I'll get him some food, or he'll move all his rocks around.' He disappeared through a door and came back with some frozen slipper limpets, still in their shoe-like shells. 'These are good – he has to work at them.'

Sure enough, the lobster grabbed the first shell and started delicately picking out the meat, transferring it to his mouth.

'Come into the office,' he said, leading her further through the aquarium. Most of the tanks were quiet and empty, but half a dozen had lights and filters on. Columns of bubbles aerated the water for a group of fish and a whole reef of different-coloured anemones and a fat starfish. The largest tank, right at the end, was filled with nooks and crevices made of coral and rocks, but it wasn't until Josh put his hand on the glass that a tentacle crept out and touched the glass on the other side. 'Hi, Harry,' he said, affectionately.

Nicole could see it was a large octopus. Large meant old,

octopi were short-lived at best. An eye peered through a hole in the coral and swivelled it around.

'I'll come back and give you a cuddle when I'm finished,' he said to the creature.

'He needs a cuddle?'

'He likes one,' Josh said, looking over his shoulder as the lights went on in a windowless office. 'Hey, don't judge. We all have different tastes in pets.'

She laughed as the octopus slid out, gliding over the edges of the corals. She put her fingers on the glass and he patted them gently. A drift of orange spots flowed over his skin, then flashed white, gold, white. 'I think he likes me.' It never got old, the magic of interacting with a wild animal.

'I think he does,' Josh grinned. He opened the freezer and dropped some frozen prawns into the octopus's aquarium. Harry grabbed each one with a different tentacle. 'It's here somewhere...' he said, rummaging again in the freezer.

He quickly located a sealed plastic bag with the frozen specimen in. With its belly distended and the fins flat against its flanks, it was hard to see what it was. 'Can you weigh it?' she said, suddenly in scientist mode.

Josh put the whole thing on some electronic scales and turned them on. It beeped. 'Eighty-eight grams,' he said. He looked around and pulled a ruler out of a pen pot. 'One hundred and eighty millimetres.'

'Big for a blenny,' she said, leaning forward. It was starting to defrost, even in a few seconds, and there was an unpleasant smell. 'How fresh was it when you froze it?'

'I found it dead, floating on the top of the tank, so not fresh.' He opened up a battered-looking laptop, switched it on. 'I did get some pictures in life, but it was pretty sorry for itself, fins all folded in and sat on the bottom.' He brought up a few close-ups, all taken through the glass of the tank. 'Sorry they aren't better.'

She compared the pictures and the malodorous body with

images stored on her phone. 'These are the best two contenders I could find,' she said, showing him.

He picked out the one from Biscay. 'That one, no – I think it's too heavy, the head's too deep. But that one, that's pretty close. What do you think, random occasional migrants, washed up in storms?'

'Probably. But then there was a similar picture in a rockpool book, by a local author.'

'Patience Ellis? We grew up on that book, it's what got me into marine life. She was my teacher when I started school, oh, a hundred years ago.'

'Well, she didn't mention that it was rare or unusual, and I think she would have if it was just a few washed up after a storm.'

He nodded. 'If we could work out where she saw it, we could go and look.'

Nicole had one of her stomach-dropping moments of remembering she had been crushed in a car accident. 'I'm not sure... rockpools are on beaches...' she stammered. *I can't walk on sand.*

'I get it, you're a bit slow on uneven surfaces. I'll look after you. You can sit on the dunes, if you like, and I'll bring stuff up for you to identify.'

The awkwardness drained away. 'Not bloody likely,' she said, with unexpected emphasis. 'I might just need... help.'

'So, I'll help you.'

She looked over at him. He was big, solid, and looked strong. Help. The word she had hated and railed against. 'I probably won't need it. Sorry, silly wobble. I'll think about it.'

'Wobbles are OK,' he said, with that lazy smile again. 'I'm around when the tides are right. You could pack something to eat, I'll bring nets and buckets.'

'All right.'

It felt like the strangest date she'd ever been asked on.

.   .   .

When Josh dropped her back at Morwen, Nicole was exhausted but refused a hand up the cobbles. Instead, she managed to limp into the pub and sit down for a cool drink.

'Hi, there,' someone called across the pub. 'Can I bring you anything?'

'Just some sparkling water and lots of ice, please,' she replied.

'Millie's here, if you want to say hello,' he said as he walked away.

'What? Already?'

He leaned into the kitchen, called her name, and Millie bounced out of the swing doors.

'I got the job!' she cried unnecessarily. 'I'm just doing a bit of training. And I'll get paid!'

'That's how it works. What will you be doing?'

'Kitchen porter. I have to go, I'm learning how to work the dishwasher. It takes like four minutes. We should get one,' she called over her shoulder as she disappeared back into the kitchen.

Nicole sipped her drink, letting herself feel the pain. She had walked on so many cobbles and slopes today, let alone all those steps. Her leg hurt – not raw, but aching. Of course, she'd had several months of being confined to bed or sitting in chairs, so both legs had lost muscle tone. Her busy day had turned into a workout.

And Josh hadn't stared at her arm. He had stared and smiled into her eyes a few times, which was nice. He was nice. He was nothing like any man she had ever been attracted to, before relationships became impossible.

18

JUNE 1941

The journey, on Saturday, was much longer than Lily had expected. Train timetables were changed at a moment's notice to accommodate troop movements, and she and Bernie were crammed into a third-class carriage with a group of soldiers who looked barely twenty. An older lady travelling alone was glad to be sitting with them when the overexcited men started singing. Lily divined from their conversation that they were new recruits about to go to the front. The idea was heartbreaking; she had seen enough sombre, quiet soldiers return from the front.

Bernie was more subdued than usual, lost in fears of what she was going to see of a young man invalided with burns. Lily had managed to send a telegram to James, to tell him she would be on the south coast, in case they could meet up. The moment she sent it she felt awkward, unsure she was ready to see him. Snippets of their last argument came back to her. *You never loved her like I did, you don't understand. I wanted to die when she died!* Words that she had meant at the time, but also were intended to hurt him. And his replies. *You're hysterical. Grace needed one of us to be strong, you were lucky to have so much time with her.*

She hadn't had a reply by the time they had left the island. They packed their bags and booked the ferry. The outside world at Penzance seemed very full of people with blank faces, grey clothes, and hats pulled down against the summer rain.

The Cornish Riviera Express had been rerouted through Bristol, and then on towards London. Lily knew there was a fast train to Brighton, then the local service to Eastbourne. She had booked a room in a women's hostel close to the hospital, and the warden knew they would be arriving very late. Since Bernie was like a rudderless boat, Lily had packed sausage rolls and the leftover pie, as well as a chunk of apple cake they had been saving for the weekend. A flask of tea and a bottle of water would have to suffice for the journey, and they might get refreshments at the stations when they changed trains.

Ten hours later, exhausted, her clothes crumpled and her hair full of smoke smuts, Lily dragged their cases off the last train into the blackout.

'Oh.' She stood beside Bernie, lost for a moment, feeling her heartbeat speed up.

'Lily.' A voice came out of the gloom. The train swept past, briefly illuminating a face, the glow from its firebox painting everything red. Her heart felt like it jumped into her throat; she had to swallow before she could speak.

'James.'

There didn't seem anything else to say, except to turn to Bernie, who was leaning on the railings outside the station. James stepped forward, but Lily's pulse was hammering hard in her ears. She was warmed by an instant rush of love for him, and something else she couldn't name.

'This is my cousin, Miss Pederick. My husband, James, Bernie.'

'How do you do?' He reached out to shake Bernie's hand in the gloom. 'I've booked a room for us at the Royal, Lily.'

'Oh. We've booked a room at a hostel in Burton Road. I suppose we'll have to get a cab.'

'I thought you might like to stay at the Royal so we can talk.'

Lily turned to look at Bernie, just making out her features. 'I couldn't possibly leave Bernie in a strange place,' she said quietly. 'We can talk tomorrow, if you like. We're off to see Oliver at the hospital; we have special permission to visit outside the normal hours.'

Lily heard rather than saw him turn back to Bernie. 'I was so glad to hear he was brought back to England.'

'Thank you.' Bernie seemed subdued.

'I would be happy to drive you. I'll just consult with the stationmaster as to the route to Burton Road.' His voice was growing cold and mechanical.

Bernie hugged Lily's arm. 'That's so kind, but we don't want to put you out.'

'We won't,' Lily said as he walked into the station. 'If he came down to speak to me, it will give him a few minutes to do so. And you heard – he's staying nearby.'

'You should stay with him, Lily. You are his wife, after all.'

Lily shivered at the thought. She wasn't ready to talk to him, listen to his anger, let alone sleep in his bed. 'No, I'm staying with you, in the Land Army hostel. They have a room with two beds, very convenient, and just a short walk to see Oliver.'

'Thank you,' Bernie breathed as James returned.

The short drive was negotiated slowly as the dimmed and masked headlights picked out just the edges of the road, parked cars and the odd pedestrian. Lily had conceded to sitting next to James, while Bernie sat with their bags in the rear.

'Are you well? You look well, from what I can see,' James said, as if trying to lighten the mood.

'I am. Living with Bernie is a breath of fresh air, and apart from the air raid drills we haven't worried about German planes.'

'Don't get too complacent,' he warned her. 'Falmouth has had several bombs, and there have been attacks all along Cornish coasts, and people killed in Penzance.'

It still seemed so small compared to the devastation in London. 'I was wondering if you knew anything more about Oliver's mysterious reappearance?'

He leaned his head a little more towards the back seat. 'Actually, I have done a little research, but he will be able to tell you more himself. I think the aircraft he was in was shot down two miles off the French coast. It was assumed by other planes in the squadron that there was little chance of survivors, but two were rescued by French fishermen, one of whom died in their care. How Oliver came back to Britain is classified, but I assume the Resistance looked after him for some time. The Special Operations Executive are constantly taking airmen and agents across the Channel.'

'Do you know about his injuries?' Bernie's wavering voice came from the back seat.

'I don't, but St Mary's is a hospital specialising in burns. He will be having the very best of care.' His voice was warmer, kinder, more like the James Lily knew.

Lily spoke up. 'When I telephoned them, they said as much. That he was recovering well from his injuries, which included some burns. We're prepared, aren't we, Bernie?'

'He was such a beautiful child,' was all Bernie could whisper.

'Well, now he is a war hero,' James added. The dull head-light beam ran across the street sign as he turned the car. 'I assume it's up here somewhere.' He pulled into the pavement. 'I'll come with you, carry the bags.'

'You don't need to,' Lily said, suddenly breathless. But she wanted him to, she wanted to spark some reaction from him.

'I'd like to.' There didn't seem to be anything to add to that.

There was a warden on duty, who took one look at Bernie's exhausted face and ushered them in. 'The gentleman can't stay, I'm afraid,' she said, frowning.

'Of course. My husband has just dropped us off.' Lily turned to him. 'Thank you, James. We have a special appointment to see Oliver at eleven. Would you be able to meet me after that? Perhaps we can go for tea and a talk.'

'Thank you,' James said, and then did an odd little bow to the other women, then stepped forward to peck Lily's cheek. 'Goodnight,' he said, vanishing back into the dark.

Lily's throat burned with all the things she wanted and needed to say. *Are you still angry with me? Do you still love me, James?*

19

PRESENT DAY, 10 JUNE

The following day there was a light drizzle, and Millie wasn't working her first shift until the afternoon.

'Do you fancy walking around the village?' Nicole asked. 'I need some gentle exercise.'

Millie rolled her eyes from her recumbent position on the sofa. 'It's not exactly a long walk.' Nicole waited until Millie realised she was serious. 'Oh. OK, then,' Millie conceded. 'Maybe I'll get some signal on the quay.' Her smile bounced back. 'We need Wi-Fi here.'

'I'm on it,' Nicole said. After the first few days of checking her phone for social media, emails, messages, calls, the habit had trailed off and she was rather enjoying the silence. No more 'But how are you *really*?' messages, or 'If there's anything I can do...'

Millie disappeared upstairs in several, ceiling-shaking bounds.

'Can you bring my jacket down?' Nicole called after her, looking out of the window.

Millie's voice floated down to her. 'The rain's stopping. You're more likely to need sunglasses.'

'Well, bring them both,' Nicole yelled back, making sure her feet were level, both shoes on properly. Millie bounded downstairs just as loudly as she had bounded up. 'It's like having a Labrador,' Nicole said, laughing, but it was lovely to see the healthy energy return to Millie. Before her A level exams, she had been closed down, totally listless.

'So, where do you want to go?'

Nicole looked across the road. 'I wanted to have a look around the graveyard – do you mind? I had this weird experience here when I was young, before you were even born, and I just wanted to check something out. I want to see Captain Chancel's grave.'

Millie and Nicole walked slowly around the graveyard, so close to the house that they could see the cottage's bedroom window. The gravestones were either carved in the local pink or grey granite, or in a metamorphosed sandstone, which Nicole vaguely remembered was called killas. The carving lasted better on the granite, and she was drawn to a huge mausoleum crafted out of what looked like imported limestone. An expensive import, especially if everything came by ship.

CAPTAIN STEADFAST WILLIAM CHANCEL.
LATE OF MONTEGO BAY, JAMAICA, AND CHANCEL HALL,
MORWEN.
BORN 4TH DAY OF JANUARY 1831 AND DIED 15TH OF
FEBRUARY 1910

She bent to read the smaller writing underneath.

AND HIS GRANDDAUGHTER, CHARLOTTE, DIED 1919 AGED
SEVENTEEN YEARS.

'Wow. Steadfast, great name,' Millie said, wiping moss off the front of the stone. A statue loomed over the grave: a huge wave with a wide ship powering through it. 'Poor girl, though, only seventeen. I wonder what she died of?'

Nicole leaned against the mausoleum. 'I heard stories about the captain when I was a student here. We stayed in his house, although it was called Sunshine Apartments then, or something equally predictable. But it had Chancel Hall carved over the front door.'

Millie perched on an adjoining grave, which seemed a bit disrespectful. 'So, what was his story? Old Captain Steadfast?'

Nicole sat down next to her, sighing with relief. 'I don't really know, except that the house is supposed to be haunted. I remember it rained really heavily, a proper summer storm, lightning and everything. Nick and I were up half the night and then water started dripping through a crack in the ceiling. There was this sound, a horrible banging noise in the loft. When the sun came up, we went to look. We had to go through a little door, only about *so* high, up the stairs. Then we got into the sea captain's study in the attic.'

She remembered the moment she had prised the lock off the wormy and broken door, and crept onto the stairs, testing each one as it creaked, in case it wouldn't take her weight. At the top was a bigger door, one of two, ornately carved and covered in cobwebs silvered with dust. She'd reached for the tarnished brass handle, shaped like a dolphin.

It had squeaked open, and for a moment Nicole imagined the room was clean and new, the dawn light gleaming off a large brass telescope and giving a golden light to the room. She soon realised the room was under a film of grey powder. The windows were set into the roof in a line of three dormers, bringing light to all corners of the narrow room.

A few rugs, beautiful woven strips of faded reds and blues, snaked down the dark floorboards, perhaps oak. Beside the desk was the telescope, three sturdy legs, also in brass, ending in ornate lions' feet which were bolted to the floor. She had turned to a window and stared through.

Through the film of dirt Nicole had seen the Sound laid out in sparkling green in front of her, blued by the sky overhead, and the islands dotted about. A single ship, just a splash of burgundy in the distance, had drifted towards St Brannock's as the captain's ships must have done a century before.

Nick and Nicole had tiptoed past a table covered with papers – old charts, she realised, bleached cream. Then, in the corner, was a screen and a chamber pot on the floor. Even if the captain had indoor plumbing, it wouldn't have reached up here. A yellowed and brittle scrap of newspaper abandoned on a desk could have been a hundred years old.

One of the windows was cracked; a small corner triangle had fallen onto the floor, letting the rain in. She had slotted it back into place, wedging it into the swollen frame.

Beside the desk was an old chair; it had squeaky castors and swivelled in her hands.

Nick had reached forward and pointed at the floor. He'd said something like 'There's the ghost.'

A dead pigeon, that had obviously squeezed in the broken window, had been beating itself against the windows, leaving feather prints like angel wings in the dust. It must have died of panic or starvation. She still felt guilty about it now, telling Millie.

'Wow,' Millie said. 'So it wasn't haunted.'

'Oh, Nick said it *definitely* was,' Nicole said, standing up and looking at the graves surrounding the imposing vault. 'We heard all sorts of bangs and creaks the whole time we were there. Nick wanted to move out, but it had the best views.' She smiled. 'That's probably why we didn't end up together. I said it was just the ghost of the pigeon, but down in the town there were all sorts of stories about the family. Apparently, the captain brought his mistress back from Jamaica to live in the house, alongside his wife. She's supposed to be buried here, too, somewhere.'

They wandered around, Nicole stepping carefully on the sloping grass. Millie read out the names as she went. 'Here's a Millicent,' she crowed. 'Oh, sad, died at fourteen months. Oh, another baby, and an eight-year-old... And a lady who died at one hundred and two, that's more like it.'

Nicole looked over the graves. 'There were a lot of sea captains and fishermen who drowned, weren't there? The waters around the islands are so dangerous.'

Millie crouched down to stare at the captain's stone again, and brushed away some of the lichens growing on it. 'Poor Charlotte.' She jumped down from the grave to the path. 'I'm going to look her up. She was my age, you know.'

'If you've got time. Now, come on, it will take you at least an hour to get ready for your first shift.'

'For Francesco? I'm intending to get ready all afternoon.'

Later that evening, Nicole was stretched out on the bed in her pyjamas after a hot shower, reading and waiting for Millie to come back. She would have gone to sleep early, but since Millie was such a klutz around the house she didn't want to be woken up when she came in. The book was starting to wobble, and the words were blurring into each other, when someone knocked on the door downstairs. She squinted at the clock: twenty past nine. *I'm not going down and I'm definitely not putting the leg back on.* She hopped to the window and pushed it open.

'Yes?' The long, sun-bleached mop of hair tipped back to look at her. The window was so low, the ground-floor ceiling so short that she could almost reach down to him. 'Josh?' Her heart skipped a beat.

'I'm sorry it's so late. You don't get a phone signal up here, do you?'

'Not yet. I'm putting a landline and Wi-Fi in soon, though, I hope. What can I do for you?'

He grinned up at her. 'I'm going to St Piran's tomorrow, to look at some stranded jellyfish. Some tourist is panicking about Portuguese man o' war, but it's probably just a blue sailor. I don't want to have to close the beaches.'

She laughed at the film reference. 'They didn't even close the beaches for a great white shark. One little jellyfish?'

'Well, a Portuguese man o' war could really hurt a child or a dog. Anyway, want a lift? I have to go on a falling tide, and I've organised cover on Gannet Rock, so there will be time to look in a few rockpools, if you like. We could have that picnic?'

One million reasons to refuse filled her up like cold water. Her missing leg, being alone on the island with him, needing to ask for his help. She took a deep breath, hugging the windowsill as her good leg started to go numb. 'You'll need help with definitive identification on that blue sailor?'

'That, and I need someone to bring sandwiches and beer.'

She laughed at him, and maybe it was because it was so late, or because he looked so funny looking up at her. 'What time?'

'I'll pick you up about two, is that OK? I'll carry the bags.'

'Great.' She pulled her head back in and closed the window. As she passed the dressing table mirror she realised she was grinning.

I'm going on a date with a lovely man.

20

JUNE 1941

Bernie was subdued as they walked through the halls of the hospital, shoes clacking on spotless linoleum, the sound echoing around the airy ceiling. They had easily found the building as it loomed over that area of the town, a red-brick castle of medicine.

'Now, I want you to be warned,' Matron said, turning in front of two doors with obscure glazed panels at the top. 'Some of our young men are very disfigured, and have not yet accepted their condition. Please try not to appear distressed or repulsed. Oliver is at this end of the ward.'

'Is he badly affected?' Bernie asked in a whisper.

'Not too bad. His flying suit protected him to some degree, then he was immersed in water. His fractures are healing, but he didn't receive the best medical care when in hiding. He's just recovering from an operation to reset his leg, so don't be alarmed by the plaster. He's recovering very well.'

She pushed open the door, and Lily looked around involuntarily. Faces like melted wax, livid skin, bandages and plaster on limbs. After the first moment of indrawn breath, her eyes filled with tears. She fixed a wavering smile on her face and said, 'Good morning,' as clearly as she could. A few patients mumbled back. One waved the bandaged stump of a hand.

'Ollie?' Bernie said, as she was guided to a bedside. 'Oh, my dear boy.' She collapsed into a chair beside him as Lily squeezed her shaking shoulder.

'Hello, Oliver,' she said, smiling. She wouldn't have recognised him; she hadn't seen him since he was a beanpole of a twelve-year-old with ginger hair and deep brown eyes, freckles everywhere.

'Cousin Lily,' he said, managing a smile, although parts of his face were covered with gauze. The clumps of his hair that were sticking out from under the bandages were a darker red now. 'How have you been?'

Her instinct was to be polite, say she was fine, but her smile faded, and she shook her head. 'My daughter died,' she managed to say.

'I heard. I'm so sorry.' The matron had brought in a spare chair, and Lily thanked her.

'But how are you going on?' she asked him.

'So-so,' he said, then started to chuckle past the bandages on one side of his face. She couldn't help smiling, too. 'Where are you living?'

'With your aunt,' Lily said, reaching out to Bernie, who was weeping quietly, and letting her clasp her hand. 'We were bombed out in London. How long do you need to be here?'

'Another few weeks, then I can come home – well, come back to the island, anyway. Until I'm ready to return to active duty, they say.'

That brought Bernie to life. 'No! Surely you have done your duty!'

His hands were shaking in their bandage mittens. 'It might not be necessary. I could have a desk assignment somewhere, or I might get pensioned off.'

Bernie shook her head. 'You'll come back to the flat, and we'll soon get you better, you'll see.'

He laughed, a shaky little chuckle as if he was still a boy. 'We hear the bombers going overhead here; they've dropped leftover bombs on the town on their way back. It would be good to get to relative safety on the island.'

'We've hardly seen a German plane – there have just been a few over the county,' Bernie said. 'And we can make your room ready for you.' She looked over at Lily. 'You don't mind sharing with me, do you?'

'Not at all!' Lily said, although she wondered how they would squeeze into the small room. 'We can probably put a folding bed in. I can sleep anywhere now.' Which was true. After months of lying awake next to James, remembering, remembering... Now she slept until the gulls woke her. 'I will leave you, Bernie. I'm sure you two have lots to talk about. I'll pop in again tomorrow, Oliver, if that's all right, before we travel back.' She stood, patted Bernie's shoulder. 'I'll be outside the hospital, with James. Take your time.'

Her heart lurched as she saw James pacing outside the main door, along a strip of lawn with a few memorial benches on it. He turned to her, and she stared at him.

He looked different in the light, his hair very short, in a military style. He looked thinner, too, his neck swamped by his suit, his collar bunched up under the sombre tie. He also looked pale; many hours stuck in an office poring over photographs and drawing maps wouldn't give him much time out in the sunshine.

'You look well,' he said, staring at her. He held out his arms for a brief embrace, a chaste kiss on her cheek. His lips were cold.

She flinched at his coolness, but he was never given to displays of affection in public.

'I am,' she said. 'I walk around the town when I can, or visit Morwen Island to help Emma. I'm only working part of the day, and so I help Bernie, too.'

He seemed to be drinking in every detail of her uncovered hair, and her face. 'I feel useless, sitting in a basement when I could be fighting the Germans.'

She put her hand on his arm. 'Please don't think like that. What you do is crucial, you know that. It must save lives.'

He looked down at her hand until she felt awkward and removed it. 'How is young Oliver?'

'Better than I expected,' she said, carefully. 'Obviously hurt, but recovering well. At least he has all four limbs.' Tears arrived out of nowhere as she remembered the man waving his damaged arm at her. 'Better than most,' she choked.

'Where will he be discharged to? Do you have room for him at your cousin's house?'

'Goodness, no! It's just a tiny flat. Big enough for two but it would be a squeeze for three.' She walked to a bench and sat in the warm sun, dabbing at her tears with a handkerchief. 'I thought I might ask to stay with Emma. After all, the house used to be a hotel, and there are lots of rooms. She might like the company, too.'

'She sounds most unsuitable,' he said, sitting as far away on the bench as he could. It was such a strange thing for him to do. 'Perhaps she would be better being cared for somewhere that specialises in looking after people like her.'

'Emma's perfectly competent, in her own way,' Lily snapped. 'She doesn't live in a narrow, limited way; she lives her own life.'

'Whereas we are limited and narrow?' He passed his hand over his face. 'Oh, Lily.'

'Well, the absurdity of changing for dinner when we've

been busy all day, and trying to cook three courses with rationing. I'm fairly sure you don't do that now,' she said.

'No. I mostly get a sandwich from the canteen, and just sleep at the office, change my shirt in the morning. Thank goodness the laundry collects from headquarters.'

'Oh, James. No wonder you look so pale and thin.' She leaned forward, grasped his hand. 'Darling, come to the islands. You must be due some leave. We could stay somewhere, and talk.'

'I can't,' he said, turning his hand to clasp her fingers. His thumb made circles in her palm. 'But you could stay with me for a few days. Maybe look around for a new place for us. I don't have time to visit anywhere the estate agents suggest.'

She tensed, slowly withdrew her hand. She felt unsettled at his touch. 'I need to take Bernie back to the island. And I have work on Tuesday.'

'Lily...' he groaned. 'Please. Are you *ever* coming home?'

She looked at his bowed head. His dark hair was so short she could see his scalp, the whorl on the top of his head. 'I want to, but we need to talk about Grace,' she said, keeping her voice calm. 'I need to talk about her. I still love her, she's...' She could feel her heart fluttering, fast. 'She's still in me,' she tried to explain. 'I think about what to get her for breakfast when I wake up, before I remember she's gone. I look in the toyshop and choose her a gift. I think I hear her laughing in the playground. She's always nearby.' She realised she was shaking. 'I wake each morning with her in my arms, sometimes just a baby, asleep on my shoulder, sometimes lifting her into bed – at the end. I feel her, I smell her.'

He turned away, his body tight. 'I can't, Lily. You know I can't talk about her.'

'When then? I can't pretend she never happened, that she wasn't the person I loved most in the world.' There, it was out.

He flinched, as if she'd hurt him. He'd always been a little jealous of their mother–daughter relationship.

'I loved her, too,' he managed to say.

'I know,' she said. 'But we need to get past this, or we will fall apart. I won't be able to come home.'

He shook his head, staring over the road opposite, eyes shining with unshed tears.

'What will you do with the rest of today?' he asked.

'I'll take Bernie for lunch, then she's going to visit her sister, Ollie's mother. She's in Brighton.'

'I could drive you,' he suggested.

She could feel her chest tightening at the thought of more difficult conversations. 'No, we will be fine. But please, think about coming to the island. I can get you a room at one of the hotels.'

'I don't think...' He tailed off. His lips were tight, the way they did when he wasn't getting his own way. 'Maybe we could get a room, if you're so desperate to talk. I'll do my best.'

'Thank you.' She stood up and he followed suit. 'Look, it's her anniversary coming up next month. I'd like to mark it in some way. Could you come then, do it for me?'

He looked like he wanted to say no, he even shook his head. But he agreed.

21

PRESENT DAY, 11 JUNE

The next afternoon, Josh was on time for the trip to St Piran's, and Nicole had been able to pack some food into a sling rucksack along with a phone and a few plastic bags in case they found anything interesting. She was hopeful she could manage with one walking stick.

The light beers she had brought raised an eyebrow. 'Low alcohol?'

'You're driving,' she said, shrugging the bag onto her shoulder and grabbing the stick. It made her face hot, but she tried not to guess what he was thinking.

'I put nets and specimen jars in the boat,' he offered, as he walked towards the quay. 'I don't know if we'll find anything, but it's good to be prepared. I have my camera, too. It's got high magnification on it. Just in case we find the fish we're looking for.'

The cobbles were easier to walk on with her canvas shoes, but the heat off the stone quay already made her wish she could wear shorts. She tried to keep up, but he slowed down to match her steps.

'Just so you know,' she said, a little out of breath. 'This isn't a date.'

'Even though there's food and drinks?' he said, feigning shock.

'I don't accept anything less than lobster for a first date,' she said, loftily. 'And champagne.'

'Neither do I,' he said, and laughed with her. 'No, it's just really nice to meet someone who knows about marine life. And cares.'

Her smile widened. There was a lot of truth in that. The fact that he was very attractive and charming was good, and he was also taking her on her first field trip in years.

The tide was going out, and she measured the step down with her eyes. It would have been difficult with her real foot – now it was just too far. He stepped in easily, standing first on the seat then into the base of the open boat. After stowing the bags and her rucksack, he turned to Nicole. He held out his hands.

'Everyone needs help getting in,' he stated, without emotion or judgement.

She put her hand in his. It felt small and pale in the sinewed fingers and broad palm, and she was acutely aware of the warmth of his skin. She put more weight on her prosthetic, feeling the resistance, the little bounce. Her physio had told her, about a thousand times, that she had to trust it. She leaned forward, moved her weight onto the good leg at the edge of the quay, and stepped forward. Her fake foot landed a bit awkwardly but she still had enough contact to move her weight onto it, clinging to Josh. He smelled good, for a moment, as she steadied herself against him. Then she was stepping down, letting go of his hand and breathing out with a whoosh. She sat down abruptly on the seat, her heart racing, facing the back of the boat.

'It's easier to land on the old jetty at St Piran's,' he said, untying the dinghy and starting the outboard. 'It's a bit rough, but the view of the evening sun is amazing.'

'We'll be staying that long?'

He shrugged, standing at the back and steering through tied up yachts and boats, and empty buoys. 'The tide's about halfway down, and we can get in and out. It will be back at this level no earlier than eight; nine o'clock would be better.' He smiled at her. 'Moonrise is about then, too. We could catch the sunset and moonrise in one evening, and the weather is perfect.'

She settled on the bench seat, starting to relax as the boat rose and fell out in the Sound between the islands. 'Maybe you *should* have brought a lobster,' she joked.

He smiled, leaned into the wind, and shut his eyes for a moment. 'It's great to be out on the water for something other than groceries and work.' He turned to her. 'Guess what my glamorous wildlife ranger job involved this morning? Taking faecal specimens from puffin burrows. I was dive-bombed every four minutes for two hours.'

'We need that information,' she said, primly. 'Parasite load is a primary indicator of stress on the population.'

'Before I came out, I also scraped a week's worth of guano off the solar panels.'

She made a face. 'I hope you washed before you came to pick me up.'

He laughed. 'I had a solar shower and soaped up, then swam around the boat to rinse off.'

Her imagination went into overdrive at the idea of his lean body, naked in the water, and she turned to look out to sea.

A hundred metres away, a glossy black head popped up and she gasped. 'Josh, look! A seal.'

It swam alongside them for a minute, staring at them curiously.

'If I stop the boat, a couple of them hop on board,' he said.

'We're trying to discourage them but some of the tourist boats have been feeding them. It's got so many negative consequences, like propeller injuries to the animals and the seals getting aggressive with tourists. Not to mention disease; they're very susceptible to canine distemper.'

The seal fell back as he revved the engine up, sweeping away from rocks barely visible below the water as dark smudges. Her imagination made them sharks or whales. The fronds of kelp trailed around them, glossy ribbons, dozens of metres long.

St Piran's island had a low profile and sandy dunes around a mound of rocks. The old jetty had suffered in the storms, and some planks were missing.

Josh tied up at the end. 'This bit isn't going to be easy for you,' he said, as he picked up the bags. 'Can we talk about it? You obviously have a bad leg.'

She shut her eyes, took a breath and stared at him. 'I have a below-knee amputation,' she said. 'I'm learning to use a prosthetic. Eventually, I should have pretty normal walking abilities, but I don't like talking about it. Not yet.'

'Fair enough. Why would you? Just put your arm around my neck. With three legs between us we should be able to climb up onto those last few planks. What do you say?'

She almost refused; the habit ingrained now. She waited for the embarrassment and rage to kick in, but it was just an ember of an old fire.

'Go on, then,' she snapped. 'But if you drop me in the water, I will literally kill you.'

She looped her elbow around his neck and stood on the seat, the boat rocking uncomfortably as he shifted towards the edge. He was strong, already taking some of her weight, and she couldn't help noticing the muscles moving under his tanned skin. 'Now, if we both step up onto that step – careful, it's slippery – and *up*.'

She swayed on the jetty, looking around the white sands

either side, the turquoise water lapping the timbers, the dart of silver fish in and out of the shade. 'I'd forgotten how beautiful this place was,' she said, and slowly let go of his neck as he turned towards her, inches away.

He glanced down at her eyes, held her gaze for a moment, then pulled back. 'We'll just have to walk these dodgy planks to the beach, and we're set for the day.' He looked up at the clear sky. 'I hope you brought sun cream.'

The sandy stretch of shore was reached easily via a footpath, and Josh extracted a rolled-up sheet of canvas and a few poles and strings to build a shelter from the sun. He sat under it while Nicole started exploring the hard-packed sand, down to the first rockpools revealed by the falling tide. She sat on the edge of one and examined it; she was so immersed in the task she didn't notice him walking over, and his voice made her jump.

'Ready to stretch your legs? I need to check out this mystery creature on the other side of the island.'

'Sure,' she said, extending her hand to let him to help her up. 'You're right, my back is stiff.'

'And your nose is red,' he said. 'That cap doesn't cover it all.' He waggled a small tube of factor fifty sun cream. She watched him squeeze out a little blob and then, as if she were a child, said, 'Look up.' He dabbed it onto her nose and chin, then she turned away, suddenly self-conscious, to rub it in. She took the cream and applied around the neck of her T-shirt, and over her exposed arms.

She could walk on the wet sand, but staggered on the dry, windblown sand, dotted with spiky marram grass at the top of the beach. She grabbed his arm to stop her falling, until they reached a wooden boardwalk creating a path through the dunes. She let go, and he smiled at her.

'So, how long is it since you got your feet wet as a proper marine scientist?'

'Far too long,' she said. 'Where do you think all your puffin poo samples end up?'

'You examine those?'

'Someone in my department does,' she said, skirting a boulder on the path. 'There are lab techs for that.'

'So, you collate the data, that sort of thing? Tell me you still work in a lab.'

She stopped, leaning on her stick for a moment, then walked to a bench up ahead and sat down. 'I work in an office. Or a boardroom, or in Parliament. I'm the person who super-vises the science.'

'From a distance.' She thought she could hear some snippi-ness there.

'I'm the person who argues for protection for those puffins,' she said. 'Who creates sand-eel reserves to protect their food supply.'

'Are you involved in the reapplication to create a Marine Conservation Zone for the Atlantic Islands?'

Nicole looked at him. There was a tension about him that she hadn't seen before. 'Someone in my department will be, yes. Not me. I lobby for developments and grants to protect the envi-ronment.'

'We're getting knockbacks from all directions.' He shaded his eyes as they came to the top of a low hillock. 'I can't see the jellyfish. It's above the tideline, apparently.'

He strode out, leaving her behind as she cautiously navi-gated the soft slope. She could see his hunched shoulders. She called out. 'Wait!'

He stopped and looked over his shoulder at her.

'Can you give me a hand? I feel like I'm going to fall.' She knew she sounded like she was trying to manipulate him, change the awkward subject. 'Don't get angry at me. You could ask me how to improve your application, focus your efforts. That's what I *can* do, that's how I could help.'

He stepped back, held out a hand. 'I'm sorry. I care deeply about this place, it's in my DNA. It terrifies me seeing what's happening to the sea, to our world.'

'Me too,' she said, trying to ignore the warm strength of his hand in hers. 'Which is why I moved to work for the government in the first place. To get things done.'

He laughed then. 'How's that working out?'

She let go as she reached the flat sand, then grinned at him. 'It's measured, but we get there in the end.' She made a face. 'Actually, it's incredibly frustrating. It's too slow.'

She looked along the edge of the sand, a line of weed marking the last high tide. Above it something blue was sticking up, like sea glass, half bleached white.

'That must be it,' he said.

They stood looking down at the creature, barely the size of her hand and bright blue. Nicole washed the sand off with her water bottle. 'Blue sailor,' she said. '*Velella*. It wasn't going to kill anyone.'

He looked out to sea. 'Is that another one? Close to the edge.'

She waded out into the shallows without thinking how her leg would perform, but apart from feeling like she was stepping down into a hole every time, it held her up. The creature was transparent blue, still alive. 'It's going to get stranded.'

'Wind's onshore, that's the problem. There's another one, already beached.'

She looked up and down the shore. 'There are a few decent rockpools on this side. The jellies could survive until the tide comes in.'

He hesitated. 'Can they hurt you? I know they aren't dangerous, but I've never picked one up.'

'I don't think they sting,' she said, lifting the creature up. Apart from a tingling against her palm from its feathery tentacles, most of it was the elegant sail, a little pyramid of dense blue jelly. The base plate was decorated with concentric circles of denser tissue. 'They're not jellyfish at all.'

'They're related to the Portuguese man o' war, though, aren't they?'

'Distantly.' She scooped another one up and handed them to the reluctant Josh. 'There's another one.' The cold water rushed over her liner and started to trickle through the outer sleeve of her prosthetic and into the sock, shocking her skin. 'Ooh!' She laughed, and he caught her elbow as she staggered.

'OK?'

She limped back towards the shore. 'Surprised. The water is freezing.'

She sat down on the warm sand, watching him scoop up another half a dozen sailors and a little moon jellyfish into the pool. She knew she ought to take her leg off to dry the skin, but was suddenly shy, although he had shown no sign of being bothered.

'Our good deed for the day,' he said, smiling as he walked back and sat next to her. 'You're pretty wet. You should have worn shorts. Or better still, a swimsuit.'

'Well, I'm still a bit self-conscious,' she managed to say, her voice coming out small. He blocked out the breeze on that side, and she suddenly felt very hot.

'Why? It's only us.'

Exactly. You're here.

'Help me get back to the shade and get some food.' She held a hand out to him, and when he stood, he pulled her close to his chest. The proximity made her breathless, and she turned away, reaching for her stick, limping back to the shelter.

She had packed a small bag with sandwiches and snacks with a cool block. He ate sandwiches in giant bites. 'Smoked salmon and cream cheese?' He opened a beer and washed the bread down with a swig. 'I haven't eaten this well for weeks. Normally I lose a stone or two living with the birds in the shack.'

'It can't be easy cooking up there.'

'I have a gas hob but, honestly? Everything ends up tasting of fish and worse. The fulmars dive-bomb me if I cook outside – they have nests on the lighthouse steps above the shack.'

She laughed and picked up a chicken and salad sandwich. She was glad she'd packed plenty; being on the beach always made her hungry, and it seemed to galvanise Joshua. He also managed two beers. The heat was easing off as the evening approached. Finally, he threw a few scraps into the grass for a couple of waiting crows and pointed out to the far shoreline.

'The biggest rockpools are out there.'

'Is that where that old book said those fish were?'

'Patience's book? Sure, there's a little pen and ink sketch that reminded me of the dune behind, although the winds sculpt it differently each year.'

'You said you knew her?'

He nodded. 'Everyone on the islands knew Patience. She was my teacher for six years. Where do you think I got my love of nature from?'

'I thought she was a lot older than that.'

He shrugged. 'Patience was coming up to retirement in the old school, before it burned down. Then we got a modular building. We thought it was very modern, for the eighties. It's hopefully going to be replaced now.'

'I need to fix my leg.' She tried to pull her wet trouser leg up, but the sleeve extended halfway up her thigh. 'I'm going to have to take my jeans off,' she said, looking around for some cover, privacy, anything.

'I brought a couple of towels,' he said, adjusting the canopy over their heads to cut off the view of the sea. 'I can have a scout

of the rockpool while you get those trousers off. They will probably dry in a couple of hours, if we hang them up.'

She stared at him, standing there on the edge of the awning
he had created. 'You're a proper gentleman, do you know that?'

'Not *that* much of a gentleman,' he said, with a lopsided
smile. 'But today isn't the day.'

22

JULY 1941

Lily, working in the library basement, teased another page free of the damp mess that the fire brigade had made when they rescued three volumes of Tudor hymnals. She had packed up two bags of belongings and was going over to Morwen to stay with Emma. May had arranged it, but Emma was still understandably nervous; she hadn't accommodated anyone else since her father died.

Gently, gently... She breathed again once the edges, which were glued together with oak gall ink that had run, separated. She was shaking inside, and she couldn't work out why. Of course, it was a big house and the way Emma talked about it, it was full of ghosts and memories. And moving there would take Lily another day closer to Grace's anniversary, and maybe even a visit from James. She had picked up a lot of Bernie's anxiety, too, as she tried to get ready for Oliver's return. They had painted his room, to freshen it up, but then Bernie wondered if Oliver would have preferred his old colour. Lily had also helped spruce up the old curtains with a border that made it easier to close them. They had already arranged help to get Ollie upstairs.

And then there was James. He had written a polite note to confirm his travel arrangements and that he was planning to train as an aircraft photographer. Then he'd dropped his guard for a few lines. 'I miss you every day, my darling, and long for the time we can resume our life together...'

She had decided to share her room with James, and maybe that was making her shaky inside. It had been so long since they had slept as man and wife.

Lily glanced again at the clock, carefully placed acid-free waterproof paper between the damp pages and left the book in the drying box.

'That's me done for the week, Mr Prendergast,' she called through to the library desk in a respectful whisper.

'Well, I'll see you on Monday, and I hope you settle in well with Miss Chancel. It's a funny house. We always called it... well you don't need to know that,' he said, his eyes creased with sudden concern.

'I think "haunted house" gives it a bit of character,' Lily said, smiling back at him.

'Do you know the history of the house? It was built out of the collapsed lighthouse stone. Two men died when the light-house was blown down, you know.'

She hefted her suitcase then her handbag. 'I've heard several versions already,' she said. 'But Miss Chancel and her family lived there for many years without incident, and my mother was brought up there.'

'Ah yes, of course she was. And how is your mother?'

Lily's smile slipped. 'She's struggling with the war. She's had a bit of nervous collapse. But she's on the mend. She's even talking about moving to a nursing home in Cornwall, so I can see her more often.'

'That's nice,' he said. 'She'd moved off the islands before I came here, but people speak well of her. Good evening.'

Lily smiled and walked through the door he held open for

her. She had visited her mother, Elizabeth, over the previous weekend and had been shocked to see her so thin and pale. But once she got talking about the old times, when Grace was a baby, Elizabeth cheered up. Lily had cried herself to sleep later, in her bed at the hotel in Cheltenham, but she felt better for it. Her mother's collapse wasn't due only to the barrage of bombs and the constant threat, it also stemmed from the loss of her only grandchild. She'd had a wonderful – and separate – relationship with Grace, teaching her baking and gardening, and walking miles through the London parks with the dogs. Lily was humbled when she understood that Elizabeth's loss was crushing, too.

One source of discord was her absolute refusal to agree that Lily should go to Chancel Hall.

'Edwin should have known better,' she had said. 'Taking his girls to live there. Four months later, one of them was dead and the other in hospital, run over.'

'How well did you know Edwin?' Lily had asked.

'Not well, he was away at boarding school when I was born. He rarely came home, but he seemed kind enough. It wasn't a surprise when he went into the church.'

Lily had often wondered about her mother's side of the family, but Elizabeth had always remained tight-lipped. She seemed to have despised her father, leaving the island for good at her marriage to stay with a distant cousin of her mother's at eighteen. She did let slip that her own mother had been seventeen when she married her father – always referred to as 'the Captain' – who had been almost fifty himself.

Lily stepped onto the ferry, a little steamer which was taking goods as well as passengers around the islands. She enjoyed the boat rides, although in the evening the wind-over-tide effect could produce a 'bit of chop', according to the pilot. Lily didn't mind, and as Morwen was the furthest out of the islands, she managed to relax into the corner out of the wind and think about her next adventure.

Remembering or talking about Grace was like the pain of toothache, sudden and distracting. But it was less sharp, and now memories brought tears to her eyes, and a longing, rather than the agony that had made her mind veer away. James obviously hadn't got there yet, but she hoped he would. She shut her eyes, savouring that first proper look at him in Eastbourne, when she recalled how she had loved him, how he had been kind to her. Maybe there was an ember of that James in there somewhere, like there had been in her. She was changed by Grace's loss: she thought more seriously, perhaps she felt things more deeply. But she was still Lily. Maybe he was still James, just changed by grief.

'You asleep there, maid?' came the boatman's voice.

'No, just thinking,' she replied, as he gave her a hand onto the side of the slipway, then passed her the two bags.

'I hear you're joining us,' he said with a grin. 'Living up at the old haunted house.'

She smiled, not wanting another lecture about funny Miss Chancel and the ghosts. 'I'm looking forward to staying with my cousin,' she managed.

'Well, it's done her a power of good, having visitors,' he said sincerely. 'She's been coming down to the quay and to the shop. Not on her usual days, neither.'

'That's good,' she said emphatically. 'Thank you.'

She looked along the shore, the sea lapping at the tideline in the sand one side of the low wall that separated the fields from the sea. The slate gravel path led past the cannery, with its stale fish smell, and she strode onto the path to the hotel. The grand house struck her as beautiful, before she got close enough to see how deteriorated it had become.

Maybe she could help Emma restore it, save it. Maybe they could rescue each other...?

23

PRESENT DAY, 11 JUNE

Nicole wrapped herself in a towel and laid another in the warm sand under the canopy. Josh came back and forth with animals in buckets. He brought a skeleton shrimp, a circular crab and a shanny for her to see, but at some point, she fell asleep. When she woke, the sea was curling higher and higher up the beach, calling to her.

It was hot, too hot. She hesitated for a moment. Josh waved to her, stripped off his sandals and shirt and dived in, so she decided to hop closer.

'Come on in,' he shouted, a hundred metres away, swimming strongly parallel to the beach.

She shut her eyes, swallowed her embarrassment, and took off the towel. She threw it up the beach and pulled her long shirt down over her underwear. Hopping down the firm sand was easier than she expected. Sitting in the shallow water, which was warmed by creeping up over hot sand, was less dignified, but the childlike freedom she felt was priceless. She pushed herself in slightly deeper, and colder water covered her hated, defective limb. The sensation was glorious, prickling with the cold, the currents tingling.

He splashed closer. 'Good, huh? Have you ever scuba-dived?'

'I have. I've done courses, and dived for work,' she said, tensing up as he sat beside her in the shallows.

He let the water flow over his legs. 'I need to do a reef dive for the ranger service. We've got permits. Fancy tagging along?'

'I might need a refresher, it's been a few years.'

'We're only going down ten or fifteen metres, you'd soon remember.'

For a moment, she wondered if she could swim with one leg. *Will I swim in circles?* The idea was funny. 'Maybe.' She turned to look at him.

'I would think diving is one thing that won't be affected by a duff leg.'

'I'll think about it. Can you give me a hand up?'

He jumped up. 'Of course.'

She was able to struggle up by leaning on his shoulder. She fleetingly noticed he had a little spare flesh around his belly and that he had a scar on his shoulder. *No one's perfect.* She flapped a hand at him. 'Would you mind... looking away? I'm in my underwear.'

By the time she had got to the towel the water was almost upon it. She wrapped it around her waist quickly and hopped up to her damp jeans. The liner was better, almost dry, and under the screen that he'd erected, she managed to put her leg back in place and roll on the outer sleeve. The jeans were much harder, still damp enough to fight back over her inflexible foot, and she was out of breath by the time she pulled back the awning.

He was standing with his back to her, up to his waist in water like he'd just emerged from it. The sun was going down, the water halfway up the beach, and the golden light gilded his body. She stared for what seemed like ages, drinking in the sight of a man she had to admit she was incredibly attracted to.

'I'm done!' she called to Josh, her voice coming out softer than she'd intended.

'It's your turn to look away,' he said, as he walked up the beach, undoing the snap fastener at the top of his shorts. She laughed, and covered her eyes.

When she heard him open the last beer, she felt she could look up.

He took a mouthful, then handed the cold can to her. 'We didn't find the fish,' he said.

'Well, we came for the sailors,' she said.

He pointed down the beach. The wind had veered a little, and dropped, and now the little creatures were bobbing in the rockpool as each wave topped it up. 'I'll let the social media kids tell everyone not to worry,' he said, grinning. 'We did a good thing.'

She looked around. 'When's moonrise?'

'Half an hour.'

She reached over for her rucksack. In the front pocket was a large bar of expensive chocolate. 'I'm only sharing this with you because I've had a brilliant day,' she told him, breaking off half.

'I'm glad. Me too.' He broke off a piece and ate it slowly. 'I'm guessing you haven't had much time to get used to showing people your leg?'

'No,' she said. 'Just medical staff. And my sister because she asked. I *hate* it.'

He shrugged, took another square, savoured it. 'Are you going to tell me about the accident?'

She ate a nibble of chocolate. 'No.'

'Fair enough.' It was cooling down now. He shrugged on a sweater from his bag over his dry shorts and tee, and Nicole put her jacket on. He lay down on the sand, staring up at the sky, facing east. 'I love this time of day.'

'Are you going to sleep at the shack tonight?'

He shook his head, the sand sticking to his damp hair. 'No,

it's too risky when it's dark. I'll sleep on the boat, catch the morning tide instead. I might pick up a few luxuries at the shop when it opens.'

She arranged the driest of the towels under her head and torso, and lay beside him. 'There's Venus.'

'Maybe it's the space station,' he quipped, lazily.

'That one's Vega,' she pointed up. 'Then Deneb and Altair.'

She could see them better now the sky was turning deeper and deeper blue, the orange glow in the west. 'I used to have a telescope,' she admitted. 'I was a nerdy kid astronomer.'

He rolled his head in the sand again. 'Me too. Geeky bird-watcher.'

'For goodness' sake.' She laughed. 'You can share the towel, you'll never get all that sand out of your hair.'

He rolled closer, sharing a corner of the towel, their shoulders touching. The moon, just coming up to full, started to show above the horizon. His arm was warm against hers. They watched in silence. She could hear his slow breathing, feel the cold seeping through the towel. The pull to turn and look at him was almost irresistible.

'We'd better get back.' She sat up, brushing sand off her clothes.

'The tide will get us soon, anyway,' he said, standing and shaking himself like a dog, the sand in his hair glistening like glitter. 'Thank you for a lovely day. And the picnic.'

'Can you round up the bags? And the beer tins.'

He packed everything away and lugged it back towards the boat. She was tired now; her leg was hurting and her footing not as secure. She stopped, almost reduced to hopping, at the edge of the damaged jetty. When he loaded up the bags, he came for her.

He didn't ask, just scooped her up like a child and carried her down the jetty. She was so surprised she could only squeak a tiny protest, which he ignored. He set her on her feet by the boat, then handed her down onto her seat.

He stepped on board, started the engine, loosed the boat. 'We might see those dolphins again,' he said, in a subdued voice. 'If we keep fairly quiet.'

She looked forward, letting him steer through the rocks using the last of the light. The dolphins didn't appear, but the boat disturbed a lot of fish in the middle of the Channel, which splashed silver. She was exhausted. She hadn't done so much physical exercise since before the accident. Her body was tingling with the cold water, the softness of the sand, his nearness.

He helped her out of the boat at the dark quay, handed her the stick and her bag. 'Are you OK to get up the hill?'

'I'll be fine,' she said, her voice coming out suddenly shy. 'Thank you for a lovely day, Josh.'

He waved as he drove the boat further up the quay to tie up. Maybe he really was going to sleep on the boat, although it seemed impossibly uncomfortable. Maybe he had a friend in the town. She turned and started up the hill, for the first time feeling alone. Lonely.

24

JULY 1941

Lily walked up to the front door and pulled the bell to hear it jangle. Emma was talking as she came to answer, and it sounded like she was arguing. Perhaps May was there? When Emma answered the door, she was red faced and dressed again in men's clothes, covered in foliage and mud from the gardening.

'I was weeding,' she grumbled, unnecessarily. 'I thought you'd be on the late boat.'

'I wanted to get settled in. It was so kind of you to let me stay. I'll be happy to help you with the garden, and you must let me help around the house, too.'

Emma stood, staring as if thinking through the idea, the stepped back to let Lily in. She banged the door shut, the light dimming in the gloomy hall. For a moment, the stories of ghosts and the sea captain with his teenaged brides and mistress crossed Lily's mind.

'May put you in Mother's room,' Emma said. 'It's by the bathroom, and it looks over the sea.'

'How kind of her, thank you.' Lily paused at the door, a small key on a faded ribbon in the keyhole.

'I keeps it locked,' Emma said, making no effort to open the door. She licked her lips and backed off down the landing a step.

'Of course.' Lily frowned as she tried to understand what Emma was thinking. 'Have you been in here, recently?'

'Not since she died,' Emma admitted. 'May cleaned it, made up the bed, but I stayed outside.'

'Oh, Emma. I'm so sorry.' She wanted to hug the tense figure who had wrapped her own arms around herself as if for comfort, but somehow didn't feel she could. 'Where do you sleep?'

Emma pointed at the ceiling. 'The nursery,' she said. 'Charlotte and I have our own rooms off it.'

Lily shook her head at the confusion of tenses. 'Did you always have your own rooms?'

'No,' Emma said, watching intently as Lily moved her hand towards the key. 'Sometimes we shared a bed, too. Go on, May made it really nice for you.'

The door swung open easily, and was revealed to be charming, if somewhat Victorian. A washstand with a marble top had a bowl on it, decorated with a rose design, and a jug with a chip at the top. A towel rail had a pink towel, rather threadbare but still useful, and the bed was a large metal one from the last century. An coverlet with an Indian design was over the blankets, and two white pillows peeped out the top.

An uncomfortable thought of James intruded, although he hadn't yet agreed to visit.

She patted his last letter, folded up in her pocket. He'd been a talented amateur photographer, much sought after in the architecture practice where he had trained as a young man. But flying over the south coast, with German planes everywhere, seemed far too dangerous to her. It seemed out of character for cautious James, almost reckless. Soon he could be sleeping right next to her under this beautiful, and possibly antique, quilt.

'This is lovely,' Lily said, running a hand over the coverlet. 'How charming.'

'May found it in the attics,' Emma said, stepping forward a little. 'It's a bit different in here now. Mother died in the hospital in Penzance. She had a stroke,' she confided, walking over to the window. 'See. You can see the fishing fleet and the ferries.'

Lily was shaken with relief that her mother hadn't died in the room, which was ridiculous in a house of this age and size, because it must have seen many deaths. The window was smeared and dusty, and she knew she would enjoy polishing it up. The glass was so old, it distorted the view a little.

'This is a good room,' she said, turning to Emma, seeing a small smile turning the corners of her mouth up. 'And I've brought some treats from the big island.'

Emma had made some bread, and Lily admired the fresh rolls that she pulled out of the restored oven. With a little cheese and a scrape of margarine, they were delicious with salad, and at Lily's suggestion, they ate them on the terrace. Lily had brought a small box of strawberries and a few early raspberries.

'This is like a picnic,' Emma said, watching the birds flap around the terrace for crumbs. She threw a crust for them to squabble over. 'When do you have to go back to work?'

'I'm going back the day after tomorrow, more to help Bernie with getting the room ready for Oliver. I'll be staying there three days a week to look after the books, but it will be a squeeze for the two nights in the flat.' At the slight frown on Emma's face she explained again. 'Bernice and Cissie are your cousins, and Oliver is Cissie's son. He's been hurt in the war.'

'But I've never met them?'

'I'm sure you have. Everyone meets everyone sooner or later

on the islands. But your father didn't have much to do with their mother.'

'I don't remember. Not since the accident. I was unconscious for a long time. Mother had to teach me to eat again, and to walk properly.' She rubbed her head. 'I couldn't do anything myself at first.'

Lily couldn't remember anyone talking about the accident, which seemed odd. 'Was Charlotte in the same accident?'

'She made it happen,' Emma said, her face turned away, her jaw tense. 'She walked into the road just as a van came around the corner. She died.'

'I'm so sorry.' Lily's life seemed full of grieving people right now, and the whole country seemed to be in mourning for someone.

'I didn't remember much about that time,' Emma said, looking out to sea. 'Charlotte used to talk to me while I was ill, teasing me, calling me ugly and stupid.'

Lily didn't understand, so she prompted Emma to say more. 'Did she?'

'When I came home from hospital, they had to carry me because I couldn't walk yet. And she came with me.' She picked a little bread off and offered it on her hand to a robin, which came closer but not quite close enough. 'He has taken food from me before,' Emma said. 'But now you're here he's too scared.'

Lily finished her food. 'Did you say you have a cat?'

'I do,' Emma said. 'I leave his food outside as he doesn't come indoors very often.'

Lily offered to wash up, but it was on Emma's diary page, so she let her get on with it. Instead, she walked out to look over the low wall to the beach. James had been on her mind all day, the memory of him, pale and thin. She could feel the pull to go back to London, to feed him up and make him walk in the park. And the nights, sleeping next to him, making love—

She shut down the idea before it started. After Grace died,

she couldn't bear to, even though she suspected it would give James solace. Early on, her mother had delicately suggested that men derived comfort in different ways. But he had been so cold, so distant, she filled up with rage at him. The anger was really at the unfairness of Grace's illness, that took her last year, and then her life. She found cold tears on her cheeks and dragged her sleeve over them. Going back wasn't an option; if she was to be with James, they had to find a new way to be together. He *had* to come to the island.

PRESENT DAY, 15 JUNE

In the four days since her trip to St Piran's, Nicole had woken every day feeling better. She had turned the memory of the day with Josh over in her mind, and wondered how he felt about her. There was something between them, she felt, some chemistry... As she lay in bed thinking about it, the smell of baking bread brought her fully awake.

Millie had started making huge and creative 'healthy breakfasts': plates of fruit and cheese and bread.

She hopped to the stairs and sat down, scooting down easily now. Her leg had suffered, not from the salt water but from the sand caught up in the sock. She had given it a few days off, using Heike's scooter to get around. She hopped into the kitchen, where the smell was more intense.

'What are you up to?'

Millie smiled at her and kissed her on the cheek. She was becoming very affectionate and relaxed, despite working ten-hour shifts until midnight some nights. 'The pub kitchen had some pizza dough left over. I kept it in the fridge overnight and – bingo! Bread rolls for breakfast.'

Nicole pushed the kitchen door open into the cool, shaded

garden. Her bare foot seemed to know every contour of the slates, and she sat in her usual chair, letting the fresh air fill her lungs. 'If you could bottle this feeling...'

Millie bustled out, carrying a tray of cups and a fragrant, steaming teapot. She had a light throw over her arm and draped it over Nicole's chair. 'Don't get cold,' she called over her shoulder as she went back in. 'And don't pour the tea yet. It needs three more minutes.'

Nicole wondered for an amused moment whether she should drape the throw over her legs like a Victorian invalid, but opted instead to wrap it around her shoulders. She leaned forward to sniff at the pot: the predominant scent was something citrussy, maybe grapefruit, and lifting the lid revealed blue and red petals.

'What is this, Mills?' she asked lazily, relaxing back, the morning sun just coming over the wall to hit her face.

'It's my own blend of Blue Lady tea. You'll like it.'

The strange thing was, Nicole generally did like the fruit breads and teas she invented. Millie came out with a platter of baked rolls of all shapes, two knives and the butter dish. 'Mum would insist we have separate plates,' she said, stepping out onto the pavers in bare feet.

'On this tiny table?' Nicole looked over at her and smiled. She watched as Millie poured two cups of tea through an ornate strainer, split and buttered two rolls and gave one to Nicole. 'So, how are you getting on?'

Millie took a huge bite of bread. 'Good,' she mumbled.

Nicole took smaller bites, but the bread was delicious, deeply flavoured and still hot. 'I was going up to the hotel for lunch today, but I'm not sure I'll need it.'

Millie took a sip of the tea. 'I'll come with you, if you like. I found out something about the ghosts.'

The Blue Lady was lovely, the grapefruit just biting through the black tea and floral notes. 'You made this?'

'The head chef at the pub blends them; they have all the ingredients. This is my version, lots of citrus, no rose. Orange pekoe tea, so plenty of caffeine.'

'The ghosts?'

'I looked up the history of the hotel on a genealogy website. I think Josh might be related to Captain Steadfast through his daughter, Elizabeth, and *her* daughter, Lily. *She* was Josh's grandma.'

Nicole nibbled a little of the buttery crust. Millie was too young to worry about the amount of butter she had piled onto the bread. 'How do you know all this?' She threw a couple of crumbs to a bold sparrow, which had almost perched on her bare foot.

'I found out about the captain online. He was married twice but there are two illegitimate children with his name on their birth certificates.'

Nicole gave it a little thought. 'It's a really unusual name.'

'There was a woman – Bertha Pederick. She had children by him. He's listed on the birth records for Bernice and Clarissa Chancel. On Clarissa's marriage certificate he's named as her father, Steadfast Chancel, sea captain, deceased. Get this, Bernice was born when Bertha was *sixteen* and a live-in maid at the house. She's listed at Chancel Hall in the 1901 census.'

'Poor kid. The captain was a bit of a dog, then, getting a maid pregnant when he was how old?'

'Seventy. Yuck! He had children by his first wife, too, but they were older, then he married another teenager and had Elizabeth, Josh's great-grandma.'

'Do you think that's the ghost, dragging herself around the attics, the pregnant servant girl?'

'Bertha?' Millie topped up their teas. 'I don't think so. It looks like she lived in the town – that's where the babies were brought up, according to the 1911 census, anyway.'

'If we go to the hotel we could ask the owners, perhaps see if they know anything?'

Millie looked at her pointedly. 'And we could ask that nice Joshua of yours, too. Since his mother was also the housekeeper, and he's related, and they lived there. Ooh, maybe his mum was like Mrs Danvers out of that book *Rebecca*, all creepy and scary.'

'I don't know when I'll be seeing him, and he isn't *my* Joshua.' She was ambivalent about Josh, not when she was with him but afterwards, thinking about him. Most of her relationships were with high-powered, educated men from the world of government science. Josh was so down to earth she didn't know how to take him. But kind, he was so kind.

'Well, very soon, hopefully. You were all glowy-eyed when you got back from St Piran's the other night.'

'Glowy-eyed? I was exhausted, I nearly fell asleep on the couch!'

'And covered in sand.' Millie gave her an amused look. 'You trailed it all through the house. I had to vacuum it up.'

'Thank you. I didn't know you had.'

'Because you were so tired, you slept through it,' Millie said, triumphantly.

'I did overdo it.' Nicole looked down at the remnants of her food and chucked a few more crumbs to the waiting birds.

'Are you going to tell me about it?'

Nicole almost said no, because she wasn't sure how she felt about the day with Josh. 'We rescued some jellyfish – well, they're actually colonial hydroids – and had a good look for this weird fish. Josh found some cool stuff, though not the mystery fish.'

'Yes, but how did you get on?'

Nicole shrugged. 'I took a picnic, we drank a few beers waiting for the tide to come back. We did watch the moon come up, it's such a beautiful spot.' She could feel her cheeks warming up. 'He went for a swim, I had a bit of a paddle. The water was wonderful.'

'*And?*'

Nicole laughed. 'OK, he was lovely and carried me onto the boat like a Victorian heroine.' She paused to sip her tea. 'I do like him.' It looked like Millie was choking on the questions she wanted to ask. 'He's nice, but we're so different. I can't see a future in it but I am enjoying myself.'

'How about your leg? How's it healing? I mean, you always keep it covered up.' Millie's face was so open and curious, like a child half her age. Nicole gave in to impulse and slid her skirt up a few inches, the residual limb in its compression sock. 'That's it, really. It takes a few months for the swelling to go down but you have to keep the muscles in good condition. I thought it needed a bit of a rest.'

'After the sand.' Millie smiled after a fleeting – and not very interested – glance at the stump. 'Looks OK to me, with that long sock thing. You don't have to hide it all the time – no one would know at first glance. Why don't you wear a dress to the hotel? It's going to be hot. I'll book a table and we can talk about those ghosts.'

They headed for the hotel around lunchtime, the mobility scooter travelling at a comfortable pace for long-legged Millie. It was good to see her so curious and engaged but Nicole was still convinced stray pigeons and creaky pipes probably accounted for the ghosts. She parked on the terrace and a young woman came out to offer them a patio table with a sea view. Millie sat, promptly reached for her smartphone and started tapping.

'See, Captain Steadfast Chancel had two sons living at home, Edwin and Jonah. Jonah was a shipping agent. Look, he was born in Jamaica! Oh, died aged thirty-three, at sea. Edwin was a prebendary – whatever that is – and he had two daughters, Emma and the tragic Charlotte.'

'Prebendaries are something to do with the church, I think. So he inherited the hotel,' Nicole said, still watching the sea as a waiter came up and took their orders. As he jotted down their choices, she spoke up. 'Do you know anyone we could talk to about the history of the hotel?'

'Well, the two owners know a bit because they were here when it was renovated. But I would ask Mrs McKay. She used to be the housekeeper for the old flats.' He pointed beyond the airy glass block that was the dining conservatory. 'She lives in the cottage on the other side of the hotel, just over there.'

Mrs McKay. Josh's mother.

'Do you have contact details for her? I can't just bang on the door.'

'Of course you can, she would probably enjoy the company.' He smiled as he moved off.

Of course you can. This was an island where people called around late and talked to her through her bedroom window. What else did she expect?

'Great, we can ask her a few questions,' Millie said eagerly. 'Maybe she's seen the ghost. Did you ask Josh?'

Nicole was surprised at her interest in everything. Millie had become more passive and inward looking as she'd settled into her teens. But now she came home from work shattered, in stained clothes, happy and often singing. 'I haven't seen him. But we can't just barge in on his mum and ask a load of nosy questions.'

Millie laughed out loud. 'Um, that's *exactly* what everyone here does.'

After their lunch, Nicole followed the patio around on her crutches, as she had taken Millie's advice to leave the leg at home. Every bit of breeze swung her skirt around her thighs, and she was acutely aware the stump could be revealed. *One day I won't care...* A gate led through a hole in a tall hedge.

'Hello?'

A woman with short white hair was standing by the side of the gate, in gardening gloves and wellies.

'Mrs McKay? My name is Nicole Farrell and this is my niece, Millie.'

'So *you're* Nicole. I've heard a bit about you in the village and of course from my son. He only has lovely things to say about you. I'm Catherine McKay, by the way. How are you finding the house?'

'It's lovely, thank you.'

'I can see you've hurt your leg. Do you want to sit down? I'm just doing some pruning in the back garden if you want to come through.'

The hall was dark and cool, leading to a room each side, both low ceilinged and with beams running across. One had a large table and a dresser covered with old china; the other was a cosy living room with mismatched chairs and sofa. At the back was a sunny kitchen, with a table and chairs and a pale pink Aga. By the time Nicole had hopped through the cottage on her crutches, and through French doors to a garden bench, Millie had thrown herself on the grass and was crooning to a dog.

'I'm glad to meet you,' Nicole said. 'Josh mentioned he had grown up here.'

'We were wondering about the ghost sightings,' Millie said, getting her chin licked as she held her laughing face away from the terrier.

'Oh, I don't hold with ghosts.' Catherine chuckled. 'It's an old building, it creaks terribly. But I never saw a ghost, and I worked there for forty years. I still do the odd spell on the reception desk in the summer, when the boys are busy with the children.'

Nicole looked down at Millie. 'So if there was a ghost, Mrs McKay would have seen it.'

'Call me Cathy, please. I don't think it's a simple as that,' she said, sitting beside Nicole. 'Some people are just sensitive. My mother used to hear things in the big house, quick steps running across upstairs, that sort of thing. It used to sound like furniture moving around in the loft. I just blamed it on the pipes, and the creaky timbers heating up and cooling down, but she always blamed her cousin, Charlotte. She died young, you know.'

Nicole related her encounter with the attic.

Cathy laughed. 'Well, there you go. A broken window, a trapped bird. I do know we were always up there, puttying the windows and putting buckets down for leaks. It was too high for my husband to repair the roof. We had to get someone with the extra-long ladders belonging to the church just to put a few slates back. The storms hit this corner of the island hard. A really bad one brought the lighthouse down in 1843. Most of Chancel Hall is built out of the stone. Shall I make some tea?'

'Oh, we couldn't bother you—' Nicole said.

'Nonsense, it's nice to have visitors. I miss my son when he's on seabird duty – I hardly see him for four months. Tea or coffee?'

While she was in the kitchen, Millie inspected the outside of the cottage. 'This looks really old,' she said, touching the wall between sheets of climbers.

'This was the first Chancel House.' Catherine's voice drifted out of the open window. 'They were just lighthouse keepers and common sailors until they made their fortune in the late 1700s.' She carried out a tray. Nicole couldn't believe that a family who made a fortune in Jamaica in the eighteenth century weren't using or trading slaves.

She stared over the end of the garden, where the edge fell away. The cottage was enclosed in a densely planted garden with hedges, but a gap had been left for a perfect sea view. Catherine could sit on her bench and see the shack on the islet where Josh was working.

'Were you working at the hotel when I was there, renting one of the holiday flats?'

'I used to be the housekeeper, and my husband was the handyman. I moved back when my father died in 1971, and Josh was born a few years later. Aunt Emma left my parents the cottage when she sold the hotel. Hopefully, Josh will take over the cottage when I'm gone.'

'And he owns the aquarium, too?'

'That he got from his dad. Ratty old building. It was originally owned by two Victorian ladies as a tourist attraction. Josh is trying to get planning permission to turn it into two flats and maybe a couple of offices to rent out.'

Nicole scooted up to make more room for her on the bench. 'He has a strange fish in the freezer there.'

'He told me about that when a tourist brought it in. I hope you find out more about it. I think he said it was in Patience's old rockpool book.'

Nicole sat back in the sunshine, her attention following butterflies looping from flower to flower, honeybees drunk with nectar and bumblebees dusted with pollen. 'I can see why people thought the captain haunted the place.'

'I think his ghost is at rest. But his son Edwin had two girls, Charlotte and Emma. You should look into them – now that's a ghost story if there is one. They say Charlotte's ghost followed Emma back to the hall.' Catherine smiled at her. 'The boys – Justin and Robert who run the hotel now – use the attics as offices and storage now, but some of the family's old stuff is still up there. If you two are interested, you could take a look. There might be documents or pictures. Someone could write it up for the local history newsletter.'

'You could do that,' Nicole said to Millie, nudging her niece, who was smoothing the dog's ears through her fingers until it was almost hypnotised. 'You used to write things for the parish paper.'

'I could do,' Millie said, squinting up at her. 'Especially if it is really haunted up there...'

26

JULY 1941

Lily and Bernie had arranged Oliver's bed in the middle of the room, so they could move around both sides like a hospital bed. Bernie had found a couple of extra pillows and a spare blanket in case he felt the cold. Local people had offered useful things like a bedpan, a commode and an invalid cup. The hospital had arranged for his notes to be dropped at the island hospital, and for one of the doctors to visit after rounds that evening.

'We haven't forgotten anything, have we?' Bernie fussed. 'Maybe I should have got some beef extract for him...'

Lily shook her head, laughing. 'I have brought some Ovaltine from Chancel Hall. You can make it up with powdered milk if he isn't hungry. But I'm sure if he is well enough to come home, he'll want home cooking.' It was her first trip back after the weekend with Emma, who had reverted to being almost silent for most of the time. 'He'll be here in a minute. Shall we wait outside? I heard the boat coming in.'

Bernie fussed even as she put on her cardigan. 'There's a nasty wind blowing off the sea.'

'He'll be well wrapped up,' Lily reassured her. 'And it's not cold out there. Remember, it's July.'

Oliver was transported, on a stretcher, off the ferry and carried up the hill to the flat. Then he was placed on a stout chair, easier since he was just skin and bone, and carried up the stairs, Lily's hands holding Bernie's throughout to stop her running forward and interrupting the ambulance men. They knew what they were doing, they were cheerful and got Ollie up the stairs easily.

'Come on.' Lily urged her to follow the men. 'Let's get Ollie settled and comfortable.'

Oliver reluctantly allowed them to put him to bed, but he insisted on getting up for the evening meal.

'We got some fresh mackerel from Mr Turner. Lily cooks it with oatmeal, it's delicious.' Bernie put a cushion on the kitchen chair, only to have him remove it with his bandaged hand. The other one had three fingers still bandaged, but the rest of the skin was healing, shiny and red like it had been painted with lacquer.

'I'll be very comfortable here,' he said, sighing. 'It's so good to be home. The French were very kind but I couldn't understand a word and was too ill to eat anything but broth.'

'How long were you there?' Lily said, deftly filleting one of the fish, feeling for hidden bones.

'They told me it was seven weeks. An English agent came to the farm where I was being held under the eaves, nearly freezing or boiling to death, to be honest. He organised getting me out, but... I couldn't cope with the pain, my broken leg hadn't knitted properly and I was almost screaming. They knocked me out with morphine to transport me in a truck with pigs going to slaughter. I think that's the closest I got to death, but at least I don't remember much. It was an abattoir transporter. I was jammed in the back behind a stall. The Nazis wouldn't let their dogs search because they might get covered with manure.'

He sighed and Bernie jumped, but he looked happy to be home. Lily went back to preparing the fish. After the meal, Ollie was happy to go and lie down, and Lily helped him to the bathroom first. He flushed bright red at needing help, but she left him to it and Bernie walked him back to bed afterwards. 'I think I'll sleep better at home,' he said, sinking into a pillow and letting Lily pull the blanket up.

'You're a lot better than we expected,' Lily said with a smile.

'Well, tomorrow the nurse will come, and I'll be rebandaged,' he said. 'Will you still be here?'

'I'm working tomorrow,' she said, sitting on the chair beside him. 'I'm so glad to see you again. I don't think we've met since you were just eleven or twelve.'

'I remember,' he said, his eyelids heavy. 'You were such a beautiful young lady. I remember your pearls and your shiny shoes.'

She laughed. 'I'd just got engaged,' she said. 'We moved to London after I got married and then I had Grace.' Her eyes brimmed with tears.

His better hand found hers, squeezed gently. 'I know. I was so sorry to hear.' Lily clung to him for a moment.

'I have a picture, if you'd like to see her?'

When he nodded, she unfolded the snap she kept in her wallet at all times but rarely showed anyone. Grace had been five in the picture, before she was really ill but after the X-ray had found the lump in her head.

'Oh, she's lovely,' he said, looking up at her, and back at the picture. 'I'm guessing your husband is dark-haired?'

'James? He is.'

'Is he serving?'

Lily glanced at him. She knew James had felt the pressure to fight, especially after Grace had died. 'He's part of the British

Geographical Section. He makes maps from reconnaissance photographs taken of the continent. He's doing some training to take better pictures.'

Oliver nodded, his eyes wide. 'We rely on those maps,' he said. His face dropped and he looked at his hands. 'Well, *relied*.'

'Of course,' she said. Then, hearing Bernie going down to answer the door, 'That's probably the doctor.'

'You don't mind me staying, do you? Will you be all right in with Bernie?' He reached his good hand out.

'Of course I will,' she said, putting out her own fingers. His skin was hot and hard, the gauze soft and tickly. 'We get on so well, and I have the room back on Morwen four nights a week. You must come and see, when you feel better.'

'They never wanted anything to do with us, the Chancels,' he said, looking small in the bed, on the banked-up pillows. He looked scared, and she could feel the tension in him.

'Well, now, young man,' a doctor said, walking into the room. 'Is this your young lady? She still can't stay.'

'No, no, it's my cousin Lily,' he stammered. As Lily shut the door, she could hear the doctor's voice.

'Now, I'm not going to pull you about too much, so don't worry. I'll just make sure there isn't any damage after that long journey.'

Lily walked into the living room and sat at the table as Bernie stood by the kettle, which was sizzling on the stove. 'Do you think he's all right?' Bernie asked. 'Did we do the right thing? I don't mind telling you, I was so glad to see him I wondered if it was just my selfishness, taking him away from that lovely hospital.'

'He was never going to get better surrounded by all that suffering,' Lily said. 'No, fresh air and good food, that's what he needs. It was what I needed, too, and look how much better I am? I had to let the waist out on my skirt.'

Bernie smiled at that. 'You were a sad little thing, when you came. Like a flower in need of water.'

The doctor came out and was able to put Bernie's mind at rest. Oliver needed good food and good company. He seemed a little down in the mouth, and the two of them could cheer him up. After a few anxious questions from Bernie, he advised her that Oliver could be left for a few hours at a time – Bernie couldn't lose time from work – and when the doctor had gone, the two women agreed to stagger their lunch hours so they could go in from work at different times.

'I can make myself a sandwich,' Ollie called out from the bed, but his voice was weak and by the time Lily took in his tea, he was already fast asleep.

27

PRESENT DAY, 16 JUNE

Nicole found herself speculating like a teenager on Joshua's movements over the next day. Was he on the islet or was he in the town? Was he thinking of her, or had she not crossed his mind? While she sorted through a career's worth of papers, chucking almost all of it into bin bags, she listened out for his footsteps on the cobbles.

She drank her coffee on the outside tables on the quay, rather than in the shaded garden behind, hoping to see him. She knew she was doing it, but it was an exercise in knowing the new Nicole, who could hop around on one leg in a dress – as long as it was a maxi.

And it was clear that the new Nicole longed for Josh's company. She'd found a friend, she rationalised. It was just a friendship with someone who shared her interests. She kept telling herself that as she chose the most flattering clothes, the hat that stopped her nose going red.

When she got up to go back to the cottage, her mobile vibrated. She'd turned the ringer off ages ago; she found she couldn't answer the questions of people who were still living in that other world. She did check the name, though, in case it was Millie.

But it was Josh. She sat back in her seat and managed to answer before it stopped buzzing.

'Hello?' She sounded quite breathless, like she'd been running. 'Josh, hi,' she dropped her voice to a normal tone.

'I was wondering if you were free this afternoon?' The line was crackly, the signal bad, even in the street.

Her chest lurched into an irregular rhythm, and she suddenly felt warm, shaky. A cynical part of her mocked her body for its reaction.

'Um. I might be,' she managed to say. She cleared her throat, took a deep breath to calm her heart. 'What do you suggest?'

'Do you know where Morwen School is?'

'I think so...'

His voice was businesslike, practical. 'I have to do a talk there this afternoon. I wondered, if I email my notes over, you could chat to the children?'

Nicole had a hideous vision of a classroom of teenagers. '*Chat?*'

'It's easy. I set up a saltwater tank there a few weeks ago, and they've collected some creatures and put them in. It's just a talk until I take them down to the sea to let the animals go.'

'I mean, I suppose I could....'

'Charlotte will be there, the teacher. You've met her, I think?'

'I have,' she said uncertainly. Some doubt must have crept into her voice. 'How many children will there be?'

'Half a dozen, probably. Maybe a few strays from another school. Play it by ear, but they're lovely kids.'

She agreed, but her morning peace had instantly evaporated, and her confidence burned away with it.

. . .

Nicole pushed the door open into the cool, quiet cottage, and shut it behind her with some relief. Millie was sitting in the garden, earbuds in, listening to music on her phone and reading a book. Nicole stashed her crutches in the hall and bumped upstairs, picking up dust on her dress. She sat in the padded chair by the window and stared out at the islet.

She had to admit to herself she had a crush on the tanned, long-haired man from her youth. Maybe she was yearning for that simpler past, full of firsts. First lovers, first projects, first independent choices. Maybe that was what it was, a craving to go back to that life, when she was vivid and alive, her emotions raw and exciting, her body young – and whole.

A moment of grief hit her then, and tears rose and trickled from her eyelids. She bowed her head and let the feelings bubble up. The horror of seeing her crushed limb when she awoke in the hospital, seeing it every colour of the rainbow, crisscrossed with lines of stitches and staples and tubes and dressings for the first few weeks. And the pain, rolling in, leaving her exhausted in the minute or so in between each wave. At first, she had believed that she had caved in to the idea of amputation following advice from the doctors and her family, but she could look back with clarity now. It was the first sight of her black, dead toes, in the light of her exhaustion and despair. She had chosen to lose the leg because it made scientific sense, because it gave her a future.

Pull yourself together. She bumped back downstairs and hopped into the garden. She tapped Millie's hand, making her start.

'Are you working today?' Nicole said, sitting in the chair.

'Not until four. Francesco and I are going for a walk before work. Why?'

'I said I would go up to the school to give a little talk. Can you come with me? To give me some confidence.'

Millie rolled her eyes. 'They're little *kids*. And it's hot, and I don't want to miss my walk.'

'You won't.' Nicole looked at the lounging teenager. 'What's going on between you and Francesco, anyway?'

'Nothing.' Millie sat up and switched off her music. 'We're just like best friends from another life. Or lovers from the past. Cesco says our souls are connected.'

'Hmm. You really like him? He's engaged, remember.'

'I know, it's not like that.' But the wild rose in Millie's cheeks said otherwise.

'Millie, please be careful.'

The girl smiled, a little sadness in her expression. 'I might have a little crush on him, that's all. All the staff do. He's just funny and nice and so *kind*.'

'Is he taking other girls for afternoon walks?'

Millie's gaze slid away. 'No, but that's just because we have so much in common. He misses Italy, I let him talk about it. And *her*.'

'So, you've done this before?'

Millie shrugged. 'Couple of times.'

'Well, be careful.' Nicole sighed. 'Don't let yourself get hurt.'

Nicole and Millie walked along to the lane and the turn-off to the school. It wasn't until she got there that she realised she hadn't worried or bothered about the walking, kicking her artificial foot out easily with each step. She had chosen a long skirt – it really was too hot for jeans – and hoped no one would notice. Josh was already there – she could see him through the panoramic windows of an old, peeling, temporary building. Charlotte, the teacher, waved her in.

There were three steps up to the door, and she had to cling to the railing and swing her leg up each time to get to the top.

'Thank you for coming,' Charlotte said, ushering them in. Josh gave them a little wave. Nicole's heart lurched for a moment, but she quickly turned to the children. Charlotte pointed to the back of the classroom, where there was a large fish tank. 'We're just getting ready to release our sea animals back at high tide. We'd love you to tell us more about them.'

'I'll try,' Nicole said uncertainly. She looked at the children. There were six kids between about five and twelve years old. She gave Josh an anxious smile. It was awkward to be businesslike after that wonderful day on the beach.

'How are you?' His local accent slowed his deep voice down, carrying over the excited squeals of the children. 'Not too much sand damage?'

'Not much,' she said, looking at the tops of the children's heads. Not her normal audience of politicians and science advisers, and she didn't know how to get their attention.

Charlotte did. In three minutes, the kids were sitting in their chairs and even Millie was waiting expectantly. Nicole walked carefully to the seawater aquarium.

A couple of squat lobsters, one brown, one more orange and barely longer than a prawn, patrolled each end of the tank. In the middle, a whelk shell wobbled, with the front claws of a hermit crab dragging it along. A few shrimps, and a few living shellfish moving over the glass made up the collection. A mound of black, grape-like objects sat near the front, on the coarse sand.

'You've got some great specimens here,' she started. 'You're going to have to come over and tell me where you found them all.'

The children crowded around her, explaining where they found them, what they had called them, naming each species correctly. Finally, Charlotte got them to sit down again and Nicole pointed to the grape-like objects.

'Does anyone know what these are?' A slender black boy

who'd been introduced as Beau shot his hand up along with the oldest child, Rhiannon.

'Yes, Beau?'

'We think they are some sort of eggs.'

Out of the corner of her eye, she saw Josh smiling.

'They are. You'll need to let all these crabs and shrimps and animals go, so that the eggs can hatch out safely. Have you got a torch, Charlotte? Quite a bright one?'

Charlotte rummaged in her desk drawer. 'How about this? Felicity, pass it over.'

'Thank you.' She looked around – she couldn't stand on tiptoe any more. 'Could I borrow that stool?'

It was about a foot high, probably used for reaching the ceiling. Felicity placed it next to the tank and she put her foot on it, pulling the artificial one next to it with a clunk. All eyes swivelled to her leg as she leaned over and shone the light through the eggs. 'Can anyone see anything?'

The children leaned forward, then Felicity pointed. 'It's got a baby animal in it! Like a little starfish.'

'It does. Not a starfish, though. Can anyone see?'

Beau nudged his younger brother. 'Go on, Billy, you say.'

'Is it a baby octopus? Wiggling.' The little boy was open-eyed with amazement.

'Nearly right. Oh, I can't get down, can you help me, Beau?'

He solemnly handed her down, helping her balance.

'Those are baby cuttlefish in their eggs,' she said.

Charlotte held up a cuttlefish bone. 'We found this on the beach last year – it's been on our nature table.'

The kids went for a look, except for Beau, who stood next to her, staring into the tank.

'When will the babies come out?' the youngest child asked.

'I think quite soon. So, we need to get all the little creatures with claws or teeth out, because the hatchlings will be very small and we don't want them to get eaten. Once they are

out and swimming, you can let them go. Maybe you can
release them where you found the cuttlebone – what do you
think?'

Millie tapped her wrist, waved goodbye and sidled towards
the door.

The children were talking excitedly, crowding around the
tank. 'I have a question.' Josh had his hand up, and the children
turned to him. 'Why are the eggs black? I mean, octopus eggs
are usually white or pink.'

'Well, octopus mothers lay their eggs in little caves, and look
after them until they hatch. But the cuttlefish have to leave their
eggs, so they squirt a little ink into each one as they lay them to
hide the babies.'

Josh raised his eyebrows and grinned. 'Is that so? I never
knew that.'

She smiled at the kids. 'Any more questions?' Hands shot
up. 'Yes, Beau?'

'What happened to your leg?'

She carefully avoided looking at the adults and spoke
directly to the faces of the children. 'I had a very big accident,
and broke my leg. Any questions about the animals before you
release them?'

Merryn, the youngest child, held up her arm. 'When I was
little, I broke my arm. But it mended.'

'I'm glad,' Nicole said, with a smile. The little girl looked
sad, so she bent down to talk to her. 'Most broken bones make
themselves better quite quickly.'

'My arm won't go like your leg, will it?' she whispered, tears
spilling over her eyelashes. 'All black and shiny.'

'This isn't a real leg,' Nicole said, and on impulse, slid her
skirt up a little. 'See, my leg couldn't get better, so they took it
away and gave me a new one. I'm going to buy a pretty cover for
it. I'm getting used to it, and one day I won't need a stick or
crutches.'

'Wow.' Billy crouched down and tapped her shoe. 'Can you take it off?'

The laughter bubbled up. 'I can, but I'm not going to! Let's have a look at that hermit crab. His shell seems a bit big for him.'

The children broke into explanations about how, outgrowing a battered old shell, he had moved into the only one available. She looked up, meeting Josh's eyes. He silently clapped his hands together and her face warmed with a blush.

After another few minutes of looking at pictures she had brought, feeding the crabs with some frozen shrimp and admiring a butterfish when it appeared from behind a rock, Charlotte ended the session with a big thank you and a round of applause. Nicole couldn't help laughing, the kids were so fresh and unaffected and interested in the sea. Josh spoke in her ear. 'What do you think, a few new marine biologists?'

'And possibly an orthopaedic surgeon,' she chuckled, looking at Beau.

'Well, we need those, too. Beau's dad is a diver – he sets up expeditions locally. I'd still like you to cast an eye over that reef we're checking out. We're going on Friday.'

'Oh.' She thought about the idea, the weightless freedom of being underwater. The awkwardness of having her amputation exposed. 'Yes, I'll come. On one condition.'

'OK,' he said cautiously.

'Can you walk me back? I brought a bag and it's awkward.'

Josh's slow smile came out. 'Any time.'

28

JULY 1941

He's coming.

James had written to say he had four days of leave. He'd also mentioned how hard he found it to talk about Grace, which was at least better than not mentioning her at all. He'd also said he missed her, his wife...

Lily's nervousness seemed to spill onto Emma as she helped spring-clean the room that Lily had been sleeping in. They scrubbed the old bathroom, even getting the plumber to fix the dripping tap that had lulled Lily to sleep. The room was very comfortable, but the wind rattled through the gaps in the window and a missing corner in the glass, billowing the curtains on stormy nights. The bed was huge, but it gave Lily pause as she decided whether to share with James or perhaps open up one of the other rooms on the main floor. *I am his wife... it's the wifely thing to do...*

She knew James would respect her wishes; he wasn't the sort to be overcome with his emotions, even when they were first married.

'Can we tidy up the attic? Next to the lumber room,' Emma had asked as they ate their evening meal – a little liver and onions with some greens gone wild in what had been Mrs May's husband's vegetable patch. Lily was staring to clear one end of the ground, and Mr Prendergast, who was always giving her produce from his own garden, had given her carrot, lettuce and onion seeds to sow and promised her broad bean plants for the autumn.

'We can make a start, if you like,' Lily agreed, finishing her raspberries, also from the overgrown garden. The door to the loft room, which Emma described as the Captain's Cabin, was always locked, but Emma thought they might be able to prise the door with an old chisel from the tool shed. 'What's in there?'

Emma just shrugged, putting the dishes and cups in the deep sink, pouring in a little hot water from the kettle. 'I haven't been up there since the accident. Charlotte and I went up to look around when we moved in, but Daddy thought it was a bit dangerous.'

Lily picked up the tea towel to help dry. Emma had just started allowing her to help. 'Is it safe up there?'

'Daddy just thought the windows were very low. As if one of us would lean out too far,' she scoffed. 'We weren't babies, we were seventeen.' Then she fell very quiet, her jaw moving as she seemed to think about something. 'Maybe he was worried *she* would push me out.'

'But you were close with your sister?'

Emma frowned as she put a saucepan on the drainer. 'Close? I suppose... we were never apart, except for a few hours at school. Mostly we were together. Charlotte was the talker. I never spoke to anyone, I don't very much now, really. Just to you.'

Lily was touched. 'And I'm very pleased you do.' She draped the tea towel over the stove to dry and the two of them gathered up some water in a bucket with a little soda in it, a few old cloths, the broom and dustpan and brush. They kept their aprons on, and Lily changed her slippers for shoes, reasoning

that there might be the odd loose nail as there had been in the
adjoining lumber room.

Emma got increasingly tense as she plodded up the stairs.
She slowed to a stop in front of the attic steps.

'Are you worried?' Lily asked, grasping Emma's elbow,
which made her jump. 'What are you afraid of?'

Emma mumbled something, opened the door and looked
anxiously up the stairs.

'What do you expect?' Lily said, squeezing around Emma
and starting up the steps.

'Something Charlotte left up there,' Emma muttered, her
voice a little slurred, as it had been when they first met.

'It will be fine,' Lily said, stopping at the door, testing the
lock. It seemed solid but the door jamb was rotted through
with woodworm. 'We need to be careful, if the floor is wormy,'
she said. By prising alongside the lock's tongue and
compressing the soft wood, she managed to swing the door
open.

It was a long room, the length of the whole house, with
three windows spilling rectangles of evening light onto broad
oak boards. They looked in good condition, and a woven runner
ran the whole length of the attic. There were two buckets under
one of the windows – perhaps there had been a leak, but the
room didn't smell of damp.

Through the dirty windows, the sea stretched away, over
the low islands and beyond. Emma followed her, shuffling
slowly, her limp more prominent.

'What's wrong?' Lily pushed a large swivel chair out of the
way, its castors screeching in protest, the leather crackling
under her fingers. A corner of the window in front was cracked
right across, and Lily could see other defects in all the windows.
'We should tape that up,' she suggested. She turned to Emma,
who was white faced. 'What is it?'

'I thought she would be up here,' Emma said, in a low whisper. 'I thought this is where she lives, after the accident. This is where I hear her talking to me, above my bedroom.'

Lily put a hand on Emma's arm and found it was shaking. 'There's nothing up here but dust and memories,' she said gently. 'Charlotte died many, many years ago.'

'I never saw her afterwards,' Emma said. 'After the accident, when I was in hospital, they had the funeral. But when I woke up, I could hear her talking to me, whispering in my ear like she did in church or at school. She did all the talking.'

'How long were you unconscious in the hospital?'

Emma shrugged. 'It was March when we had the accident. I woke up in September, properly, but I had been moving and crying in the summer. I just don't remember it.'

Lily was shocked. 'That was a terrible time for you all. You must have been very badly hurt.'

'Afterwards, I asked for Charlotte, all the time. I know they kept telling me she was dead, but I couldn't believe it when she spoke to me every day. I just couldn't find her.'

It sounded impossible, but Lily knew it wasn't. 'After Grace died,' she said, a lump gathering in her throat, 'I heard her call out my name. If I went to the park, I could hear her laughing on the swings.'

'So, you understand?'

'I think I do. You and your sister were so close, being twins, you expected to hear her all the time. So your mind gave you what you were expecting.'

'And the dreams,' Emma said, staring out of the window. 'She's there in the dreams, too...'

'I wake up with Grace laughing, or crying, or in my arms,' Lily said, aware now of the sheet of tears running down her face. 'Last night, I said: "What a little lump you are" to her, because she's grown. She did grow, before she got ill. Then I woke up and she was gone. It was just a dream.'

For a long moment, Lily and Emma stared at each other, Emma's hand reaching for Lily's, squeezing, letting go.

'Perhaps we should put flowers on Charlotte's grave?' Lily suggested, a painful wrench at the thought of how far away her daughter's grave was.

'I don't think she'd like that,' Emma said, her face closing down, and she turned away.

'Maybe she would. We could get some of Mr Barker's carnations for her.'

'She does like flowers,' Emma said, doubtfully. 'But she'd prefer sweets.'

'Well, we'll take sweets as well,' Lily said, wondering how she was going to find sweets in wartime, on an island where the shop was half empty at best. 'I could make something,' she offered instead. 'We could make a bit of toffee, or fudge.' She mentally thought over their ration allowance for sugar.

'It's so far down,' Emma said, leaning over to look through one of the dusty panes. 'Look.' She had a dreamy look on her face.

'Are you hearing Charlotte?' Lily said, with a sharp note in her voice.

'I think she would want me to jump. She wants us to be together.' Emma looked up, her face tearless, blank.

'Oh, Emma. Does she often ask you to do that?' Lily asked, her heart beating faster, her arms tense with the effort of not grabbing Emma. 'Do you hear her a lot?'

'Most of the time, she's there.' Emma stepped closer to Lily, as if for comfort. Lily put her arms around her until the dark head dropped onto her shoulder. Emma looked heavy because she wore several layers of clothes; up close, she was frail as a bird. 'It's just me imagining, I know that really, the doctors explained.'

'She's not real,' Lily managed to choke out.

'Grace isn't real, either,' Emma said, lifting her head to look straight at Lily.

'No. It's terribly sad, but they are both gone.'

A bang downstairs made them both jump and Emma gasp.

Lily turned towards the door. 'Let's go down. We can always come back another time. There's lots of family mementoes, but there's definitely no one up here. And no way in, unless you're a seagull.'

Emma turned to go back onto the landing. 'I feel better now,' she said, looking over her shoulder at Lily. 'Isn't that stupid? It wasn't a ghost, it was probably just something banging in the wind.'

Lily still shook off a shiver, perhaps from the draught coming in the broken windows. 'Let's look in all the other rooms, to prove to ourselves that there's no one here.'

Emma almost smiled, her lips twitching. 'Even in Charlotte's room?'

'In *all* the rooms.'

29

PRESENT DAY, 18 JUNE

Nicole soon realised that Beau, the little boy at the school, had essentially outed her to the whole island. The local people now felt free to ask about the accident she had undergone three months of therapy even to mention. Now all she needed was a gin at the pub or to sit on the quay and someone would come along and ask her about it.

Except Josh. He smiled when she mentioned her leg but didn't pursue it. Even when she asked about wetsuits with only one trouser leg, he smiled.

She did meet Ash, the diving instructor, a slim guy in his thirties with the same dark colouring as his son, Beau. He sized her up straight away for a wetsuit and told her he would just tape up the spare bit of leg. 'Have you dived in cold water?' he asked, as he was checking her height. 'You're a good fit for this yellow one,' he said.

'No, I've only dived in tropical water.' The Red Sea, that had been amazing. She'd been constantly anxious about diving in Australia, but she had never even seen a shark. 'At least the wildlife won't try and kill me here,' she quipped.

'No. The cold water might, though,' he said, tagging the suit for her. 'So, we need to be careful. It's so beautiful, it's easy to forget to check your core temperature. The water around here is freezing.'

'The sea off the beach was lovely.'

He shrugged one shoulder. 'Because it had come up over hot sand. But once you get offshore, the temperature drops. And we still have sharks and jellyfish that can scare you. More accidents happen in diving because someone panics than anything else.'

'Sharks?'

He smiled. 'Seeing a basking shark loom out the blue will give anyone a heart attack. Once you realise that they are just after the plankton, you relax, but they are huge.'

'Have you ever seen a dolphin underwater?' she asked, checking out his storeroom in an old canning shed on the shore.

'A few times. We see seals much more often. They're so nosy. They do bite your fins, sometimes, but they're just exploring. Like puppies, they don't have hands, so they feel things with their mouths. I take my camera – we get fabulous shot of birds diving at this time of year.' He glanced down at the stick. 'I think it might be fun for you. You won't need crutches down there.'

She smiled, rueful. 'I'm not sure how I can get back on the boat.'

'Same as me. There's just one foothold. You sit on the gunwale, swing your legs – leg – in. Charlotte said you were cool about it at the school.'

She sighed and sat on the only chair. 'To be honest, I was only cool about it with the children. I haven't entirely processed it all myself. A bit of post-traumatic stress. I was originally talking to a counsellor, once a week. Now I talk to nosy people in the village three times a day, it's getting easier.'

He laughed. He tagged another wetsuit with the name Josh. 'I'm ex-navy,' he said. 'I've work with quite a few amputees.

One was my instructor, a great bloke called Cappy. He loved the freedom. I think you will, too.'

She looked around the room. 'Charlotte said you haven't been here long?'

'About a year.' He turned around to the weight belts and gas bottles. 'I love it. I had to fight for custody of the boys, so stayed around to be with them. I've found so many opportunities here. A house, which we've just extended; jobs, which I've cobbled together. And Charlotte, of course.'

So you and she haven't been together long?'

'Moved in a few months ago. But we've been involved for a year.'

'Congratulations. You look like a happy family. So, where does Josh want to dive?'

'Deadman's Reef.' He smiled. 'I know, it sounds like something out of a pirate movie. But there are literally *hundreds* of wrecks caught on the rocks, which are covered with corals. I think Josh has identified a problem.'

She walked back along the shore, leaning less on her stick for support and more for balance. She stopped to sit on the low wall separating the beach from the fields alongside the hotel. Close to shore, a small motorboat was creating a little wake behind it, two people laughing or talking, then leaning in to kiss. She felt a shock of recognition when she saw Millie's swimsuit and the colourful skirt she'd been wearing that morning. Even her mop of gingery curls, blowing around her face. And the tall, black-haired young man could only be Francesco.

She was shocked. Millie, if she hadn't actually lied, had been playing down the relationship between the two. She didn't know whether to broach the subject – no, she had to trust Millie, treat her like an adult, not a surrogate child.

She was finding it difficult to talk about her own feelings for Josh, after all.

. . .

The next day, the phone company installed the new landline and internet. Nicole shot an email around friends and family with the new number and waited for their calls to come in. It was lovely to hear from people. Some had been wary after she had been so depressed and uncommunicative at the hospital. As people did call, she had found herself apologising a lot.

Within hours, Kim, a friend from work, emailed and asked if they could chat. Nicole suggested a time and the phone rang on time in the early evening.

'Nicole, it was great to hear from you!'

Her voice was rich and warm. An environmental lobbyist, they were usually on the same page, but she was more political and budget focused than Nicole. 'I wondered how you were coping.'

'I'm good,' Nicole said, doing a mental health check. 'I'm really bouncing back.'

'That's good news. Look, I'm in your neck of the woods next week. I wondered if we could meet up, maybe in Cornwall, have lunch, chat over things?'

Nicole's emotional antennae twitched. 'I'm off the job completely, now. If you're looking for information—'

'No, not at all! Last time I saw you, you were so miserable and fragile. I want to see your recovery with my own eyes. And moan about Ben and Lisa, obviously.'

Nicole uncramped her fingers from the handset. 'I'm about thirty miles from Penzance, in the Atlantic. I'm not sure...'

'There are helicopters. I looked up the schedule. You get to the helipad in Penzance, I will send a car. Next Tuesday.'

For a moment, Nicole remembered the wonderful car services, great hotels and excursions companies provided for conferences and fact-finding missions. 'Well, that would be great. We can't meet too far out of Penzance, though. I can only be away for a few hours. I'm looking after my niece.'

'I'm going to be staying in a little place in St Ives, overlooking the sea. It has a great pool – bring your swimsuit. I'll book you a room if you like.'

Nicole shut her eyes. 'I'm not sure, I'm not a hundred per cent yet.' *Millie – and Francesco? Would she be all right if I go away overnight?* She didn't want to precipitate an escalation in the young lovers' relationship.

'I know, I know. But it would be lovely to see you, and honestly, I could do with a bit of a handover. You left so abruptly. The company will pay, you know.'

The company. The government. Kim had a point, the accident had abruptly ended her career, not because she couldn't do it, but because she couldn't imagine going back to the life where she'd nearly been killed. No, she had to trust Millie's common sense.

'All right, then. One night.' She'd tell Jade, who got on well with Millie. Maybe they could have a girls' night in together.

They arranged the details even as Nicole wondered what she was getting into. When they rang off, she sat in the slowly darkening room, thinking about work. For months she hadn't even been able to remember the place with any kind of objectivity. Which was daft; it wasn't her job that caused the accident, it was an idiot of a driver who had just forgotten for one moment which side of the road to drive on. She felt bad even thinking of him as an idiot – he'd died in the crash, his wife injured.

The accident. The dark road, just at dusk, nose-to-tail traffic for miles, then opening up and everyone raising their speed. The car on the outside lane had seen his exit and just pulled straight in front of her. She recalled being calm, tipped forward by gravity in slow motion as the windscreen shattered into thousands of stars, the seatbelt catching her as her limbs and head carried on forward, the impact of the airbag. There wasn't pain, just increasing pressure until it was almost unbearable, then the slumping back of her seat as the vehicle rang like a bell, and the front of the car slammed into both her legs.

Then the pain building up as the sounds returned: car engines, car horns, more screaming of brakes, squealing of tyres on the road, more distant crashes.

She shook away the images, not willing to fall back into the recollection of pain and fear and rescue and the first few days. She'd had a head injury and had been placed in a therapeutic coma, the merciful sleep. Time passed differently. She was woken up a week later into more pain and demanding people. *Squeeze my hand, just cough, swallow this.* The smell of antiseptic, the mask, oxygen.

She stood up in an attempt to leave the memories in the armchair, and limped into the hall, holding onto the walls. Millie was out, so she couldn't talk to her, and images and sounds were replaying like a recorded nightmare. Her mother's face, the repeated surgeries on her leg, the endless physio.

There was another handset on the counter in the kitchen and she picked it up. She had already put some numbers in – the shop, the pub for Millie, Josh. *Josh.*

She called his mobile. When he answered, she almost folded from the pain in her middle, whether of memory or relief, she couldn't tell.

'Uh, hi, Josh,' she managed to stammer out.

'Nicole?' His voice was sharp. 'Are you OK? What's wrong?'

'No.' The word slipped out, desolate and childlike. 'I mean, I'm OK, I just remembered—' She lost her breath again.

'Take a breath. Sit down and tell me.' She could hear the screaming of hundreds of birds in the background, probably settling into their nests before the sun went down.

'I didn't want to bother you.'

He laughed at that, a soft chuckle. 'What do you think I'm doing on the rock? I don't have a TV, it's not like I'm watching the football.'

She smiled through unexpected tears, and unclenched her

fist before her nails cut into her palm. 'A friend from work phoned today. It just reminded me of... of *before*.'

'Of the life you lost?'

Put on the spot like that, Nicole didn't know what to say. She sat at the table, thinking. 'I didn't give in my notice just because of the accident. I'd been unhappy for a while.'

'Why? What did you do on all those scientific committees?'

It was her turn to laugh. 'It didn't matter what we did. The government didn't follow through. Not enough, anyway. Otherwise you'd have your Marine Conservation Zone.'

He puffed out a frustrated breath. 'We spent years putting the application together, only to be told they needed more information. We gathered it for six years, then they refused it anyway.'

'You need to apply again.'

'I don't know what I need to change to get it through.' He paused. 'You could help me.'

She took a deep breath. 'I'm only here for a year, remember.'

'Well, think how much you could guide us in a year.'

The idea of working with him on the seas around his incredible islands was exciting. 'Maybe. We could talk.'

'In the meantime, you're upset.'

'I was.' She tipped her head on one side. 'I am. You're probably going to tell me to live in the moment, to leave the past behind.'

'Do something mindful and useful. Take my meditative practice this evening. I cleaned the solar panels, emptied the composting loo and heated a can of chilli over one gas ring, until the bottle ran out. I ate it lukewarm. Simple tasks cheer you up – when you stop, anyway.'

She looked over the kitchen, checking in the cupboards for dried fruit and flour. 'I suppose I could cook something for Millie. Maybe teabread for breakfast.'

'You can make teabread?' The longing in his voice made her laugh.

'A six-year-old can make teabread! But I don't know if Millie even likes it. And I can't eat a whole one by myself.'

'I will be there, eight o'clock sharp. Save a piece for me.'

30

JULY 1941

James had persuaded Lily that she did not need to meet him at the ferry, so he turned up at the town hall on Friday morning, dusty and tired, dragging a leather kitbag. Mr Prendergast immediately brought him down to where Lily was working, setting a chair for him.

'We're so very glad to have you here,' he gushed, his accent more Welsh than usual. 'Let me organise a cup of tea for you. You must be absolutely parched.'

Lily looked up, holding two pages with bone spatulas. 'James!' she breathed. 'Sorry, I'm stuck here for a few minutes.' When Mr Prendergast bustled out, she leaned forward for a quick kiss, just a brush of their lips. She couldn't think whether she was more excited or apprehensive about his visit, but her heart was racing. 'I can get off a little early.'

'No rush,' he said, looking around the room. She had put up various pieces of information around the walls – expert advice for each book – and he studied a couple. 'I'd like that tea, first. The last ferry to Morwen is on the hour, apparently.'

She checked her watch. 'Oh, that's plenty of time.'

When Mr Prendergast returned with a tray for two, he asked about the journey.

Lily concentrated on the pages while the two men made small talk.

'Will Miss Chancel be at the house while you're there?' Mr Prendergast asked.

That made her jump. 'Of course. Why wouldn't she be?'

'I just thought...' He went quite red, smiled, gave a little half bow, and then retreated to the safety of the library upstairs.

James rested his hip on the end of the worktable and laughed. 'I think he's concerned that Miss Chancel might play gooseberry for the whole weekend.'

Lily laughed. 'It's her home! Anyway, she's my cousin, you should meet her. If we want to talk in private there are some lovely walks nearby.' James looked like he wanted to say more, but Lily changed the subject. 'I'd like you to meet Oliver, too. And Emma hasn't met Bernie. The two branches of the family were never in touch.'

'That's hardly surprising.' He sipped his tea, raising an eyebrow. 'This tea is very good. Not like the muddy water we've been getting in the office.'

Lily let the pages settle, checking that the glue was dry and that they weren't going to weld themselves back together again. 'I know Emma and I are from the captain's legitimate children, and Bernie's mother wasn't married, but that isn't Cissie and Bernie's fault. Emma needs all the family she can get.'

He shrugged. 'People don't forget or forgive that easily. Perhaps less so on the islands where all the scandals played out in the open.'

'Bernice's mother was sixteen when she got pregnant,' Lily said, covering her work with delicate shrouds of muslin. 'She was a maid at the house. Her master was nearly seventy and his wife was living in the house, pregnant with my mother. I think that's the captain's sin, don't you?'

'But she went on to have another child, and he paid for her to have a house.' He drained his cup, poured a little more. 'She was his mistress. You can't expect people to overlook that.'

Lily picked up her light jacket and her work satchel. 'Maybe not back then, but nearly fifty years on? I think people would be a lot less judgemental.' She smiled at him. '*We* can, at all events. The war has made this a new world.'

The trip on the ferry was quiet, the noise of the engine and the splashing of the choppy waves making conversation difficult. James stepped out at the quay and put a hand out for Lily to help her, more of a habit than needed. His hand felt cold, bony, and was ink stained from his work. It was alien and yet strangely familiar. He retained it as they thanked the driver and she started along the beach path.

'I'm so glad to see you,' he said, his voice soft. She pulled him to a stop, and moved into his arms for a kiss. It took her back to their first kiss, eight years ago, in Finsbury Park. For a moment she was lost in the past, full of promise and anticipation. It wasn't until he pulled away a little that their history unlocked itself. *Grace.*

She couldn't speak for a minute, but managed a lopsided smile and started along the path again.

'What's that smell?' he said, his nose wrinkling.

'It's the cannery. They're working around the clock at the moment. Tinned fish isn't on ration so it's very important work.'

He smiled. 'I'm a bit sick of sardines on toast at my digs, to be perfectly honest. It's one of the few things my landlady can make.'

'Don't you eat out?' She knew he had an allowance.

'I don't have time.' He sighed and looked at the ground. 'To be honest, I feel sick a lot of the time.'

'What?' She pulled on his arm so he faced her. 'Are you ill?'

'I don't think so. Nothing physically wrong, anyway. I just ache all over, can't sleep. And a bit thin, but who isn't?' He nodded to her. 'Except you, you seem to be returning to normal after...' His face fell. After a moment he said, 'They gave me sick leave.'

She shook his sleeve. 'Why sick leave?'

'The Cartographic Branch is busy, but we are waiting for a load of new photographs of German and French lines. My manager thought I had some leave coming and the department medic signed me off. He says...' He looked over at the sea. 'He says grief can create a weakness of concentration.' He looked back at Lily. 'So that's why I'm here, to improve my concentration.'

'That was kind of him.'

James started along the path past the cannery. 'I'm sorry, Lils. I still can't talk about it. Her.'

'I know.' Lily caught him up and he took her satchel, too, after a little tug of war. 'I spoke to Mother on the phone. She's much better. And *your* mother visited her, she said it was a comfort for both.'

'Mother said.' As they turned along the seawall, the house started to loom over the corner of the island. 'It's big!'

'It's not too bad. Four main rooms on each of three floors and two attic rooms. Emma and I went all over it the other day.'

'Find any buried treasure?'

Lily smiled. 'More broken windows and a leaky roof. It needs a lot of work.'

He started up the steps to the terrace. 'Does she have the kind of money to do that? It's grand, isn't it?'

'I have no idea,' Lily said, following him up the broad limestone steps. The terrace had been weeded a few weeks ago, but dandelions were already squeezing new leaves from every crevice. 'James, stop.' When he turned to her, she tried to explain. 'Look, Emma's a bit different. She copes, which is amazing, but she can't manage too many new ideas. Please don't go around criticising what she's doing. It's her house.'

'Even if she's letting it fall into disrepair?' He put his free hand on her shoulder. 'Lils, don't you realise? If Emma dies without issue, you might be the last heir to this place.'

'No.' Her eyes were wide, her heart bumping uncomfortably. 'Don't say that. She can do what she likes with it, I never thought...'

'I know. But you are her nearest relative.' He waved at the grand façade of the building. 'It's got to be worth something.'

'I think the best thing she can do is sell it,' Lily said sadly. 'Her cleaner, May, agrees, and she's known Emma since before the accident. Maybe she would be better in a more manageable cottage somewhere, without all the memories of her sister and parents.'

'Lily, listen. We're literally homeless. Where will we live in our old age? That great big house would be worth enough for us to get somewhere lovely, for us, for our children...'

Maybe it was something in Lily's face that stopped him; she could feel every muscle in her body tense, her chin lift. 'That is Emma's business, Emma's history, Emma's house. I don't want to talk about it again.' Her voice came out so hard, she barely recognised it. 'Let me take you in, introduce you.'

She was still taut as she walked in through the unlocked main door, through the hall, which was still covered decorated with the dusty glass domes full of birds, and into the kitchen, where she had managed to persuade Emma to let her wash the whole room, polish all the silver and clean the china.

Emma rose from her chair by the stove, and Lily saw her through James's eyes. Her hair was a bird's nest of frizzly dark curls, her face lined and not made-up and her clothes were layers from her father's wardrobe. She was taller than Lily, but James dwarfed her, standing with his face frozen.

'My dear cousin, Emma Chancel. Emma, this is my husband, James Granville.' He put a hand out but Emma put hers behind her back, looking at Lily, shaking. Lily walked over to her. 'Emma and I have made a cake,' she said, putting her hand over Emma's arm and squeezing gently. 'To welcome you. Shall I take you upstairs to unpack? Perhaps Emma could fill a kettle and put it on for some tea.'

She could feel Emma nodding and walked past the table to lead the way.

'For God's sake, Lily—' he started to say, and she shushed him.

'It's up here, on the right. The bathroom's opposite.'

He followed her up the stairs and she pushed the bedroom door open. 'As you can see, Emma has given me – us – the room with the best view.'

'Where does she sleep?'

Lily walked over to the window. 'Upstairs, in the old nursery. Where my mother grew up.'

She expected him to start arguing again but he didn't. Instead, he put the case down and joined her at the window.

'It really is a fantastic view,' he said, and there was something she hadn't heard in his voice since before Grace died. He sounded defeated, like the spring that drove him had broken. 'She's pretty impaired,' he said, turning to Lily. 'I don't like the idea of you being a carer for someone you hardly know.'

'She's very shy. She's lived a completely isolated life. But she copes really well.'

'But the state of the hall, the condition of that front wall. Water must be getting in.' He stretched his fingers out and she took them on reflex. 'She needs some help.'

'And you trained as an architect. I understand how you might think it's a crying shame to let a beautiful house go to waste.'

'But, you're right. It's her house. Do you think she'd at least let me advise her? Once she gets over being so shy.'

Lily broke into a smile. 'Maybe. I'll show you around, you could tell me your opinion. Then we'll see if Emma is ready to hear it. If May comes, I think she will. You'll love her. She's Emma's old cleaner but she's more like a grandmother.'

'I'll help if I can.'

Lily put her arms around him, and after a moment, he hugged her back. When he pulled away to look out to sea again, his eyes were red.

31

PRESENT DAY, 19 JUNE

After the best night's sleep she'd had since the first night on the island – unbroken by Millie's clumping on the stairs at midnight – Nicole woke up to listen to the gulls on the roof. Something had changed, the chicks' voices sounded muted. She glanced at the clock.

Ten to eight? Josh was coming in ten minutes – no, nine. She shot out of bed in a panic. That was hardly time to do anything, to dress, put her leg on, brush her teeth, hair, maybe a bit of make-up so she didn't look like a ghost...

She hopped to the bathroom and looked in the mirror. A slimmer face looked back, browned by every breakfast in the garden, all the time in the sun, that day on the beach on St Piran's island. Her hair had grown, too, a little wavier than usual, with strands of grey in the dark chestnut. But it looked good on her, the tan made it look more sun-bleached, rather than just – older. She dragged a brush through it, cleaned her teeth, interrupted by Josh banging on the door below.

She hopped back into the bedroom to look out of the window. 'I'm running a bit late, I'll be another minute. Hang on!' Without waiting for a reply, she threw on a dress from a hanger on the back of the door and caught her crutches up to bump down the stairs. She let him in, only a little out of breath.

He was holding a baby gull under one arm, warding off a panicking adult with the other. 'Sorry,' he said, holding the chick out as it struggled. 'I just need to relocate him to your back garden. I think they've fledged a bit early, and a fox or dog is going to get him otherwise.'

He squeezed past her as she hopped back, and walked through to the garden, where the other chick was sitting on the outside table. 'Mum and Dad will feed them until they can fly,' he called back over his shoulder, gently dropping the chick beside its nestling. He ducked inside as a murderous adult flew at his face, screeching.

'No breakfast in the courtyard, then,' she said, resigned. 'Oh, Josh, look at the mess they've made!'

'I'll clean it up once they're flying,' he promised. He was wearing worn shorts and a faded, torn T-shirt. 'It's all plant food.' He grinned, one snaggle-tooth showing.

'I'll hold you to that promise,' she said, turning back into the kitchen. 'I'll shout for Millie. I can't believe she slept through all that.'

But Millie didn't answer when she called. Josh stood behind her, perhaps picking up on her tension. 'Do you want me to go up, have a look?'

'Back bedroom,' she said, suddenly cold, remembering the two kids in the boat the other day.

He came back down. 'She didn't sleep in that bed, I'm pretty sure,' he said. 'Did she stay over with a friend?'

Nicole picked up the phone to check for a message, finding just one from late the previous evening. 'She's left a message saying she was sleeping over at the pub,' she said. 'I must have been asleep. Are any of the boats out? I saw her in a small turquoise and white boat, a couple of days ago, with a boy.'

'Old Bingo?' He shook his head. 'It belongs to the pub but I passed it on the way in, moored up. Try her mobile, she might get a signal down at the pub.'

Nicole got through to the answerphone, and left a message for Millie to call her back. She tried to keep the worry out of her voice.

He sat at the dining table. 'Maybe she just stayed over with the staff. They bunk in over the week. The pub closed late – I could see lights until gone one.'

'Maybe. It isn't like her to leave me fretting, though.'

Francesco. Maybe things had got out of hand. She remembered that feeling as a teenager, of emotion sweeping her away.

'She'll wake up and realise you're worried. After breakfast.' He smiled hopefully and she hopped on her crutches through to the kitchen. Both baby gulls were standing on the table now, fluff sticking up from their heads, some of their feathers half grown. They started piping hopefully when they saw her.

'How long before they fly?' she asked.

'Not long. It's harder for them to take off in these little gardens, but the foxes won't be able to get in. I'd be surprised if they are here more than a week.'

She put the kettle on and set out cups. 'Tea or coffee?' she asked, looking back at the gulls. They were rather endearing, she had to admit. 'Do I need to feed the chicks?'

'No. We don't want them to associate people with food. The gulls in some places are really aggressive; they've been known to attack children for their ice creams.'

'Greater black-backed gulls,' Nicole mused. 'Amber status, aren't they?'

'That's it. You're personally helping the population. We have lesser black-backed gulls on the islet, too. You mentioned teabread?'

They were halfway through a piece of the fruited loaf when the door banged open.

'Millie!' Nicole couldn't stop her anxiety making her voice shrill.

'Hi, Auntie Nicole. I'll be down in a second.' Her feet beat a drumroll on the stairs.

'Back to auntie,' she said softly. 'She's feeling guilty about something.'

'Worrying you, I imagine,' he said. 'What does she drink? I'll make her a cup.'

'I'll do it,' Nicole said, fighting with a mixture of rage and fear. 'I didn't realise I'd get so... worried.'

When Millie came down she was wearing a conservative blend of jeans and a T-shirt Nicole had bought for her birthday. Nicole concentrated on making her a cup of hot chocolate as Millie greeted Josh.

'Wow. Did you come over just for breakfast?' she said, teasing him.

'She made teabread, I couldn't resist. Oh, don't go in the garden, you've got baby gulls.'

Millie walked over to Nicole to look out of the tiny kitchen window. 'Maybe they won't make as much noise in the morning, now,' she said, glancing at Nicole, their eyes meeting for a second. 'I'm sorry I didn't come home. I did leave a message.'

'I missed it, I was asleep. I just didn't know where you were for a moment. I thought you might have gone out on the boat. Again.' She looked down as she mixed the chocolate powder into hot water, topped it up with milk. 'I panicked a bit.'

Millie put her arms around her and squeezed. 'I am really sorry. I just couldn't get away. There wasn't a good time, and then I was a bit drunk, and Philly said I could stay over in her room, so I just phoned the message through.'

'That's OK, it's fine, you're a grown-up after all.' A tear splashed onto the work surface.

Millie hugged her harder then let go. 'You've had enough disasters. I'm not surprised you thought the worst.'

'That's it,' Nicole said, suddenly reassured, the fear ebbing away. 'But you can stop calling me "Auntie". I've told you before, it makes me feel about a hundred years old.'

By the time Millie had consumed two slices of the teabread and drunk her hot chocolate, the ease was back in the room. Millie started washing up, Josh poured himself another coffee and dried up, while Nicole checked her emails on her laptop. It felt strangely homely.

'When do you have to get back to Gannet Rock?' she asked him, as he hung a tea towel on the rail.

'About half an hour. I was just going to pick up a bit of shopping. The water's too high for dog walkers and hikers at the moment.'

'But there's a huge sign prohibiting dogs.'

He shrugged. 'None of them realise that their gentle Labrador will wander about sniffing and the adults will abandon half their chicks. One dog, a season's breeding lost. They can walk over there with my blessing in September, although the gates will still be locked.'

'But you still have to be there until then?'

'Yesterday, a jet skier's engine seized up. He was washed up on the shore near the jetty. I had to tow him off. He got dive-bombed by a lot of angry gannets – he could have lost an eye. He didn't have a life jacket on, either. I gave him a proper reprimand. One of the fishermen took him back in, for fifty quid.'

She glanced out of the window. 'I hope you have a good day. It's a bit overcast.'

'It will be fine, just a bit choppy on the way back. I rarely get stuck on the islet in the summer, but I need to stock up on gas bottles and beans.'

She laughed as he stood to leave. She followed him to the door. 'It was good to see you.'

'Are you feeling better now? You sounded wobbly last night...'

'I'm much better. And you being here stopped me having a meltdown at Millie.'

'She's in love,' he said, smiling at her. 'Who can blame her for making some impulsive choices?'

Before she could stop him, he leaned down as if to drop a kiss on her cheek, then stalled, pulled back, smiled crookedly. 'I'd better get on. Tide.'

She watched him lope down the cobbled street, then turn and wave at the quay before disappearing.

Millie was in love, it was obvious. And *her* heart was still racing from Josh's little gesture. She walked back to the kitchen, Millie staring out at the gulls on the table. They were being fed something disgusting, regurgitated by one of the parents.

Nicole sat back down and picked up her cup. 'Do you want to refill the kettle, Mills?'

'Sure.' Yep. Millie definitely was feeling awkward.

'So, you and Francesco. It is serious?'

Millie snapped back. 'You and Josh, is *that* serious? Did he stay the night?'

'Of course he didn't. I thought you were going to be here.' She immediately questioned her own thought. 'I mean, we're not romantically involved, we're just friends.'

'Well, Cesco and I are just friends, too. Only yesterday he took me out on the boat, and we stopped on West Island, and pulled up on the beach.'

'OK.' Nicole talked herself down from the first three things she wanted to ask. 'And you're... all right?' she asked. *Is she even on the pill, does she know about safe sex, is she being manipulated by an older boy?*

'He kissed me. Then he talked for ages about Maria, this girl he's engaged to. Then he brought me back.' She shrugged, but Nicole could see hurt there, too. 'So, I stayed after my shift and drank too much tequila. I don't even *like* tequila. He's confused, and he's confusing me.'

'So, you didn't...'

'No.' She sighed. 'I wouldn't have, anyway. Not like that.'

'And definitely not on sand,' Nicole said with a smile.

Millie grinned. 'Not good, huh?'

'I had my first serious relationship on the islands. Having sex with my boyfriend on a campsite wasn't good, but the beaches were worse. I'm not going into details,' she said, mock-serious.

Millie burst out laughing, then her smile faded. 'Why did he kiss me if he is so in love with her?'

'Because he's young and stupid and a boy, and you are beautiful and charming, Mills,' Nicole said. 'He can't help himself. Why did *you* go, if you knew all that?'

Millie leaned on the sink, looking out at the chicks. 'Because I really like him.'

The heartbreaking bleakness of her voice echoed something inside her aunt.

32

Lily woke up in a cloud of well-being. The freshly changed sheets, the sunlight just creeping over the top of the heavy curtains, the soft hiss of James's breath on her back as he lay alongside her. Then she remembered.

She hadn't intended to make love, and he hadn't asked, just looked at her in the half shadows, his dark eyes overflowing. It was to give and take comfort, it was love, and it was the first time she had felt like that since Grace even became ill. When she was looking after Grace, her whole being – mind, body and soul – belonged to her daughter. Now she felt different, not a girl any more as she had been when they married. Grace's slow, quiet death had burned away a lot of small things in Lily, leaving stronger, darker feelings. She had long admired James, ten years older and with so much life experience. Now that seemed irrelevant. She had held him while he sobbed in the dark, calling out Grace's name. She could feel his grief, dark as blood, echoing her own loss.

His arm was over her waist, and she hugged it to her, enjoying the peaceful moment of calm before he woke up.

She must have dozed off again, because he turned over and woke with a startled 'Oh.'

'Good morning,' she said, and stretched out.

'I forgot where I was for a moment,' he said, then snuggled into her, breathing in her hair. 'I like your hair longer,' he said, his voice muffled.

'I've just got used to tying it back. But I fancy a smart crop, so don't get attached.'

'Don't I get a say?' he mumbled.

She pulled away to sit on the side of the bed. 'Not really,' she said, amused. But when she thought about it, she'd always run her fashion and hair choices by him in the past. 'I'd just like a change.' She turned to look back at him. She could see his ribs now he'd taken his pyjama top off. 'We're going to have to feed you up,' she said, grabbing her towel and heading for the bathroom.

By the time he had shaved, and both of them were dressed, her shyness had crept back. 'So, what are the breakfasts like at this hotel?' he asked, smiling. He was really staring at her; it made her uncomfortable but somehow it was nice, to have someone look at her like that again.

'I think we can guarantee toast and home-made jam from Emma, and if you're *very* lucky, you might get a boiled egg.'

'Well, that's better than porridge, no milk, hardly any sugar,' he said. 'I live on snacks at work.'

They descended the stairs, James looking around. 'This needs a good clean,' he said.

'We know. But it's hard for Emma to go outside of her habits. She's come a long way already. She's been brilliant, so kind. Come and see her at her best, among her pots and pans.'

Emma looked very serious at the stove, heavy kettle already sizzling.

'Good morning, Miss Chancel. Or may I call you Emma?'

James had a little teasing note in his voice, but Emma didn't take any notice.

'Suit yourself,' she said, without looking at him, getting a cloth to lift the heavy kettle and heat up the teapot.

Lily started laying the table. 'Well, Emma is my cousin, so she's also your cousin by marriage.'

'Emma it is,' he said, looking around the room. 'I see you have a cat bowl. Do you have a cat?'

'I do,' Emma said, spooning out the tea carefully and filling the teapot.

'He's a bit shy. I've never seen him,' Lily said, putting freshly washed cups with mismatched saucers.

James lifted one, showing Lily the bottom. 'This is Spode,' he said. 'Around 1800, I think. My grandmother has a few pieces.' He looked at the saucer. 'Royal Worcester. Top notch.'

'They's just cups,' Emma said, putting the pot down for Lily to put a knitted cover on.

'Exactly,' said Lily, looking back at James. 'And these are just saucers.'

A smell rose from the pan Emma was using and both turned to stare. 'Bacon?' Lily laughed. 'Where on *earth* did you get bacon from?'

'May got me some, for your man – your husband. For James.'

'Well, that's marvellous,' James said, smiling. 'The last pig-based food I had was tinned ham and it was... horrible.'

The bacon and eggs Emma cooked were divine, matched with some fresh bread she had got up early to bake, and some real butter. Lily was almost in tears at the effort she had gone to. While Emma didn't directly look at James and never tried to use his name again, she looked pleased that they were so thrilled, although it got a bit much for her after a few minutes. After she had eaten, she disappeared to leave Lily and James to finish the tea between them and eat the last pieces of toast.

'Did you bring walking shoes?' Lily asked, putting the dishes in the sink and sliding the half-filled kettle back onto the heat.

'I did. Are you going to wash up?'

'It won't take long. Find your shoes and a light jacket. You might need a hat; it gets very sunny at this time of year. You don't want a burnt nose. You don't look like you've been outside at all.'

She washed up the china carefully, dried and replaced it, then left the heavy frying pan to dry on the drainer.

'Are you going out?' Emma was standing by the door in her gardening gear, which was simply gumboots and fewer layers.

'I thought I would take James down to the cove, to see the sea. He's been stuck in a building all these months, working.'

Emma made a face. 'I can't imagine that. How big a building?'

'Oh, huge!' Lily said. 'Bigger than here, many times bigger. And they don't have many windows.'

Emma nodded. 'Tide's coming in,' she said, turning away.

'We'll be careful,' Lily called after her, but she knew Emma was oblivious once she was focused on something.

James met her in the hall. 'These birds,' he said, brushing the dust off one. 'It's all a bit Miss Havisham, isn't it?'

'The problem is, her father made a list of daily and weekly chores for her. He forgot to mention the hall. The main rooms were pretty tidy and clean – at least, the bits she used.'

He followed her through the door and took her hand as they walked past the house to the steep lane that led up to the old lighthouse base on the northern corner of the island. 'I mean, she's nice, in her own way, but she's a bit mad, isn't she?'

Lily stopped, pulled her hand out of his. 'She's odd, of course she is, she had a terrible accident. But she's no more mad than you or I.'

He stopped, too, halfway to the steep path, and looked around. 'What's that?'

'What do you mean?'

He pointed at the ruined cottage beside the house, tucked into its nest of brambles and saplings. 'That looks like a roof. Fallen in a bit, but that's the gable end.'

Lily stared at him, her anger fading. 'It's the original house. Before they were rich, the Chancels owned a smaller cottage. That's what's left of it now.'

'It's a sensible size,' he said, and she could make out more of the structure now she had identified a gable end and a curved roof line, a few jumbled roof slates. Above the end was a chimney, which she had first thought of as a tree.

'What are you thinking?' Lily allowed him to take her hand again as he half pulled her up the hill.

'Well, Chancel Hall is a monster. It would cost a lot to repair, it needs good heating, and it's too big for one person. It was designed for half a dozen servants.' They came to the top of the path, to a clearing with a white platform. 'The cottage would be a better size for your cousin. What is this?'

'It was a lighthouse. It fell down in a storm, and the family used the stone to build Chancel Hall,' Lily explained.

Even in the summer's day, the wind swirled around them. James had brought a hat, and he was holding it on. 'Look at that view,' he said. The sea swept away in greens and blues, shadowed by clouds overhead. He took a deep breath, then another. 'You wanted to talk about Grace,' he said, turning to her.

'I did. I do,' she said.

He took another deep breath, shut his eyes. 'This is how Grace made me feel,' he said, 'when I first held her.'

Lily smiled at the unexpectedly poetic words. But he was right, there weren't ordinary words to describe having their daughter. 'Me too.' She looked over the white-topped waves.

'I can't talk about losing her,' he said. 'I just can't.'

'I know,' she said, sighing. 'But I need to talk about her. Can you listen?'

He seemed to think for a long time, as the wind tugged at her hair.

Eventually he said, 'I will try.'

33

PRESENT DAY, 21 JUNE

The trip to the mainland had to be organised with precision. Corinne was driving the ferry and could get Nicole to the big island in time for the helicopter. As it took off, it wheeled around the archipelago, giving her a perfect shot of Josh's roof, of fishing boats heading out to the crabbing grounds, pretty cottages on each of the islands. Most were hunkered on the eastern coasts out of the predominantly westerly winds.

Nicole had smartened up for the trip, and she'd even allowed Jade to trim and colour her hair a little, closer to the highlights she'd been used to. It was still longer; she was enjoying the way it fell around her face. Jade had also promised to keep an eye on Millie.

Josh had been busy for two days, which had given her time to think about their almost-kiss. She decided he hadn't meant to raise her expectations, it was just a random stumble, soon corrected. She'd reacted like a Victorian teenager about the whole thing by obsessing and reliving it.

Wearing the prosthetic was both hot and heavy. She'd quite enjoyed hopping about without it and the skin had healed further. The swelling had gone down so much the leg was almost loose, ready for a refitting. She had dressed up a bit, in smart trousers and a linen blouse with a delicate bird print, from a trip to Thailand. Her suitcase had been impossible to carry with her stick and handbag, but Corinne had helped her on.

A car will be waiting at the heliport, Kim had texted. *Looking forward to seeing you!*

The drive through Cornwall was slow as holiday traffic was heavy in places. The scenery was lovely, even if several sunny weeks had dried out a lot of the fields. The roads were narrow, lined with stone walls, and the air conditioning in the car was welcome.

The driver was funny, a northerner who was fascinated by the scenery. He dropped her right by the hotel door and a young man rushed out to carry her bags.

'Your colleague is waiting in the bar,' he said, 'if you want me to take your case to your room?'

Nicole would have preferred to tidy up after the journey, but she had become increasingly nervous on the boat. She took a deep breath and decided to get it over with. 'Thank you,' she said. She stood up straight, leaned lightly on her stick and tried to walk as normally as she could.

Kim was sitting on a stool by the bar, sipping something tall and fruity. She glanced over as Nicole walked in.

'Oh, you're here!' She put her drink down and ran over, hugging her. 'Oh, thank goodness. I was just starting to get a bit tipsy.'

'Tipsy? *You?*' Nicole let go carefully, making sure she was balanced. 'Can we sit on a proper chair?'

'Of course. I almost forgot; you look so great. Come out and sit by the pool, isn't it lovely?'

The blue ripple on the water was lovely – but artificial.

Beyond the edge of the pool, over a glass barrier, lay Carbis Bay. The turquoise water pulled her attention.

'You look fantastic,' Kim said, sitting opposite. 'Have you been in the gym? Or a tanning salon?'

Nicole laughed. 'No! Just walking around with crutches is a workout, and I'm outdoors a lot. It's great not being stuck in an office all the time.'

Kim stared at her. 'Last time I saw you, you were so pale and ill. I can't believe you've recovered so well.'

Nicole ordered a fruit juice with ice from the waiter. 'I had just come out of intensive care. I was still fairly concussed and banged up.' She started to wonder why Kim even wanted to see her. They had never been that close outside of work, and she'd only made one visit to the hospital. 'So you're here for work?'

'Sort of.' Kim dragged a folder out of her bag. 'I actually have a proposal I want to run by you. Recruitment is something you're better at than me.'

'Are you trying to choose my replacement?' Funny, the idea hurt even four months after she had resigned. 'I'm pretty irreplaceable.'

'Not really. We've been offered an opportunity to apply for funding for *this*.'

She handed over the folder. The first pages were a job specification for a new role, with a not-for-profit environmental group. They were looking for a project leader to run an independent, joined-up agency. She took her time reading the first few pages, the last ones were full of details for the proposed job.

'Where's the funding coming from?' Nicole asked eventually. 'It doesn't look like one of ours.'

'It's not British government at all, it's independent. It's being funded by multinational agencies through the World Bank. It's save the planet time. Well, the *oceans*, anyway.' Kim rolled her eyes. 'I don't know how much good it can do, but this is better than every organisation doing something separate.'

Nicole recognised some of the lines. 'This is... I wrote this.'

'Yes, it came from your Green World speech two years ago. Some people – important, rich people – were listening.'

'Who's going to head it up?' Suddenly, she cared. This had essentially grown out of her own ideas, her synthesis of other people's research and concepts. 'Luke Sanderson could do it. Miyaki Takeda and that guy she partners with, they would be great, too.'

'They don't want Luke or Miyaki, although I think it would be great to get them on board.'

Nicole racked her memory banks, dusty after so long away, a little hazy after the bang on the head. 'McMillan, Maeda, Saint-Germain and Ostler.'

'All possible.' Kim leaned forward, touched her knee. Nicole was instantly annoyed; it was the bad leg. Maybe Kim felt the padded sock underneath, she lifted her hand quickly. 'They want you.'

Nicole's mouth dropped open. For months she had been pulling back, cutting links with the past, selling her home, feeling utterly changed by the accident. She had resigned to get away from the world of corporate science with all its politics. '*Why?* I mean, I've been out of action, I've been ill...'

'Don't get me wrong, I'm massively annoyed that they didn't ask *me*.' Kim laughed, an insincere little chuckle. 'But they're right, you've always had the broad overview even with the tightest research. You're the right person to advise global initiatives, global companies. Big oil, manufacturing, mining – they all want to know how to look good to their customers. Who knows, some of them might even care about the planet.'

'I have memory problems, Kim. And I've lost a leg.'

'Are you brain damaged? Really? And how does losing a leg stop you working with people?'

Nicole shook her head. 'I forget things, I sometimes use the wrong words.' The truth was, she had stopped having those problems when she came to the island. 'The doctors said it was emotional, maybe PTSD.'

'But can you still read research papers?'

Nicole smiled to herself. 'I've been reading my own PhD research. And I've been looking at an application for a Marine Conservation Zone.'

'Well, you don't have to be that academic for this role, anyway. It's about talking to people, getting them on board with doing things that might cost them money just to save dolphins or coelacanths.'

'I do love coelacanths,' Nicole said, grinning at Kim. She had swum with the prehistoric, pre-dinosaur fish in Indonesia.

'Apparently, they taste disgusting,' Kim said, and sipped her drink.

Nicole laughed and shook her head. 'They can't be serious about this. How many other people are they looking at?'

Kim stopped, glanced up at her. 'The company is dead serious; they want a Brit in the post. Someone who knows all those lovely and clever people you just named, who can work with them.'

Nicole felt cold inside. This was the dream job. This was a fantastic opportunity to push a whole-ocean agenda. 'I don't feel ready to go back to work.'

'It will be fine, because you will appoint me onto your team, helping you find somewhere to live, getting you to your wonderful new office. It can pretty well be anywhere you like. I'm thinking New York, actually.'

Nicole looked again at the sea. A fire had been lit inside her, but alongside it was a shaking, terrified shiver. 'I'm not ready.'

Kim nodded. 'The job starts next year. They will make sure you get all the necessary information. But they want you to submit a proposed plan of action, for the first three years. You'd be working on it up to Christmas.'

'Why didn't I know about this until now? Surely this has been in the pipeline for years—'

'Because the person who's bankrolling it was captivated by your speech two years ago. They have been stalking you since. And no, I don't know who it is.'

'So, they know what happened to me.' That feeling of being disempowered by the damage done in the car was fading.

'And they still think you can do it. I guess. You'd have to meet them, but please say if you do that I can go with you.' Kim was laughing. 'As your personal assistant, sidekick, anything. I'll carry your spare leg.'

Nicole gave her a hard look. 'What's the pay like?'

'OK. A bit more than you're used to, but they don't want you to look greedy. The expenses are stellar, though. And, as I said, office in New York? Or South of France? Even Australia?'

'I'll think about it. Who do I talk to for more information?'

'Georgia, at the ministry. Then *this* guy, one of the money people.' She pointed out a name at the bottom of the first page. 'He'll contact you directly, probably jet you to his summer home. Again, I'll carry your luggage.'

Kim would be a very good assistant. 'What about Ben and Lisa?'

She made a face. 'I think I'm over both of them. Throuples are so 2020. We had a good run, but I think Ben's seeing someone else and Lisa's getting a bit needy.'

Nicole shook her head. 'I couldn't manage *one* partner at a time.'

'So you and that IT guy...?'

'We were over well before the accident.' And un-mourned, she realised. At the time it had left a hole in her life, but now her life was different. Josh's face sneaked into her mind, to be severely banished.

'Well, I'll hand you the full proposal to have a look at later. But now, you fancy a swim?'

Nicole took a painful breath. 'I haven't... I didn't bring a swimming costume.'

'They sell them. What are you, a size ten now? Go and look. You'll love it.'

'I haven't shown anyone... I'm not ready.'

Kim shrugged. 'Who cares? I'm the only person who knows you. Anyway, it's quiet. Everyone's on the beach.'

Nicole found she didn't mind as much as she thought. 'Will you help me if I can't get out?'

'No, love. I'll leave you to flounder until the staff rescue you.' Kim rolled her eyes.

Nicole laughed and let a little flame of positivity and confidence warm her. They wanted her to head up a huge project. People still wanted what she could do. Maybe when she met the benefactor who had proposed her as team leader, he would change his mind. Maybe she was fine on the island, getting better.

But the water really did look so inviting...

JULY 1941

It took another day for Emma to relax around James, and he seemed to find her flat little statements amusing.

'We have a surprise for you, for today,' Lily said to James as he finished his breakfast. She nodded to Emma, who brought out an old picnic basket with a flourish. 'I thought you'd like to go over to another island. So, bring your trunks.'

He laughed and protested, and it took a joking discussion of buying some pre-war ones from the shop on the quay before he conceded that he had brought them. 'But the water will be freezing,' he said.

'But as clear as glass,' Lily said. 'At least come prepared in case the urge takes you.'

What neither had said was the date. The anticipation of Grace's first anniversary had been excruciating. Now it was here, perhaps the actual day would be easier.

The boat was operated by a skinny boy, who immediately ordered them to their places so they wouldn't unbalance the craft. Then he was quiet, just answering questions with yes and no, ma'am, when required. He expertly eased off the oars, shipped them, and ran to the bows to catch the side of the small jetty on St Piran's island.

The sand was glowing white under the morning sun, and he tapped his watch. 'You'll be here until four o'clock. There's the village over the hill, that way. You can get water there, or food if you need it.'

'Is there a restaurant on the island?' James asked as he balanced in the centre of the boat then stepped out carefully. He reached back for Lily's bag and the hamper, then steadied Lily, too.

The boy guffawed. 'No rest-au-rant, no. The post office sells crackers and could make you a sandwich.'

James didn't answer, but Lily could tell he had withdrawn. Her heart sank. She handed over two shillings and a third as a tip. 'Thank you, and you'll come back for us at four?'

'Me or me dad, yes, ma'am.' He let the boat go, and lifted a single oar to scull back away from the sand. 'Enjoy your day.'

'So what are we going to do all day?' James said, shading his eyes and looking over at the distant shadow of the other islands.

'We are going to walk along the ramparts,' Lily said. 'They have an old fortified town. Well, it's only about forty houses, but it has Napoleonic gun emplacements all along it. Then, we are going to have our picnic – it's a lot more delicious than you seem to think – and I have the guide to the church. But first, I'd like to sit on the sand in my swimsuit and spend half an hour soaking up the sun.'

'And splashing about in the shallows?' His voice was snappy, impatient. 'Honestly, Lily, you're such a child.'

The word crashed down between them like a bomb. She choked down the first things that flew into her head, blinked away tears. 'Just because I can enjoy the simple pleasures of life does *not* make me a child. Why don't you sit in the shade, and I'll put the towels out?'

A low wall offered a little shadow from the morning sun, and Lily, eyes smarting, carefully unrolled a towel for herself and one for James. The connection they had felt, the hours they had spent in each other's arms, felt as far away as ever. Deliberately not looking at him, she sat down, slipped off her sandals and pulled her homemade sun dress over her head, to leave her swimming costume. She pulled on her cap to save her curls, and walked across the crystal sand, warm against her soles, almost too hot.

I wanted to bring Grace to the sea for a proper holiday. Ever since she first got ill...

The water was like ice rolling between her toes, tickling the top of her feet. It was almost painful, the burning cold of the water straight off the Atlantic. She persevered, even as the thoughts of Grace intruded: in the park, walking Grandma's poodles, singing in the bath. The water lapped her knees, the sand underfoot slipping away a little, letting her sink another few inches.

On this day, at eleven forty-two, exactly one year ago, Grace had smiled. 'I'm just sleepy, Mummy...' She had fallen into a doze that got deeper as the minutes went on, drifting into unconsciousness, then coma. If Lily had known then that those would be her last words... She couldn't stop tears rolling down her face, but concentrated on keeping her balance as tiny waves rode higher up her thighs, onto her swimsuit, taking her breath away. Finally, she let go, dived forward into the water, into the agony of her memories.

The water was green underneath, the surface silver, bubbles rising from her costume like mercury. She stared around her, the salt stinging her eyes. She could stay here, she could imagine becoming a fish, a mermaid. Maybe she would find Grace here, doing somersaults underwater, grinning at her to do the same.

The burning in her chest made her surface involuntarily. She could hear James yelling, but ignored him. She'd always been a strong swimmer, so she front-crawled parallel to the shore. She swam as far as a rock formation that ran up the beach, then turned and breast-stroked back. As the water deepened, she saw a flash of something golden under a moored boat, and dived down to have a look. In the shadows were fish, looking surprised to see her. She waved at them and they dispersed, and she surfaced, holding onto the side of the boat. James was standing at the edge of the water, staring out at her. His mouth was opening and shutting, but her ears were full of water. She began swimming back lazily, the water feeling warmer as she acclimatised.

She walked out past him, heading for her towel. His legs and feet, in those neatly pressed linen trousers and leather shoes, were soaked.

'Didn't you hear me?' He stood over her, his face twisted into ugly rage. 'I was worried!'

She shook her head, used the corner of the towel to pat her face, then roughly dried her hair. 'You can't just shout at me like a dog,' she said calmly. 'You upset me, and I went for a swim. Actually, it helped. I feel better, even though my child *died*.'

He froze, and sat down, his back turned away a little. '*We* lost *our* child, Lily. I loved her too.'

'Maybe you did,' her own anger making her cold, 'but would it hurt you to show it sometimes? You were barely even there.'

He turned to her. 'I *was* there.'

'Not when she was conscious, saying her goodbyes. Not when we needed you.'

He stared out to sea, his strong profile taut. 'Grace always knew I loved her.'

Lily wrapped the towel around her as she started to shiver. 'We always seem to argue about the same thing.' She sighed.

He dropped his head. 'I wish I had been there more. I wish I had never had to leave her side. In fact, I wish I could have given her my own life.'

Lily put a hand on his shoulder, and after a moment he reached up and squeezed it. 'I feel the same,' she said, her voice cracking.

After his outburst, Lily couldn't think how to speak to James about anything meaningful. He had closed down, diverting her with questions about her mother, giving a little information about his own mother, his job. They walked around the walls of the old defences, just rambling stacks of stones in places. Lily was numb. She couldn't think about the future; she couldn't seem to care about anything.

The sandwiches she and Emma had prepared were as good as rationing would allow, and the sausage rolls had hardly cooled down since baking early this morning. Every few minutes through the day, Lily had a moment of memory, crisp and focused. Of Grace's hot hand in hers, the doctor's grave face, her mother's relentless sobbing out in the hall. It was as sad and calming as the cooing of doves; it was the backdrop to Lily's waiting. Hours of whispering to Grace, of her lying curved into her mother's body like a baby. Part of her wanted to share it all with James, but he was more distant than ever, a polite stranger.

When they reached the church, she knew she couldn't hold it in any longer. 'I need...' She couldn't finish the words, just nodded to him, and walked inside and found a pew in front of the lectern, in the light of a stained-glass window.

Gracie, Gracie, are you here? Are you with me all the time? Because I feel you are.

She could still feel the halo of stuffed toys around her from that day, not just Grace's but Lily's childhood dolls, James's stuffed horse and bears. The sweet smell around Lily as her body closed down. Her porcelain skin, lashes fanned over the curve of her cheeks.

When grief came it was a scalding wave. Lily wrapped her

arms around her empty belly and wept. Her mind still called out to Grace. It was several minutes before she felt James squeeze in beside her, wrap his arms around her, soothing her like he would have comforted Grace. She could feel him shaking.

'Please, Lily, I can't bear seeing you like this. I can't talk about it, but I can't cope when you cry...'

The words slowly filtered through her own feelings. She relaxed into him, the sobs stopping. She rummaged in her pocket for a handkerchief, mopped her tear-soaked face and blew her nose.

'It's not always going to be like this. This is a bad day,' she said, carefully. 'This is a special day. A year ago, she was still alive.'

She glanced at her watch. It was time. She waited for – what? She had waited last year, too, as she took a breath and waited for Grace to do the same. Then Lily hissed in another breath and Grace didn't, and Lily's cry had been in realisation of what was happening. James had just held her back then, put his fingers over hers, peeled them away from Grace's little hand. She was curved against Lily, she had felt him as he'd dragged her away, held her back.

'She's gone,' he'd said, and the doctor had stepped forward to confirm. From then on, there wasn't time to do anything. The nurse was there, the doctor, everyone telling her to step back, let them tidy Grace up – as if she wasn't perfect as she was. The doctor had given Lily something to drink as she sat in a corner of the room, and later James had had to half carry her next door to the bedroom. When she woke up, many hours later, Grace had been taken away.

The minutes ticked by, and James still held her lightly as she wrestled with her rage and pain. Eventually, he let her go.

'Do you want me to wait outside?' he asked, his voice gentle.

'Please.' She turned to the centre of the church. She shut

her eyes, trying to pray, but, as usual, found herself talking to Grace instead.

Gracie, don't leave me. Where are you? I need you.

For a moment she knew exactly what Grace would say, as clearly as if she had heard her say it.

Poor Daddy.

35

PRESENT DAY, 22 JUNE

The next day, Nicole got back to the house to find Millie entertaining Jade from next door, cooking in the kitchen.

'Oh, you're early! I wanted to finish this.' Millie flung her arms around Nicole and hugged her. 'Did you have a good time on the mainland?'

'Very. I even went in the pool a couple of times. Hi, Jade. What are you two up to in here? It smells amazing.'

'We're making a lemon and poppy seed cake with a grapefruit buttercream,' Jade said, as if she was narrating a cooking show.

'And look how much the chicks have grown in two days,' Millie said, pointing out at the garden. One of the baby gulls was on the ground, scratching the last of the down off his head, the other was on tiptoes on the table, flapping his ungainly wings ineffectively. 'We named them: Tia and Maria.'

'So they're girls?' Nicole asked, smiling. 'I'm going to unpack.'

'Let me take your bags upstairs. Watch the timer, Jade!'

As Nicole followed Millie upstairs, on foot rather than

bumping up on her bottom, she sighed with satisfaction, and some exhaustion. 'Don't let me lie down, I'll fall asleep,' she said. 'Kim took me out. I even danced, sort of.'

'And walked up the stairs?'

Nicole sank onto the side of the bed. 'I walked everywhere. No blisters, just tired. It was nice to feel a bit more normal, do normal things.'

'And swimming?'

Nicole unzipped her case and brought out a two-piece swimsuit. 'Shorts and bra top. What do you think?'

Millie's eyes widened. 'Maybe you should let Josh see you in that get-up.'

Nicole swatted her. 'Josh is just my *friend*. We share an interest in marine wildlife. Like those man-eating baby gulls.'

'The chicks are OK, but the adults will tear you to bits if you go out there.' Millie looked over at the large folder among the clothes. 'Is that work?'

'No, not really.' She waited until Millie sat next to her on the bed. 'Maybe.'

'What's up? You were so upbeat a second ago. Shouldn't I mention Josh?'

'Should I mention Francesco?'

Millie half smiled. 'No future there.'

'Exactly. I'll have to go home one day, find another job. I can't just retire at the peak of my career.' The decision to leave her job had been a jumble of emotions, at the worst of times. She really hadn't thought it through.

'Why can't you spend as much time as you like with Josh? Mum says you could live off the compensation from the accident.'

That hit Nicole in the chest like a fist. 'Maybe. I've got enough money from the sale of the house for now. But I won't be here forever, and Josh... I just can't see a future in it, Mills.'

Millie leaned her shoulder against Nicole's. 'But you're not rushing off yet.'

Nicole smiled. 'Not yet. Now, let's check on this cake. It smells amazing.'

She hadn't expected to hear from Josh straight away, so was surprised when he turned up an hour later when Millie, Jade and Nicole were on their second slice of cake.

'Did you tell him?' Nicole asked, pretending outrage when he knocked on the door. 'That I was back?'

Millie rolled her eyes. 'He can smell the cake from miles away.'

'I saw the water taxi from the islet,' Josh said, as he sat down on a dining chair. 'Is there a sliver for me?'

Nicole cut him a large slice and got him a fork.

'We're going down to the beach in a minute,' Millie said. 'Do you want to come too, Nicole? You could try out your new swimsuit.'

Nicole shot her a hard stare. 'Go away. Thank you, girls, the cake is amazing.'

They left, chattering and joking like a pair of parrakeets.

'Swimsuit?' Josh mumbled through his cake.

'Yes. It turns out I still love the water since my little paddle on St Piran's.'

'I'm glad. And Ash is ready to take us out to Deadman's Reef tomorrow, if you're game.' He smiled at her. 'I'd like your opinion on something that might add to our application. Which reminds me, I wanted to show you... these,' he said, pulling a sheaf of papers out of his rucksack and smoothing them out on the bit of the table without plates or cake.

She quickly cleared more space. They were plans, for two floors of the old Victorian aquarium.

'You're converting it into flats?'

He shrugged. 'I'd love to keep the old building, but it was built as a warehouse; it has no real foundations to speak of. The inside walls are holding up the top floor – it would cost more to retain the original.'

'But it had such a good story. The ladies setting up their aquarium. Did you know Dorothea's father was a famous natural historian? He got her to draw all the plates for his books. But he didn't even credit her until his third book. She was an expert in peering down a microscope and creating etchings of the tiny organisms she saw. Plankton, single-celled things. Amazing.' She looked at the plans. 'See, you have to underpin anyway. You could keep as much of the building as you can. I think her history is worth preserving.'

'You looked her up?' Josh grinned. 'She was a bit of a pioneer in lesbian relations, too. Even wrote a little book about life with Ursula.'

'She was a pioneer in female science. It just seems a shame that her history won't be preserved.'

'Well, if I don't get planning permission, I'll apply for a blue plaque until the building falls down.' He looked down at the plans. 'I can't afford to keep it on,' he admitted. 'I would have loved to keep the aquarium going, but it's too much work, and kids don't care that ours was one of the oldest aquaria in the country. They just want to go to Plymouth and see sharks and rays.'

She looked again at the plans. 'You've included an office on each floor?'

'Demand for small offices with facilities is high. And the flats would sell well. I'll live upstairs, probably, and rent out or sell the bottom one. The offices will bring me in some income, too.'

She looked again at the dimensions. 'It's a really large building.'

'It is, but the world moves on. How long do you intend to hide out here on the island?' he asked.

She looked down at the cake. 'I suppose that's what I was doing,' she said slowly. 'I originally intended to sit in the cottage, entirely alone, and live on frozen meals until... I don't know. Everything became clear.'

'And did it?'

'Well, Millie turned up and I've met loads of people.' She looked back up at him and everything became less clear. 'I don't know. I have ideas, opportunities. I don't want to go back to the world I had before, but I can't sit here, staring at my navel.'

'So, go explore some ideas. I'm assuming you're not running out of money? You did hire the cottage for a whole year.'

She smiled fleetingly. 'No. I'm just confused. Everything's changing very fast. I'm a bit unsure what to do.'

'If you want to talk about it—'

She cut him off. 'I just need to think. I'm looking forward to diving with you and Ash. I might go down to the beach some day and swim, if it isn't too busy. I know the summer holiday crowd are arriving soon.'

'We can always go to West Island or St Piran's. Much quieter beaches. I could take you over.'

She smiled. 'Maybe, but I also need get around by myself, maybe rent a boat. I should look for that fish. Millie would probably come with me, I know you're busy.'

His face was cool, arrested, as if he'd been hurt. 'Of course. Let me know if you change your mind. I'm on St Piran's at the weekend.' Before she could backtrack or apologise, he stood and looked out of the window. 'How are our nestlings?'

'Losing their fuzz,' she said, feeling horrible. This man, this lovely man, had been nothing but kind and she'd dropped him – why? She wasn't sure herself. 'Thank you for rescuing the chick. The parents are looking after them.'

'Well, I'd better be off,' he said, scooping up the blueprints. 'I'll see you tomorrow; Ash will give us a time.'

'Yes. Thank you.' She felt as stilted as a duchess, as he bowed his head a little and disappeared up the hall.

Suddenly, she felt a horrible urge to cry.

36

JULY 1941

Lily and James returned to the house sandy, hot and upset. James suggested, over a ham salad Emma had prepared, that he could help her go through nearly four years of unopened correspondence. Lily held her breath, but Emma surprised her by considering the offer seriously.

'Lily did offer,' she said. 'Maybe we could do it in here, together, bring it in here to stay warm?'

Even in the middle of summer, the shaded part of the house cooled down quickly, the sun setting in the kitchen windows.

'That's a lovely idea,' James said, and Lily passed a tea towel over the table to wipe it. The evening was beautiful, the heat softened by the sea breeze drifting in the French doors. Lily had caught the sun a little across her shoulders on the beach, and it made her feel even warmer. Emma brought out a wooden apple box filled with letters and even a few parcels.

'These brown ones are from the bank,' James said, picking up the ones on the top. 'You should look at these, they are private.'

'Don't want to,' Emma mumbled, so Lily took a couple and started opening them for her with a letter opener Emma had found on her father's desk. It was made of bone, and had a cross carved into the end. 'The bishop gave him that,' Emma said, then disappeared back into the study.

'She literally hasn't opened anything since he died,' James said, baffled.

'Because they weren't addressed to her,' Lily said. 'I suppose that was why – and her grief.' She unfolded the first bank statement, a simple document showing a weekly account, paid by cheque, with the shop, and a small amount of interest added. 'James, look at this.'

He glanced down at the balance. 'She won't be able to live here more than a few years, if that's all the money she has.'

Emma returned, lifted another box onto the end of the table, and added a shopping bag overflowing with letters.

Lily waved the letter at her. 'Emma, is this your only bank account? Do you have any savings, or shares, that sort of thing?'

'I have a few pounds in my National Savings account,' Emma said. 'I use it for treats, for my birthday and Christmas.' She turned and reached into the dresser drawer. 'I can't read numbers very easily,' she said. 'Since the accident.'

Lily struggled to read the amount in the savings book – the cashier had entered the total in very curly writing. She squinted at it. 'One hundred and eleven pounds, eight shillings and seven pence,' she announced. 'And about eighteen hundred in the bank. But that's it?'

'Maybe we'll find something in the boxes,' James said to Emma. 'Don't worry, I'm sure there's more. What did your father do?'

Emma relaxed a little. 'He was a retired dean. He used to look after the books in a cathedral library.'

Lily turned over more letters. Some of them looked like condolence cards. 'Perhaps he left you a pension somewhere.'

As the evening wore on, Lily shut the blackout curtains and lit all the lamps and candles, the room starting to smell like paraffin and melting wax. Emma made tea, unable or unwilling to open any letters. She did read a few once Lily or James had opened them first. One came from Lily's mother.

'Look, Emma,' Lily said, reading the familiar handwriting. 'This is from my mother, asking if she could come and visit you to help, if you need it. She's your Aunt Elizabeth, you know.' She sat back in her chair. 'She's always said she would never come back to the island.'

'She hated Grandpa, that's what my father said.' Emma took the letter and looked it over. 'I never met her. She ran away to get married when she was eighteen, after her mother died.'

'She did.' Lily picked up a large letter, with large, florid writing on the front. 'Goodness, this is addressed to The Present Owner. You could have opened this one, Emma.'

Emma shrugged into a hunch. 'That's the builder, the one I told you about. He wants to buy our house.' She handed it to James.

He opened the letter and his eyes widened. 'He's offering twelve hundred for the house and – get this, Lily – all the attached lands and buildings. It must be worth five times that, maybe much more.'

Emma shuddered. 'He came here, banged on the door, but I didn't answer, so he just walked in. He was so cross, telling me it was a good offer because the place was going to fall down unless he did a lot of work. He said it was a good price, and island houses are cheap, especially if they are so old.' She looked upset, leaning forward so Lily couldn't see her face behind her hair. 'He came in, and I kept telling him to leave, but he wouldn't. He called me some names. He said he was going to get a solic... someone to say I was mad, and put me in a hospital.'

Lily jumped up, furious. 'He had no right to even come in here, let alone threaten you! Let me see that letter – I've a good mind to write to him myself.'

Emma managed a smile, but she still left the room and shut the door behind her.

James didn't say anything until she had gone. 'He's got a point, though. She might not be capable of making complicated financial decisions, and no one can deny the house needs a lot of repairs. There's a letter from the council, too. They want to send an engineer to see if it's safe.'

Lily swung around to stare at him. 'How can you? She's managed up until now, and her father decided not to make those repairs. Or was he incompetent, too?'

He frowned. 'Maybe he couldn't afford to make the mainte-nance. Maybe he was aware he was running out of money. What happens when it *does* run out? I doubt she has more than three or four years here, and then where will she go?'

'She's lived here for nearly thirty years, most of her life. We have to help her.'

He opened another letter. 'This is a mess.'

'She's my family. I have to try and help.'

He picked out another letter from the builder. 'He's offering a little less this time, a year ago. He says he will renovate the cottage, that outbuilding, for her to have the use of in her life-time. She could stay there, and she wouldn't have this great big monster to look after.' He pushed it across the table. 'It's still low, but she'd be able to stay here.'

'She calls it the gardener's cottage,' Lily said. 'It was for servants. She wasn't brought up to live like that, and anyway...' How could she explain to him how resistant to change Emma was, how fixed in her ideas?

'We could help her design a house she can easily look after, make sure she gets a good garden and some sea views. It could be lovely, Lily. I've been over the shell of it. It was a good house.'

The argument made sense, even to Lily, but she couldn't imagine Emma making that decision. 'He may call her mad, but that's just because she isn't doing what he wants, or you want. It's her house, she can make her own choices.'

He dropped his voice to a whisper. 'She's impaired, Lily. That accident left her injured. She needs a guardian who can protect her interests properly.'

'Someone like you, someone who will force her to move, force her to leave all her memories behind? She's not mad, she's just... different.'

'She talks to her dead sister all the time – I must have heard her say Charlotte a hundred times. She rambles on about a cat no one has ever seen, she even feeds it outside although I'm pretty sure a fox takes the food every day. She can't adapt to change. She'll need a lot of help, Lily.'

Lily was shaking with anger. 'You hardly know her. I've been here for weeks, I've got to know how resourceful she is. You're just thinking that she will leave it all to me one day.'

'Leave *what*?' he hissed back. 'I don't want my wife living in a wreck that could fall down. I don't want you to be taking on the care of an impaired woman who fills your need to look after someone now Grace is gone.'

The silence stretched out between them and Lily couldn't breach the gap. In this moment, she hardly recognised the hard-eyed stranger across the table.

'I think it's time you went back to London,' she said, standing tall.

'I have something to tell you, about what I'm doing with the reconnaissance photography unit...' he said, also pushing back his chair and standing.

'I don't care to hear it,' she said coolly. 'I will sleep in one of the other rooms. The first ferry is at eight – I think you need to be on it.'

'I'll write. Maybe when you calm down—'

'I won't calm down. Not about this,' she said, surrounded by the letters, the proof of Emma's incompetence and fragility.

He nodded then turned away. Lily called him back.

'You will be careful, won't you?' she said. 'I mean, back in London. And in the planes...'

He half smiled at that, held out a hand. 'Come to bed, Lily, please. I won't talk about your cousin any more. And she has been a kind hostess, I'm grateful for that.'

She looked at the mess they had made on the table. 'I'll be up in a minute,' she conceded. But she felt a coldness in her chest that hadn't been there before.

37

PRESENT DAY, 24 JUNE

The moment Nicole dropped backwards off the boat into the clear waters above the reef, she felt a wave of happiness and freedom. It felt like coming home. She'd been scuba-diving since she was a teenager, and it was only in the last hectic decade of boardrooms and press and meetings that it had slipped away. Just the odd tourist dive, full of hand-fed fish and tame seals.

This was raw and exciting. She could feel the current tugging her, and had to give the odd kick to keep Ash in sight. Every move allowed a drop or two of the cold water in at the neck, making her shiver. She'd changed into her wetsuit in Ash's store, and he'd taped up the dangling leg without comment. Clem Ellis, who must have been in his eighties, was driving the boat. He gave one glance at her leg, shrugged and looked away. The others didn't seem to notice at all.

Underwater Nicole could swim in lazy loops, catch up with Ash, easily manoeuvring in three dimensions. She'd overestimated her weights for the dive, forgetting she had lost a stone and half a leg, so the belt was a bit heavy. She smiled inside her mask, following a group of small fish in front of her. As they descended a few more metres, she began to see the dark shape of Deadman's Reef. On the edge, the water fell off into deeper greens, a hundred-odd metres deep. Josh had unemotionally given her a quick update on the reefs. They were high points on the seabed with peaks that rose close to, or even above, the surface of the water at very low tides. They were two miles long and almost a mile wide, and the group were diving close to the edge of the western end, near several large wrecks.

The reef was covered in seaweeds of different species and colours, from green, through red to almost black. Silver flashes of fish swimming into cover and several brightly coloured cuckoo wrasse shimmered by, like tropical fish in bright orange and cobalt. She checked her depth: eight metres. Perfect.

Josh, in a blue wetsuit, waved her forward to the surface of the reef, which was covered in life. She swam close and saw delicate brittle starfish crawling over goose barnacles as long as her hand, hundreds of soft corals, dead man's fingers in peach and white, and pink sea fans branching up off the stone. Josh beckoned her on, so she swam onto the top of the reef and saw what he was pointing at.

Tramlines of damage. Smashed corals, exposed rocks with broken bivalves and crab shells. Someone had been dragging scallop dredgers over this protected and precious habitat. Reefs like this were nurseries for dozens of species of fish and crustaceans, even the very scallops they were taking.

Her heart was racing as she followed the damage along, finding crossing lines, some many metres long, fading into the green water, perhaps for a lot further.

Ash swam towards her, touched her wrist, pointed to the left. A tangle of gear, a wire and rope cage that had been snagged by a rock and torn off its tow rope. Josh's diver's knife flashed as he started to cut the rope to pieces. Without doing so, animals would crawl in to eat the dead creatures inside, only to be trapped themselves, repeating the cycle until the heavy rope broke. Worse, it was polypropylene, which would take decades to erode away. She snagged loose bits of line as Josh cut, and put them in the bag at her waist to take to the surface.

As she worked, she sensed that they were being watched, and kept looking over her shoulder. Eventually she saw it, a shape dipping in and out of the shadows in the murky water, as if stalking them. She had one heart-lurching moment – *Shark!* – before liquid eyes in a rounded face shot past her, nosing at what they were doing. A seal, elongated and fast, was buzzing around them, another joining it. Josh tapped her mask, pointing up as a young seal, half the size of the adults, raced overhead, turned sharply and flowed back towards them. Fish – young pollack over a foot long and in a tightly packed shoal – were being herded by the seals. They chased the fish, racing to the silver surface after them. One was throwing a fish around at the surface, dropping it and chasing it again until it was comfortably head-first for swallowing.

Josh interrupted her, tapping his diver's watch. She checked her depth gauge: still under ten metres. Technically possible to slowly ascend without a stop. But they had already agreed to stay five minutes on the anchor line at six metres. From there, she could watch the seals hunting below her, more and more joining as the shoal of silvery pollack got corralled. Finally, starting to feel the cold, she broke the surface of the water, pushing the mask up.

Josh surfaced beside her, and she couldn't help but laugh at him, his hair pushed up by the mask, wide eyed.

'That was amazing!' she cried, laughing. 'Thank you so much!'

Ash surfaced too. 'Watch your fins, the seals are playing.'

With that, a sharp tug on Nicole's fin pulled her chin lower in the water. She started swimming for the boat, just twenty metres away. 'That was incredible. Those seals!'

One popped up by the boat, staring at her with its huge eyes before disappearing.

Josh smiled back. 'They make me laugh. They're much more interested in us than in catching their dinner.'

'They were pretty good at that, too,' she said. She reached up for the rail and pulled herself onto the underwater step. Ash was right – she could easily sit down on the side of the boat, swing her leg over and shuffle onto the seats.

'You saw the damage?' Josh settled next to her, unzipped the top part of his wetsuit.

'I did. This area is part of the exclusion area, isn't it?'

'Except for free-diving scallop fishermen, yes. We have two locals who swim down for them, but they only take adult stock. Those dredger nets kill everything: juveniles, corals, crabs, lobster.'

Ash shucked the top of his wetsuit down and took two towels off Clem, the driver. 'Wrap up, both of you. It's surprising how hard it is to warm up after a dive, even in the summer.'

She followed suit, revealing the top of her brightly coloured bikini, and folded herself in the towel. 'Wow. I'd forgotten how amazing our own coastline can be.'

'Forgotten?' Josh frowned. 'Aren't you one of the people who's supposed to be protecting it?'

'I mean, personally. As a diver. Of course I know how important the ecosystem is.'

Ash changed places with Clem and helped him pull up the anchor. He had deliberately chosen a spot off the reef to protect it, so it took quite a lot of hauling up. Josh swapped with Clem for a few minutes.

Josh's words had stung, because she knew that there was some truth in them. Designating protection zones and conservation areas only worked when everyone respected them. But overseas interests, illegal fishing and vandals undermined all the legislation. Without policing and proper fines and consequences, the marine park status was a joke.

Back at Ash's store, the men gave Nicole some privacy to strip off, have a quick – and very cold – shower, and get dressed in her long skirt. She felt different about people knowing about her leg now. They were either unbothered or mildly admiring at her overcoming her disadvantage. She walked outside to sit in the sun while the boys changed.

Clem, the boatman, was sitting on a bench by the beach, in a patch of sunlight that had broken through. 'See what you needed to see, maid?' he asked. 'Proper mess down there. Not that I want all fishing stopped off the islands – we got to look after our own fishermen.'

She sat next to him on the rickety seat. 'But there aren't many fishermen left.'

'More's the pity,' he said, with absolute certainty. 'We used to have a fishing fleet of a hundred ships, before the war. Now there are twelve between the islands, and most of those go way off in the Channel or the Irish Sea. My own family is giving up.'

She was too tired to argue, and let the sun warm her face. 'How long have you been a fisherman?'

'Sixty-eight years, man and boy,' he said. 'But we don't go out all the time, now. Just when the catch will be worth the fuel and wages. My grandson Tink smokes mackerel, but we can buy that in fresh.'

She turned to look at him. 'You must have seen some changes.'

'Them ministry people, they come with their fancy surveys and do their tests and inspect catches. But what about the rest of the year, when they're not there? We know what goes on then – people like Joshua, they see it all. Why don't those so-called experts come and talk to us? We'll tell you how some birds and fish are getting smaller, because they don't get enough food when they hatch. How some species eat their own young, how dolphins and seals have bad years where they get aggressive, chasing fishing boats for their catch.'

She stared at him. 'Do you have proof of all that?'

He nodded and put a pipe in his mouth. 'See, them London folk, they weren't born with wet feet. Their fish are covered with crumbs or batter.'

She smiled at that. 'You may be right,' she conceded. 'So scientists – people like me – should be spending much more time in fishing ports?'

'Rather than in some office somewhere? How much can you learn from a week on the quay, measuring lobsters?' he said, and lit the tobacco. The smoke was a dense cloud that almost concealed him. He coughed loudly for a few moments.

'Maybe you should cut down?' she said.

'Don't you start. I got Mrs Clem on at me day and night. I'm going to end my days with a pipe between my teeth.'

Josh joined them, wrapped up in a jumper. 'Are you warm enough? I brought a spare.'

Nicole was touched. She thanked him and draped it over her bare shoulders. 'Clem was just saying, he thinks scientists ought to be here much more often.'

'He's right,' Josh said. 'You need to monitor for a whole year round, maybe several. The sea has its own cycles. Years when certain species spawn, and off years when they do far less. Years when we see killer whales, or no dolphins, or swarms of jellyfish. It changes the whole seascape.'

She felt compelled to reply to the accusation. 'We gather information from rangers, like you. We read fish returns, organise censuses.'

He turned to look at her, his face bleak. 'The last full seabird census you organised was twenty-three years ago.'

'We are doing one at the moment,' she snapped back.

'You can't count birds or fish or, more importantly, plankton every twenty-odd years. They are all in decline, they need help *now*. Surely you have enough evidence that the time to act is yesterday?'

She couldn't argue with that. She looked out to sea, clenching her teeth. 'My entire professional career, that's all I've done, Josh.'

'It's not enough. You need to listen to everyone, then you need to protect much larger areas of the British Isles, and you need to encourage the whole world to follow suit.' He stood up. 'I'd better get back, tide's coming back in. I had to pay someone to keep an eye on the causeway.' He smiled then, a little apologetically. 'I promised Millie twenty quid and an ice cream if she sat in the shack for a few hours.'

She pulled the jumper off her shoulders. 'Here. I'm warm now, thank you.'

'OK.' He took it, waved, shouted goodbye to Ash and Clem, and headed back to the quay.

She was furious, embarrassed and sad, because everything he had said was true. And inevitable.

38

AUGUST 1941

James had left, and Lily was still feeling hurt and angry. She concentrated on finding out what Emma could do about the rambling, crumbling house.

After canvassing people in the village, Lily had two recommendations for builders who could advise and quote on the worst defects of the hall. Both were in agreement: the building needed an overhaul which would wipe out all of Emma's savings, leaving her nothing in reserve and nothing to live on in the future. Both gave Lily private but helpful estimates of its worth, after the war was over, if the circumstances were right. An eyewatering sum.

Emma seemed relieved that James was gone. He had been like a smouldering fire most of the time he was there, ready for a flare-up at any moment. But Lily started to miss him. Now she craved his hugs, his kisses, the way he looked at her. She found it harder to travel back and forth to the big island, to work on the boxes of books arriving from bombed-out libraries, museums and churches.

Much of the drying work could be handed on to an assistant, and she was thrilled to be able to take on a young woman from the islands – May's granddaughter, who aspired to study English. That left time for Lily to properly restore some volumes, saving detached pages or whole signatures, folded sheets of pages, and replacing broken threads. The covers, the ornate leather-covered boards, would go to a special restorer, and it was Lily's job to safely preserve and detach these where needed. It amused her that in the little town hall with its combined library and office, there were books worth many thousands locked behind a single basement door. The work was satisfying, and staying with Bernie and Oliver a few nights a week was a contrast to the strange world of Emma Chancel.

She would head home – a walk of less than three minutes – and shout up the stairs, 'I'm home!' Usually, Oliver would answer, either sitting in bed or reclining on an armchair with his feet on a stool. Bernie popped in regularly during the day, and Lily took her lunch with Ollie, so he was rarely alone for long. He slept a lot during the day, but Lily often heard him crying at night. He denied that he was in pain, not bad, anyway, but admitted to having nightmares. He couldn't talk about the moment his plane was shot down, but he clearly remembered it.

'I've brought you a surprise!' she said, reaching the top of the stairs and hanging her cardigan up. 'The last Lord Peter Wimsey. It's about his honeymoon, I think.'

'Racy,' Ollie said, smiling. Most of the bandages on his face had been reduced to small dressings, but the burnt skin had healed hard and red. It pulled down the corner of one eye, but otherwise he could eat and talk easily now. The nurse changed his dressings and applied washes and ointments every other day. 'I'm glad you're home. I can't quite open the window and it's hot in the afternoon.'

Lily leaned over him and reached up easily to push the top sash down a few inches. 'Enough? I can do the bottom sash as well...'

His hand circled her free wrist. 'Lily...'

She let go of the window and sat in the chair beside him. 'What can I do?' she asked, smiling.

'You know how I feel about you.'

Her smile faded. She knew he was fond of her. They had got on well as children, although she was six years older. 'Oliver...'

'No, don't say anything. I know what a wreck I am.' He put one hand, shaking, over his eyes. 'I'm sorry.'

'No, don't be.' She wanted to reach for him to comfort him, but knew she couldn't. 'I care for you deeply, you know that. Like a younger brother. A friend.'

'I don't see you that way.' He looked up at her with his good eye, the other still bandaged, as blue as a dunnock's egg. Her father had collected eggs as a boy – there had been a tray of them in his study when she was a child. Some of Ollie's hair was growing back, rusty patches starting to droop onto his eyebrow. He'd always been a good-looking boy. 'Of course, no woman would want me now. Even if we weren't sort of cousins...'

'You're still so young,' she said, feeling like she was older than Bernie now. 'And you have so much healing still to do. There will be someone for you, too.' Even as she said the words she checked them. She did care about James, she wanted him to be safe and to come back to her but... There was no softness or sentimentality about it, as there had been when she was a romantic girl at her wedding.

'James went back. Bernie said you had a big row.'

'That's what married people do, sometimes,' she said, as gently as she could. 'But I still love him.'

'I'm sorry,' he said, trying to smile. 'I'm just feeling a bit low, mawkish really. My youthful good looks are forever gone. I'm destined to be alone.'

'You don't know that,' she said with some heat. 'After every-thing you sacrificed, everything you went through? You're a hero, Oliver. Some girl will be very happy to fall in love with you, I promise.'

'Not someone like you,' he said, rubbing his eyes like a child. 'I'm sorry, I'm just tired. I ought to go back to bed.'

She heard Bernie opening the door downstairs, humming a tune. She had been so much happier since Oliver came home, she hadn't seemed to notice how sad he was.

'Hello, Bernie,' Lily shouted down the stairs. 'I'm just making Ollie's bed up so he can go back to his room.'

She ignored Oliver's weak protests and got clean sheets out of the airing cupboard. They washed and ironed his sheets every day, to reduce the risk of infection. His wounds still wept through his bandages in places, but much less now. She could smell something delicious, and heard Bernie talking to Ollie.

'Just a few chips, my dear, and a little rock salmon caught in the harbour this morning. It will strengthen you.' She raised her voice. 'I have a little treat for us all, Lily.'

Lily dragged the old sheets off and rolled them into a bundle. 'I'll be there in a minute.' She quickly shook out the new sheets and tucked them in tight. The visiting nurses had given her lots of tips to make him as comfortable as possible.

'There. I even got extra vinegar on the chips for you,' Bernie said to Lily, sitting beside Oliver. 'I know you like it.'

'I do,' Lily said, sitting at the table. 'I was wondering, Ollie, if we might try and get you out of the flat one day? When the weather's good and you feel up to it.'

'I'm not ready,' he mumbled. 'I don't want to be seen like this.'

'I thought we could sit in the tea shop, in the corner that sticks out by the quay, look out over the water. No one's going to stare at you, but you could get a change of scenery.'

'I don't know,' he said warily.

At that moment, Lily was overcome with an odd sensation. At first, she took a couple of deep breaths, thinking she was just dizzy, maybe she stood up too quickly in Oliver's room... the smell of the fish brought acid into her throat. 'Oh, I'm sorry—' She dived into the bathroom, slammed the door and barely lifted the lid before she was sick. She sat on the linoleum, her head spinning.

'Lily? Are you all right?' Bernie sounded panicked through the door.

'I'm just tired,' Lily managed to say. 'I'll just sit here for a few moments. Perhaps I'll just have the chips.'

When she came out, the fish had either been consumed or tidied away, and Bernie had buttered a slice of bread to go with a plate of chips, warming under the grill.

'Too much vinegar,' Lily joked, while Oliver looked at her with wide eyes. 'But a chip sandwich will be perfect.' She didn't argue with the glass of warm milk Bernie pressed on her at bedtime, although nothing was said.

Maybe it was nothing, or maybe it was something and it wouldn't last. But maybe, she thought, just maybe another baby was growing in Grace's place.

39

PRESENT DAY, 25 JUNE

Back at the cottage, after months of apathy, Nicole was fired up by the idea of making a difference to the marine environment.

The next morning, she cleared the table so she could spread out the proposal Kim had given her. It was full of profiles of possible collaborators, outlines of suggested projects to fast-track, up-and-coming technologies that could help preserve the seas. Each page was a new, powerful idea, waiting for support and funding. But where would the money come from?

She read article after article about different grant-making bodies looking for projects and offering seed money. She sorted them into piles: projects already started, projects needing leadership and funding, and brilliant ideas that needed development.

She immediately wanted to talk them over with Josh. But her impulse made no sense. He had none of the political experience she had. But he did have a foot in the real world, working in the environment, hearing stories from people who worked in it every day.

That was what a lot of her governmental work had lacked. By the time the research had been added to many other studies, and statistics applied, all it told them was how species were diminishing, the environment was deteriorating, what was wrong. It gave no guidance about what to do about it. Politicians with funding behind them just looked at their holiday sea and saw what they had always seen – a rich, beautiful, constant rolling ocean.

'*I* could make a difference,' she murmured to herself, lining up two projects that would complement and support each other. But the idea of going back to London and leaving this idyllic island was painful. She had spent her entire career working to support the oceans, yet here she understood the interlinked food webs, the importance of clean water, and how crucial it was to conserve even the tiniest organisms – from free-floating algae, up to dolphins and sharks.

She could be surrounded by people as passionate as she was; she could travel around spreading the word like an evangelical scientist. But she wouldn't be able to paddle in the cold water, or swim with playful seals, with the man she—

Her mind shut down at that point. She was very attracted to him, naturally. But it was more than that. For all his enthusiasm for nature, there was something deeply rooted in him that wanted to do something, be part of the solution. He didn't have paper qualifications; his whole life had been immersive research into the sea.

Millie walked past her and put the kettle on. 'Are you OK?' she asked, her voice softer than usual.

'I'm thinking,' was all Nicole could answer.

'I wondered if you and Josh have fallen out...'

'No,' Nicole said, not sure. 'I don't know. Maybe. I'm not sure we ever fell in.'

'Only, he was acting odd last night. He was a bit drunk, chatting up some tourists in the bar, then Tink had to drive him back to the islet. He seemed pretty upset. The boss made him eat a basket of chips to stop him getting too drunk.'

Nicole started stacking up her papers. 'He accused me of not taking the environment seriously enough.'

Millie put a mug of tea in front of her. 'Well, that's daft,' she said, pulling up a chair. 'That's all you do. Did.'

Nicole sighed and dropped her head on her hands. 'No, I hate to say it, but he's horribly right. The further you go up an organisation, the slower the actions become.'

'Oh.' Millie sipped her tea. 'So, what do people do?'

'For example,' Nicole said, patting the papers, 'we could create a beach-clean project. I read about a local village that's going to clean up the plastic and plant some grasses in their depleted dunes to protect the shoreline. Many people will volunteer, it just costs a bit to tractor sand about and plant a few thousand eel grass plants.'

'OK. Well, what's the problem?'

Nicole looked up at her. 'Local politics: who's going to monitor, supervise, check if the plants survive? If the new dune causes a local pub to be flooded at high tide, who pays for that? Bigger politics: if a thousand seaside towns need to be doing this right now, which ones get funding? How much time is spent by environmental groups on the ground competing for money, how many members of parliament are going to beg me to favour their constituency? What committee is going to ask me how cost-effective it is, on each beach?'

'No wonder you jacked in your job,' Millie said, grinning. 'So, how do we do better?'

Nicole patted the papers with both hands. 'With this project – One World, Blue. Which potentially could include me.'

Millie's face dropped. 'So... you'd go back to London?'

Nicole managed a crooked smile. 'That's the sticking point for me. I hate the idea of going back to living in a concrete world. I don't think I could do it, not after living here.'

'You'd be able to travel, though?'

Nicole shook her head. 'I grew to hate that. Posh hotels, gorgeous locations. And armed security, press everywhere, protestors, endless meetings, every meal an appointment with some bigwig. The novelty has definitely worn off.'

'So, what do you want to do?'

Nicole flapped a hand at the papers. 'This! But from an anonymous location, actually by the sea. Maybe from a less built-up coastline.'

'They'd have terrible internet,' Millie said, hovering a hand over the fruit bowl and pulling out a nectarine.

'I know.' She sighed. 'If you're going to eat that, get some kitchen roll. They're so juicy.'

'Or you could run it from here?' Millie suggested. 'You could rig up my room as an office, once I'm gone.'

Nicole felt a physical lurch at the thought of Millie leaving. 'I'd need staff, computers and screens, maybe a laboratory. Definitely staffers to read and collate all the research. And partnerships with on-the-ground researchers, fishing communities, navies, shipping companies, seaside communities.'

'Well, I think you'd be brilliant at it.' She checked her phone. 'Oops. Better go.'

'Early shift?'

Millie's face went pink. 'Actually, no.'

Nicole was worried – it wasn't like Millie to be so evasive. 'You don't have to tell me.'

'I'm just going out to meet Francesco. Just as a friend.'

'Well, great. Have a good time.'

Millie came back with more kitchen roll and chose another nectarine. 'For Cesco,' she said, smiling.

Nicole went back to reading the small print and looking at individual projects online.

A bang on the door interrupted her a couple of hours later.

Without waiting, someone opened the front door. 'Nicole! Nicole!'

'Tink?' Nicole walked into the hall and recognised Corinne's partner. 'Are you OK?'

'Is Millie here? Do you know where she is?'

'No. Why?'

'Can I use your phone?'

He vanished into the living room. Nicole stopped for a moment, then hopped to the stairs to get her leg on. While in her bedroom she looked at the islet. She could just see Josh's boat swinging gently against the jetty on Gannet Rock. She limped downstairs and found Tink standing by the door.

'Tink! What's this got to do with Millie?'

'Someone said they saw her on a boat heading into the Sound. It's not the best time to be on the water. The tide's about to change and the pub says the boat's low on fuel.'

'What boat?' Nicole asked, panic rising in her chest.

'The pub's boat, just a sixteen-foot open fisher.'

'Francesco...' she murmured. 'I saw them out on it the other day.'

'The lifeboat would launch the rib, just in case, but it's out at the moment. People are keeping an eye on the boat. It looks like it's heading to St Piran's.'

She limped back to the house, climbed the stairs and looked out. There was a small boat, looking like it was drifting in the tide, slowly turning. Maybe they had lost power.

Tink shouted up the stairs. 'Can I use your phone again? Josh might be able to help.'

'Of course.'

She hopped downstairs, catching Tink's half of the conversation, the concern in his voice. 'What's happening?'

'They're drifting, the wind is pushing them onshore. Josh is going to tow them back.' He rolled his eyes. 'Honestly, kids.

Who doesn't go to White Beach on St Piran's for a bit of canoodling.'

She could feel a blush starting. 'Can you let me know if she's OK?'

'Straight away. It's getting a bit rough, now the wind is up and the tide's turned. It's cold out there in the water, so hopefully they'll stay in the boat.' She followed him down to the quay, where he waited for the smaller lifeboat. When it came, the skipper let Tink on board and spoke to him over the sound of the motor.

Tink shouted back. 'Josh said someone's in the water.'

Nicole's heart, already racing uncomfortably, lurched painfully. 'What?' she whispered, as the rib took off.

Someone touched her arm. 'Are you OK?' Ellie, from the cottage up the lane, her baby in a buggy.

A million things flew around Nicole's brain. *She'll be fine. Josh knows what he's doing.* 'No. I feel a bit sick. I'm just worried about Millie, she's not a strong swimmer.'

'The coastguard are aware, and the lifeboat is going out as well. Josh will pick them up in no time.' Ellie's hand, gently rubbing her shoulder, was strangely comforting.

'I couldn't see if she had a life jacket on her—'

'Josh will make sure she does, and keep the boat stable. He's pretty well piloted a boat from birth.'

'OK.' Nicole's heart flip-flopped uncomfortably.

Ellie dropped her hand. 'They'll be back soon, probably with a flea in their ears from Josh. That's Francesco from the pub, isn't it?'

'The currents out there aren't swimmable,' Nicole said, her mind still racing.

Ellie pulled her gently to one of the benches. 'Let's sit down. Then we'll hear the good news as soon as it comes in. Josh has got this.'

Josh. Kind, intelligent Josh, who had started making her

think about a first date, maybe staying around to see what happened. The job offer seemed far away. She didn't feel ugly with him, just shy and awkward, which was all coming from her.

The quay filled up with locals; some tourists were milling about, too, asking what was happening. Someone passed a lifeboat's donation tub around, and it was a quarter full by the time the rib returned to Morwen's quay, with Josh's boat just behind.

The lifeboat got a cheer as they sailed back towards the big island, Millie and Francesco soaking wet walking up the slipway.

Despite her concern for Millie, she found her attention wandering towards Josh as he tied up alongside the quay, a silver blanket around his shoulders but presumably unharmed. She found herself wanting to check he was all right, to apologise for their disagreement. She reached for Millie when she stumbled towards her, wailing like a child. 'I fell in! I was so scared. Cesco grabbed me, and then Josh helped me get back in.'

'You idiot,' Nicole said, holding Millie's face in her hands. Her lips were blue, she was shaking, but she seemed all right, just very upset.

Josh lifted a hand in greeting in her direction and walked over. He took off his life jacket as he walked, and she realised he must have gone into the water, too.

'Are you all right?' she stammered, alongside a chorus of other voices, Millie sitting next to her on the bench, still crying.

'Just cold and wet,' he said, smiling at her. He turned to address the crowd. 'Kids are both fine. I'll need a lift back to the islet around five, if anyone's free? My prop busted on the beach.'

A couple of people shouted, and he gave a thumbs up to one of them. He looked back at her.

'Were you worried about me?'

She realised there were tears in her eyes, that she was shaking.

'We were worried about you all,' she said, sniffing back the tears. 'Do you want to come back, dry off, warm up?' It was only then that she remembered they had left things uncomfortably angry. 'Of course, you probably want to go home.'

'No, your place would be great.' He looked around, high-fived a couple of teenagers, shook someone's hand. She realised he was shaking with cold, too, hugging the silver blanket around him. 'Thanks, everyone.'

People were still patting him on the back as he walked, slowly, across the quay, his teeth chattering. She kept her arm around Millie, who had gone quiet and was leaning on her.

'For goodness' sake, are you two warm enough?' Her fear had somehow made her unreasonably angry.

'I've been much colder than this,' he managed to say. 'It wasn't that... that bad. But the kids were going blue.'

She opened the door, pushed Millie inside, and Josh followed. She half dragged Millie upstairs. 'You need a warm shower,' she said, helping Millie undo her summer dress.

'Not too hot,' Josh called up the stairs.

She set the water running, and Millie slid off her swimsuit and stepped in. 'Thank you. That's brilliant.'

'I'm just getting a towel for Josh,' Nicole said, grabbing one off the rail.

Alarmingly, he was sitting on the bottom of the stairs. 'I think it's mostly adrenaline. The currents there are—' He grimaced and shook his head.

There was a thick blanket on the sofa so she brought that, too, and when she came back he was struggling to remove his soaked T-shirt. She helped him and he fumbled with his shorts. By the time she had got his socks and shoes off, and he was in his underwear, she could wrap him up.

'Are you sure you haven't got hypothermia?'

'I'm not that cold, but it sucks the energy out of you. I was only in the water a few minutes, boosting Millie back in.'

She offered him both hands, and pulled him upright. 'What do you want to do?'

'Can I crash on your sofa for an hour?' he said, his voice softer than she had ever heard it.

'You can do better than that,' she said. 'You can have my bed.'

'I'd still love a hot drink,' he said, walking up the stairs almost as slowly as she did. 'Thank you.' He lay down on top of the quilt, and she covered him in the coverlet.

'I'll get you a coffee.' She felt his chest, under the blankets. He wasn't too cold, but he was still shivering.

'They did say drink plenty and wrap up warm.' He smiled up at her, already half asleep. 'Mine's a pint of Pirate's Shilling.'

'You'll have coffee and we'll take it from there.' But he was already falling asleep.

She returned to Millie, wrapping her in the biggest towel she had, and putting her to bed, too.

40

SEPTEMBER 1941

Lily woke with a strange feeling of weightlessness, her insides wobbling and her body slamming back onto the edge of the bed. And then the thunderclap of a bomb. She opened her eyes to gritty smoke and complete darkness. She hadn't heard an air raid siren, she couldn't hear a plane. Bernie started shouting and swearing.

'It's all right!' Lily said, putting one foot carefully onto the floorboards. They were there, but the floor was covered in glass. She reached down for her slippers, shook them and fitted them on. Through the coughing – her own, she realised – she could hear a noise, like the keening of an injured animal.

'Careful of the glass,' she shouted to Bernie over the siren. 'I'll check on Ollie.'

Outside, through the kitchen window, a red glow was lighting up the living room as she staggered to Oliver's room. All the doors had been blown open; she could see the white shape of Ollie, sitting up in bed, screaming hoarsely, wheezing in the plaster dust. She reached for a torch from under the sink as a fire engine, bells ringing, inched past the house.

'Ollie,' she said, pointing the yellow light at him. Only his mouth, wide open and red, showed in the heap of dust, his hair, face and blankets all covered. He cried out again, a guttural scream. 'Fire!'

'Ollie, it's all right.' She reached the bed, touched his ankle through the blankets. 'Oliver!'

'Fire, fire!' he bellowed. 'Bail out, bail out...' His words petered out to a mumbled ramble, then he started coughing.

Lily shook his shoulder. 'Ollie, you're home! It's an explosion in one of the houses out the back.' He opened his eyes, wiped his face. He still looked dazed.

'Bernie?' Lily shouted. 'Mind the glass!'

More coughing from Bernie. 'It went down behind the school, in St Michael's Road somewhere.' Another bell sounded, another emergency vehicle. 'That's from the aerodrome,' Bernie said. She stepped into the doorway and Lily could see the blood running down from around her ear. 'There are a lot of people living up there. And it's on fire.'

Lily lifted Ollie's chin and pushed the dusted sheets down to see his arms and chest. 'Are you hurt, dear Ollie? Can you stand up? We're going to have to get out.'

Bernie lit a candle and put it on the table.

'Anyone up there?' someone shouted up the stairs from the street door.

'Three of us,' Lily shouted back. 'We're all fine, just a bit cut and bruised.'

'The building is damaged, you need to get out. Muster point is the tea shop. Mrs Keiller is doing tea and biscuits all round.'

Bernie leaned into the stairwell. 'Is anyone hurt?'

The man's voice dropped to a rumble. 'It hit the nurses' home. Hopefully, some were on night duty.'

The siren died away, leaving a horrible silence. There were some shouts in the distance, but now she could just hear the hissing of someone's breath. Ollie was shuddering in waves of distress, cold and clammy in her arms. 'We have to get you to the tea shop,' she said, with her firmest voice. Then it hit her.

The baby. She'd been so focused on the terrified Oliver she'd just assumed if she was all right, so would he or she. Maybe this was her last chance to have a baby, Grace's brother or sister, if James was shot down.

Bernie came in holding out Lily's coat. 'I have a sweater for Oliver, and a warm jacket. Poor boy, you're shocked and no surprise. Come on, lad, let me help you wrap up. I'm afraid you're going to have to walk down, but Lily and I will help you.'

Despite his slimness, he was heavier than Lily had expected as she supported some of his weight from behind while Bernie walked him down, one step at a time.

Someone banged at the bottom of stairs. 'Everyone out,' he shouted. 'The front of the shop looks like it might go.'

'This is all of us. Help us, Harry, we need a hand with Oliver.'

Between the three of them, with Lily feeling increasingly dizzy, they managed to skirt large chunks of masonry and a covering of glass. She was frightened to look too closely, remembering the fire brigade covering up a detached hand with a handkerchief back in London. But there didn't seem to be anything too awful.

The tea rooms on the corner at least had one window intact, although the glass in the door had gone. 'Come in, come in.' Mildred Keiller waved them in, her curlers half covered with a scarf. 'Oh, my dears. Come in please, straight away.'

A kerosene lamp made the place smell dreadful, over the smoke and the sharp stink of something chemical. The explosive, Lily thought. 'Press this to your head, my dear,' Mildred said, handing Lily a pressed gingham napkin. 'To your forehead,' she prompted. Lily lifted her fingers to find a sheet of stickiness running down the side of her face.

'I didn't know,' she said, gently placing the pad there, in case there was still glass. The bleeding had stopped.

'There's at least one dead,' she heard someone say. 'Up at the nurses' home, one of the poor Jenkins girls.'

Lily closed her eyes in a moment of shock, sadness, maybe prayer. She could feel something warm, like the memory of Grace's hug.

She turned to Oliver, hunched in his chair, tears washing tracks through the plaster dust on his face. 'Is this a dream?' he asked. 'Are we all dead?'

She tried to smile at him. 'No, my dear. And we'll all be fine.'

She felt the nausea inside her, and staggered to her feet and through the doorway to vomit in the gutter.

41

PRESENT DAY, 25 JUNE

After the rescue, the house seemed very quiet with both of them asleep, and a bang on the door made Nicole jump. It was Tink.

'How are Millie and Josh?'

'Tired, but they'll be all right. They're asleep.' A creak in the floorboards over her head suggested that Josh, at least, was waking up. 'I'm just so cross with Millie.' She felt cold at the thought of what could have happened.

'Kids don't realise that the wind will be stronger, even, than the currents. As you get close to the shore, the waves start breaking. They knocked the boat over.' He smiled. 'Josh was nearby. He saved the two kids from getting too cold. Or even drowning. He understands the danger.'

She was strangely proud, just being his friend. If that's what she was, his friend.

He looked up at the ceiling. 'Tell Josh, George is doing the shack shift today. Keep them warm and hydrated, then feed them. They'll be fine once they sleep it off.'

· · ·

For the next couple of hours, villagers called in ones and twos. A friend of Josh's, who was about the same build, brought a few dry clothes – Josh's were still in the washing machine. People had brought cake, beers, notes and his favourite macaroni cheese. When she heard him moving around upstairs again, she called up to him.

'How are you? Max brought you some dry clothes. I'll leave them on the landing.' She dropped them outside her door and checked on Millie, who was just stirring. Nicole suggested she come down, too.

She put the kettle on, and Josh came down a few minutes later. He looked paler than usual, but his lopsided smile was back.

'Thank you for the use of your bed,' he said. 'I need to get back or I'll miss the tide.'

'Someone called George is over there now,' she said. 'Come into the kitchen, have that hot coffee.'

'Thank you. Honestly, I'm not cold any more. Feel my hands.'

She took the proffered hand, the dry, warm fingers. 'But you've had a big shock,' she said. 'Tink suggests drinks, rest, something to eat. We have macaroni cheese.'

'Amy's? From the café?'

'She brought it round herself.' She pulled out a chair for him at the table. 'How about that coffee now?'

'Plenty of milk, please,' he said, turning to look at the pile of papers on the table, the glossy brochures. 'I've heard about this group. Aren't they funding research?'

Millie bumbled in, wearing flannelette pyjamas, looking about twelve. Nicole put a hot chocolate in front of her, without comment. The girl wouldn't meet her gaze – clearly she was embarrassed.

Nicole pulled the job proposal folder out but pushed the

rest over to him. 'Sort of. Not exactly. They are interested in funding real-world interventions with ongoing monitoring. Like your islands, only on a much bigger scale. Creating an army of environmental rangers from coastal communities.'

He wasn't looking at her, and she stared down at the lines where his hair and sunglasses had left his skin paler, her heart beating a little faster.

He didn't just have a quick look, he started reading. He read until a plate of hot, cheesy pasta was served with a few grilled tomatoes and some peas. Millie unfolded from her chair and took a fork. Nicole had felt oddly relaxed while he read and she concentrated on cooking. He was a peaceful companion.

'OK,' he said. 'I'm not completely convinced, but this shadowy figure behind it all is saying the right things. Is it a Texas oil billionaire?'

Nicole smiled. Hanami Tsai was as far away as she could imagine from an oil billionaire. '*She* is a brilliant scientist and philanthropist. She's decided to throw her personal fortune into conservation and rewilding and regreening the seas. Fortunately, she's one of those people who can persuade Texas oil billionaires to help.'

Millie mumbled something, picked up her plate and vanished upstairs, holding her phone. Francesco, presumably.

He laid out the glossy brochures, side by side. 'Why are you reading these? And why can't I look at *that* folder?'

Nicole picked up her fork then put it down again. 'It's marked confidential. And I haven't known you for very long, Josh.'

He took a huge mouthful of pasta before he answered. 'Long enough, though.' He glanced up her, his blue-green eyes gleaming in the last of the sunlight as it went over the house, brightening the back rooms.

She looked down at the papers, her appetite gone. 'I've been offered a job,' she said, in a small, wooden voice. 'I wasn't expecting it. I cut all ties with my previous work before I came here.'

'What job?'

'I'd be responsible for one of nine areas of marine conservation.'

'Wow. Areas as in geographical areas?'

She shook her head. 'Areas of expertise. I'm an expert in food webs. I look at the knock-on effects of tiny changes.'

'So you'd be leaving the island? Because I think we have unfinished business.' He pushed the plate away and stood up. She followed suit. 'Don't you agree?'

Before she could finish the whispered answer, he reached for her and they kissed. She lost herself in the moment, forgot all the problems looming in the future. He was a good kisser. He was also taller than she was, and her neck started to ache. She pulled away, laughing at his serious face.

'Can we move this to the sofa? I can't look up all the time.' She was breathless, shocked by how much she was affected by him.

He smiled, took her hand and led her into the front room. She thought how much with Josh was without words, just a smile or a look. It wasn't until she sat primly on the edge of the couch that she felt suddenly shy. 'I do think I have to take this job,' she said.

'But not this minute,' he said lazily, leaning back against the cushions with a sigh. 'That cold really took it out of me. Snuggle up.'

'Just a cuddle. To warm you up,' she warned, although the idea of taking him upstairs was intoxicating. But Millie was home and she didn't know him *that* well.

She was curled against him half an hour later, the hated leg discarded to stand in the corner of the room. She hadn't hesitated to unroll and unhitch the prosthetic in front of him. The light was fading outside when she thought of something

'You can't stay here.'

'Can't I?' he groaned, rubbing his eyes. 'It feels like I can.' He stretched. 'I'd be asleep in two minutes, Scout's honour.'

'No, it's too complicated. Millie, the neighbours, everyone on the island would know.'

'Everyone on *all* the islands,' he said, sighing. 'And there would probably be gossip in Penzance.'

'Can you go to the hotel cottage, to stay with your mother?'

He sat up and rubbed his face. 'I suppose so. I'll call her first, though, if that's OK. It's getting late, after all.'

She handed him the phone and hopped to the door. She could hear his low rumble as she washed up the few things in the kitchen. She was very close to inviting him to stay.

He almost filled the doorway when he came in, yawning. 'Did they bring anything for breakfast, or does their gratitude only extend to today?'

She opened the fridge. 'There's a whole carrot cake in here. There's a tin of flapjacks – your favourites, apparently. And a lopsided cupcake with "Jossh" iced on it. Look.'

He laughed. 'That's from Flora,' he said. 'My four-year-old niece.'

She stood back. 'I'm sorry. I thought you were an only child.'

'I am. Flora is my sister-in-law's youngest. My wife's sister.'

It was like ice running down her spine. 'Your wife?'

'Kellie. She died eleven years ago, but I kept her whole family. Her sister's eldest, Jackson, sometimes works with me. Good kid, but won't scrape the solar panels.'

'I didn't know you'd been married.' She was rocked, shocked by her own self-absorption when she'd first met him. Like he'd been just sitting on the islet, waiting for her. 'I guess I don't really know anything about you.'

'What you see is kind of what you get,' he said, his mouth downturned at the edges. 'Uneducated island boy.'

'Conservation warrior,' she said, looking into his eyes. 'Hero of the hour.'

'See you tomorrow. Hold that cupcake for me.'

He kissed her then, and it was darker and full of promise.

42

SEPTEMBER 1941

The day after the bomb, two fishermen helped carry Oliver, on a stretcher, onto the inter-island boat to Morwen. He endured the pain, saying nothing. He had hardly said a word since the bombing.

The news was dreadful: two nurses dead, just in their twenties. Many people were injured. Even Lily needed two stitches in the cut in her forehead but, mercifully, the baby seemed fine. Lily managed a quiet word with the doctor at the hospital and he confirmed that she was likely to be pregnant, and should be well. Bernie was very shaken; the structural engineer who had shored up the front of the shops had allowed her a few minutes to pack a couple of cases but that was it. Her only home was off limits.

'Where will we go?' she had said, crying. 'I don't know what will happen to us.'

'You'll come to Chancel Hall with me,' Lily said firmly. 'I can't get in contact with Emma in time, so we're just going to have to turn up and, if needed, I'll put you both in my room. Please don't worry.'

'But I don't know Miss Chancel.' Bernie seemed over-whelmed at the idea. 'Her family despised mine, remember?'

'Maybe there was animosity decades ago, before you or she were born. But all that's gone with that generation,' Lily assured her.

'I won't know how to behave in a mansion,' Bernie said, in a stage whisper at the end of the boat. They were both squeezed in to make room for Oliver.

'It's no mansion,' Lily said. 'And it's not a haunted house, either,' she said, casting a warning glance at the boatman who had opened his mouth to speak. 'She's just a pleasant, reserved, woman, much your own age. It will be fine.'

As the journey went on, her own doubts surfaced. She wasn't sure whether her cousin would take them in, especially Oliver. Emma would probably not turn away a young man injured in the performance of his duty; but she could be unpre-dictable and strange.

When they got to the quay, Oliver was carried into the Island Queen, one of the local pubs. The landlord was very welcom-ing, making him comfortable in the quieter of the two saloons, and sitting Bernie down with a nip of brandy as she was looking both sick and frightened.

'I'll just go ahead and warn Emma. She probably won't know about the bomb yet,' Lily said, squeezing Bernie's shoulder and looking at Oliver. His eyes were open, but he was staring at the ceiling, unmoving. 'It won't be long, now, Ollie,' she assured him gently.

As she walked towards the door, the landlord stopped her. 'We'll get a few of the army boys to drive him along to the hotel,' he promised. 'They have a lorry. He'll be safer there and it does look like it might rain.'

'Just give me half an hour to get a room ready at the other end,' she said.

She pulled her raincoat around her and ran from the front of the pub past the churchyard and along the path. The sea was right at the top of the tide, tossing its head angrily, a thousand white curls. A little spray caught on her lips, bitter salt. She ran straight to the hotel and opened the door.

Emma came out of the kitchen in her apron. 'Why are you here? Is it Friday already?'

'No, Emma. Look, something bad has happened.' She walked through to the warmth of the kitchen, to the smell of baking. She quickly explained.

Emma seemed to grasp it, slowly going over the main points with Lily.

There was a bomb? Lily was hurt (she examined the stitches). Her other cousins were coming here, and Oliver was burned in the war. They needed to stay.

'But we haven't cleaned a room and May doesn't come until tomorrow.' She twisted a cloth between her hands. 'And I'm cooking a cake for May to take to the British Legion tea party.'

'I can help you with that.' Lily looked around the kitchen. 'Perhaps we can put Ollie in the sitting room, just to start with?'

'It's warmer in here. We could put the rocking chair in the window,' Emma suggested, sounding more than a little dubious. 'Won't this lady Bernie be angry with me? My mother was rude to her, I think.'

Lily smiled. 'I'm sure she was rude *about* her, but I don't think they met often, if at all. Bernie will like you.' Strangely, now she looked at Emma she could see some similarities, in the round face and thick, wiry hair. 'I can put Bernie in my room, if you like.'

Emma seemed to recover her confidence. 'No. We'll clean out the blue room, it's next to yours. But what about this young man?'

'Could he sleep in the end bedroom?'

Emma thought it over. 'Come and see,' she said eventually.

Like most of the rooms it was locked, but had a key in the door. The room was painted a rich green, almost a match for the sea, and being on the far corner of the house over the study, it was smaller. A single, high bed was pushed against the wall, and a few boxes and a huge wooden trunk took up most of the room. Emma touched the curtains to draw them back and the fabric ripped, bleached in strips.

'This was my father's room,' Emma said, her voice soft. 'I know he would have given this boy, Oliver, his room. He would be proud to.'

'Well, we'll make Ollie comfortable downstairs first and then we'll scrub this room out and make up the bed.'

'And the room next to yours will be fine for your cousin. You won't have to share.' Emma nodded, looking pleased. 'They can stay. Like you stayed. But only if they are nice to me,' she added, a quiver of uncertainty back in her voice.

'You'll like them,' Lily said, and despite knowing how much Emma avoided contact, gave her a quick hug.

Emma froze and went red, but didn't seem to mind.

43

After Josh left to go to his mother's house, Nicole sat among the papers and plans spread over the table. When she had first met Josh, she hadn't even asked if he was seeing someone or was married. She liked him and he seemed to like her. But she'd never imagined he was widowed.

She looked Kellie up on the archived Island News website. Kellie McKay died of cancer eleven years ago. There was a picture of a younger Josh, just as good-looking, his arm around his wife. His love. She burned with a moment of jealousy.

She wondered if there had been other women since, but after stalking him on social media, she couldn't find anything. Just loads of pictures of his nephews and niece, a few of his mother, and, every year, a different picture of Kellie on the anniversary of her death. One was just a month ago – he hadn't said anything. For such a chatty, gossipy island, no one had said anything in the community, either. He'd had seventy messages of remembrance and support, though.

She opened the purple file. It was the outline of a job but, in reality, she could design it herself. She'd already thought of a few people she would love to work with again, people who would do more good on the front line than back in government, talking about the environment.

Josh.

She hadn't felt this attraction to someone since she was last on the islands in the heat of first love. She missed Millie coming into the room, and was surprised when she put the light on.

'Why are you sitting here in the dark?' Millie curled up on a spare chair. 'Is Josh still here?'

Nicole sat back. 'No.'

'Everyone knows about you two. There are probably people watching the house to see when you go to bed.'

'He is safely at his mother's,' Nicole said. 'I simply let him get changed and warm up here, that's all.'

'You really like him, don't you.' It wasn't a question.

'Yes, but...' Nicole tried to qualify it, but couldn't. *We live in different worlds, I'm moving away, we're so different. He's widowed.* 'Anyway, what happened today with Francesco? How about you two?'

'We were just going swimming. I think he was showing off. We ran out of fuel.' She rubbed her face, like she did when she was a tired toddler. 'I think he does really like me. Even though he's marrying *her.*'

'Of course – you know he likes you.' Nicole brushed a few of Millie's wild, auburn curls, like springs, out of her eyes. 'How could he not? He'll remember you forever. We do, we look back at those first loves with such warmth.'

Millie's eyes shone with tears, but she lifted her chin. 'How about your first love? Why didn't you get married?'

Nicole shook her head. 'Apart from Nick, my first real relationship, I was never tempted to get hitched.'

'Have you been yearning for him every day since? Was he the one that got away?'

'No! We grew up, found we had less in common, got bored and annoyed with each other.' She gathered up the papers. 'I've loved my freedom. I don't have to worry about children, a partner.'

'But you like Josh.'

Nicole propped her chin on a hand. 'Josh *is* different. Did you know he was married, before?'

'Someone told me today, while we were hearing how brilliant he had been. He used to be a lifeguard when he was my age, he's a brilliant swimmer.'

'He still is, apparently.' Nicole stood, forgetting she didn't have her leg, and had to clutch at the table to stop herself falling over. 'I am so tired. Bed, sweetheart.'

Millie said, 'I thought we could clean up the garden tomorrow. I think the birds have stopped coming down.'

Tears sprang into Nicole's eyes as she remembered Josh rescuing the struggling chick. *How ridiculous.* 'See you in the morning. There may be cake for breakfast.'

Millie looked down. 'I'm really sorry. Are you going to tell Mum?'

'Do I have to?' Nicole grabbed her cardigan from the back of her chair. 'I think you've learned how dangerous the sea can be.'

Millie hugged Nicole. 'Thank you.'

The next morning, Nicole had been up for hours before Josh arrived. Perhaps his mother had persuaded him to have a lie-in. She'd scraped and scrubbed the table and the yard, and brushed the chairs with some bleach until the furniture and slate floor gleamed, even if it did smell a bit antiseptic. She then felt able to launder and hang out the bedsheets. She used the nervous energy she seemed to have accrued to blitz the kitchen. Finally, she could shout for Millie and make an enormous pot of her latest blend of tea – orange blossom oolong.

'Morning.' Josh walked into the house and through to the

courtyard. He was followed by Millie, who shuffled into the garden in pyjamas and a halo of hair.

'Hiya,' Millie said sleepily to him, as he looked around the yard.

'Looks good. I meant to help you clean it up.'

'Tea?' Nicole asked, following him out with a tray of cups and the pot, treading carefully. 'Or I have coffee?'

He watched Millie pour herself half a cup. 'I'll try some of that watery stuff, if you like.'

Nicole went back inside to arrange some slices of cake and his huge iced cupcake on a plate. He laughed when he saw it.

'I can't eat all of that, I'll be sick. Millie, do you want to share? Nicole?'

She shook her head, but Millie held out a delicate bone china plate Nicole had found in the cupboard.

While the two were sharing the cupcake, Nicole poured herself a cup of the fragrant brew, shutting her eyes to enjoy the perfume.

Millie drained her cup. 'I'll have one more tea – ooh, is that carrot cake? – then I'll leave you two. I guess you have stuff to talk about.'

'Nothing you can't hear,' Nicole said, trying to smile. 'Will you be going back to the islet, Josh?'

'I've got it covered until this afternoon.' He sipped some of the tea. 'Not your best, Mills.'

'Well, it's not real ale,' she said, holding up the cup. 'But I like it. I'd like to concoct tea recipes for a job.'

'I love it,' Nicole said. 'You could organise a tea tasting at the pub. They do gin tastings, after all. Maybe do an afternoon tea session.'

Millie laughed. 'I will suggest it.' She glanced at Nicole. 'I've got to go. See you later,' and dropped a kiss on her cheek, waggled fingers to Josh and disappeared.

Once she had gone, the atmosphere was awkward.

'So, this is what a holiday romance feels like,' Josh said, but his lopsided smile was humourless. 'Only I thought there would be sex.'

'I've never really had a holiday romance,' Nicole said. 'Holiday sex isn't the same.' She looked at his puzzled expression. 'Whatever this is, it's different, for me.'

He poured himself another cup and sipped it. 'I don't know what you want.'

Nicole gripped the edge of the table tightly. 'I would like to get to know you better.'

He shrugged. 'But what's the point? You're going to leave, and I'm going to be hurt.'

She shook her head. 'Unless we find out we really like each other. Then we would find a solution. That's what I do, I solve problems.'

He smiled sadly. 'I don't think my feelings are a puzzle to be solved. I don't know how to talk to you about this stuff. I don't understand it myself.'

Nicole touched his hand, and after a moment, he pulled it back. He cleared his throat. 'I've got to get some supplies. We have a regatta going on over the weekend, and I'll be on duty the whole time. We have so many new baby birds in the water, I don't want some jet-skier ploughing through them.'

'Of course.' As he stood up to go, she felt a wave of sadness, loss, something new. 'Could I come with you? Help?'

'Stay in a wooden shack for the weekend? I can't really get away much. You'd be stuck. And I only have one bed.'

'I'll borrow an air bed. I'll sleep on the veranda.'

He started laughing. 'When I first met you, you looked like you'd been dressed by a magazine. You looked like one of the rich tourists.'

'I am a rich tourist,' she said, grinning at him. 'I'm also a marine biologist on a mission. Let me stay, and I'll make myself useful. I could help with your daily counts.'

He stared at her, his smile fading. 'I'm already hurt at the thought of you leaving me.'

She grabbed his hands, squeezed them. 'Well, this might put you off me altogether. Or maybe, we'll find something and we'll both want to stay.'

'Despite the dream job?'

She never would have thought anything would be better than the perfect job, but just standing in the kitchen, her whole body fizzing with the contact, was close.

'It might not be a dream job,' she said slowly. 'And you may not be the right guy. But I'd like the opportunity to find out.'

44

OCTOBER 1941

Within days, Bernie had taken over Chancel Hall as an informal housekeeper. She wouldn't admit to it, but she was too rattled by the bombing to go back to the big island, and the old shops had cracks and shattered bricks that would need urgent repairs before they could think about reopening. Ollie was able to walk from the bed in Emma's father's room to lie on a sofa in the front parlour, consuming book after book from the study, or to sit in the rocking chair in the corner of the kitchen. He and Emma formed a friendship easily; she was as unbothered by his scars as he was by her stumbling memory.

'Look it up in the diary, Em!' he would call across the kitchen, and she would laugh it off.

Lily found herself feeling closer to Emma as the days went on. She returned to her workshop at the library just to retrieve equipment and books so she could work at Chancel Hall. She had one book spread out in pieces on the dining table, folios detached and spread out over old rags and newspapers. The nausea was worse than she had experienced with Grace, and one day she barely made it through the back of the house to the outside privy.

'Are you ill?' Emma was standing outside as she walked out. She was twisting her hands together so hard she was leaving white marks on them. 'Are you hurt?'

'No! I'm fine.' She looked at Emma, who didn't look reassured at all. 'Look, can you keep a secret?'

'Of course I can,' she snapped. 'Anyway, who would I tell it to?'

'Well, May, or Bernie, or Ollie. And I don't want people to know just yet.'

'Know what?'

Lily took a deep breath, feeling a little light-headed. 'Let's sit on the bench.'

She closed her eyes and took a few deep breaths until the dizziness wore off. She could feel the seat sag as Emma sat on the other end. 'I'm pregnant.'

'A baby?' Emma's voice sounded so strange. Lily opened her eyes to look. 'A *baby*?'

'I know. It took me by surprise as well. And I haven't told anyone yet, because it might not last. Babies sometimes don't grow properly, and they can be lost. I'll tell James when I'm absolutely sure.'

Emma turned towards the sea. 'A baby.' She sounded completely in awe. 'Is that what's making you ill?'

'Just a bit sick.' She laughed at Emma's expression. 'It doesn't last long, I promise.'

'Then you'll get fat.'

'I will.' Lily laughed again. 'I was so fat with Grace. Then the baby will be born.'

'Is it a boy or a girl?'

'We won't know until it's born,' Lily said, smiling to herself, even as thoughts of miscarriage still lurked at the back of her mind. 'Let's get a bit further along, before we tell anyone.'

Emma's face dropped. '*He'll* take you away. I'll never see you again.'

'*He* will do nothing of the sort. He will want me to be as safe as possible.' It occurred to her that she might use the news to pressure him from flying. 'Maybe James will want to spend more time here,' she mused, although nothing seemed solid any more.

'Maybe he could live in the old cottage,' Emma grumbled, standing up and walking to the wall overlooking the beach. 'Since he likes it so much.'

'Without a roof?' Lily joined her, finding a flat patch on the rough stones and sitting down.

Emma shrugged. 'He said he could repair it.'

'He did draw up some plans. He thinks it might make a lovely home for you, when it's rebuilt,' Lily said, keeping her eyes on Emma's face. 'If you decided to sell the hall.'

'If I sold the hall, I would want to move to the big island.'

Lily rocked back with the surprise. 'What? I thought you loved it here.'

'But I don't know anyone here.' Emma picked a loose weed from between the stones. 'I've lived here all this time, but I've only known May and Mr May. People don't like us.'

'Maybe.'

Emma ran her hand over another plant. 'The cottage is separate. But I'd have to walk through the garden of the hall every time I left it.'

'That's true.' Maybe that would be hurtful.

'And I'd still be able to hear Charlotte all the time. And Bernie and Oliver live on the big island, and maybe I could visit them there.'

That made Lily smile, and stupid, pregnancy tears fill her eyes. 'I would visit you all the time, too. Who knows, after the war, we might all come and live on the islands.'

'What about the baby? Will it be my niece or my cousin?'

'Hmm, I don't know – second cousin, I think. Do you want to be called Auntie Emma?'

Emma shrank back but she was smiling. 'Just Emma. Or Em. I like Em.'

'So maybe you will leave here, after all?'

Emma stood taller than Lily had seen before, not easy as one of her legs, broken in the accident, was a little shorter. 'I must. I need to live my own life,' she stammered as she explained. 'Not like Daddy or Mother lived. It's different now. The war makes it different.'

'That's right.' Lily reached out her hand, and after a hesitation, Emma put her fingers into Lily's palm, helping her stand. Emma's hands were brown, from being out in the sun or digging in the garden all the time. 'The war has made everything different.'

45

PRESENT DAY, 26 JUNE

Josh left the cottage to buy supplies, while Nicole packed up a few basics, a couple of pieces of equipment, and left a note for Millie. Knowing there was very little electricity, she went optical for the microscope, a small box at the base of her bag. She also packed extra socks and her warm jumper. Despite what he thought, she had once been an outdoorswoman. She threw a couple of extra liners and socks in, but wouldn't need to wear the leg once in the shack. She also included her camera, which travelled everywhere with her and was battered but high quality.

She met him on the quay, with crutches, bag, sunglasses and sun cream. He handed her a life jacket – not the low-profile uninflated one he wore, but a bulky orange one that looked like it was meant for kids. She opened her mouth, then shut it again, complying. She managed to step into the boat herself – she'd mastered that much – then he handed her the bags, including a carrier of shopping. She could see a lot of tins through the plastic.

'Is this a good time to mention I'm gluten-free and a vegan?' she said, watching his face freeze. She laughed. 'I'm kidding!

But I did pack the rest of the carrot cake *and* some of Millie's rolls.'

That made him grin. 'OK, you got me.'

The tide was coming in, and the engine made hard work of pushing against the current to reach the islet. Josh manoeuvred the boat close to the shore, taking advantage of the slack water on the inside of the bend. She'd driven boats enough to see he knew what he was doing, threading the boat through eddies and irregularities in the water. He grabbed the rope and jumped ashore, timing it perfectly. He leaned down to help her out, and in the spirit of being compliant, she let him. She felt steady on her foot. The physio had told her that one day her sense of where her body was would extend into the prosthetic, and today she began to feel that. She walked up the first few steps without the crutches, then waiting for him to get everything out of the boat. She accepted her rucksack, grabbed both crutches for balance, and the shopping bag, leaving her case and another bag of supplies for him.

She found the steps were easier this time. She'd had to walk everywhere since Millie had returned the scooter to Heike, being given a continental coffee and a slice of cake in exchange for a bit of chat. Friendly gossip really was the currency on the island. The last few steps were bigger, and she had to take her time climbing each one.

When she reached the rocky terrace where the hut was situated, she was out of breath but triumphant. 'Next time, I'll do it without the crutches,' she panted.

He didn't comment, but half smiled. He pulled the veranda up; it was a wooden canopy that blocked the whole front of the cabin. It slotted into permanent supports either side with sturdy poles at each corner. He stacked her bags on the bed and opened all the windows and the main door, to let the heat out. There were two folding chairs, which he put under the shade of the veranda, then waved his arms as if doing a magic trick.

'There! Home sweet home.' Fresh air blew away the smell of bird mess from inside.

'Very lovely,' she said. He kept it neat. There was a washing-up bowl stacked with clean plates and mugs. The composting toilet – she'd forgotten that – was neatly stashed in the corner and didn't smell. The books and binoculars on the long desk in front of the window looked ready to be used. At the very end was a small frame with a faded picture in it. A blonde, smiling girl with flyaway hair.

'Kellie,' he said.

'I guessed. She was very pretty.'

'She was lovely. Beautiful, friendly, and everyone loved her.' He smiled as her face dropped. 'It was a long time ago. And nobody's perfect, right?'

She smiled back sadly. 'I suppose not.'

He lifted a water bottle and filled a kettle. 'The stove's over there, if you want to make some tea. I have to get on with my bird count.' He opened a wide folder filled with a close-lined chart.

'Do you do counts at the same time every day?' she said, working out the camping stove and lighting it.

'No, at the same time of the tide. It produces much more consistent data. Plus, I can always see birds entering the water when the tide's high.' He was counting birds plummeting into the water, swimming and submerging. It was hypnotic watching the gannets slide effortlessly, almost without a splash, to disappear for a minute or so then reappear with a fish.

She made him a strong tea. A small cool box had been freshly packed with ice blocks and a couple of bottles of milk. One was frozen solid. She picked it up and rattled it. 'That's a clever idea,' she said. 'How long does milk last in there?'

'Four days, three on hot days,' he said, still scanning the surface of the water. 'The shop freezes it for me in the summer, and I can change my ice blocks over, too.' He wrote something. 'Manx shearwaters, look.'

She stared at the black and white birds, banking and flying around the edge of the cliff. 'And a couple of petrels,' she said.

'Listen to you, getting your bird nerd on,' he said, laughing, noting them down in another column.

'How many species will you—' She took a sharp breath. 'What was *that!*' Water had swelled into a hump in the water and a blunt light shape appeared. It dived, leaving a large slap of a light grey tail and a plume of spray.

'They're back,' he said, grinning. 'They came by about this time last year, too. Risso's dolphins. They're huge – three to four metres long.'

She walked out to the veranda to lean over the guard rail as three shadows swam around the deeper water off the islet. 'I've never seen one in real life,' she breathed, to herself. *This is what we need to protect.*

'I'm surprised. They like it down in the south-west, although they're usually out to sea. They come inshore chasing summer octopus.' He leaned out of the window. 'Yep, that's Draco, the white one. Old male. I don't recognise the other two, but they're younger, you can tell because they're darker.' They didn't have a beak, just blunt, friendly faces, looking like they were smiling.

She leaned on the rail, eyes welling with tears. 'I wonder if they'd let us swim with them.'

'Not here,' he warned. 'The water around this rock is seriously protected, even from the wardens, and the tide is brutal. They occasionally follow boats, though, especially if common or harbour dolphins are playing with them. I had an encounter on the reef two years ago.'

She couldn't imagine how wonderful it would be to study these beautiful creatures up close. 'How about killer whales, orca?'

'They used to be regular visitors, apparently, but I've never seen one here. Fisherman report them occasionally.'

She smiled back at him. 'When we were working on the rockpool study, we went out fishing and we met a small pod. Amazing to see orcas in the wild. That, and terrifying – they bumped the boat a few times.'

She unpacked her bag; the only place to lay out her equipment was on the narrow bed. Investigating it further, she realised it was just apple crates turned over, covered with plywood and a makeshift mattress. 'One-star accommodation,' she joked, grabbing her old camera.

The Risso's dolphins were idly swimming around in front of the shack, avoiding the submerged causeway. She managed to get some good shots from the top of the stairs, then grabbed a stick to go back down to the waterline to see if she could get a better picture. After twenty minutes of sitting still, one finally approached, pushing his blunt face up, looking at her. Just as she got the shot, Josh yelled something, and she turned as the dolphins vanished.

'I was just getting pictures—' she shouted, but something in his body language stalled her. He was pointing out to sea, on the other side of the causeway, where the tide was running fiercely.

'Stay in the boat!' he bellowed to someone, out to sea, then he came bounding down the steps. Before Nicole could do more than struggle to her feet, he stopped above the jetty. Halfway down, he launched himself off the stairs, diving right over his boat into the deadly currents below.

46

OCTOBER 1941

James had sent a telegram to say he was flying to the island. Lily, who had moved into a room above the newsagents just to help Mr Prendergast out at the library for a couple of days a week, felt unsettled. The skies seemed very dangerous, with poor Ollie's plane having caught fire and then crashed in the sea, and a bomb indiscriminately wiping out two girls' lives and altering several more. Even though the stitches had come out, she still touched the angry red mark on her forehead, her own tiny war wound.

She almost sent a telegram back to put him off, but she wasn't sure he would listen. Or even see it in time. Their letters had become shorter and shorter, factual. She carried the telegram around in her pocket and looked at it several times in the day. Even with just a few words, it sounded friendlier, more energised than his dreary letters: 'Looking forward to spending time with you.'

The pregnancy was settling down, and she relaxed as she passed three months. But she still hadn't told James about the baby. Bernie had guessed, she was sure of it. Ollie was lost in his own feelings and hadn't noticed anything at all. Emma and he shared an interest in games, and he could play for a while, but holding cards hurt his hands. She also walked with him, the two of them exploring the tideline looking at jellyfish and crabs and seabirds.

She couldn't imagine what James was doing. He had said he was training people, young men who would risk their lives hanging out of a plane to get the very best photographs of the ground for the cartographers to translate into new maps. So why was *he* in a plane?

The boat to Morwen would be on a late tide, so she would wait for him at the aerodrome. She stayed at the library for two more hours, just sorting new books packed in two tea chests from the mainland. The chests smelled like fresh tea leaves, straight from Assam or Ceylon. The books, many of them old, had taken up the fragrance, which made cataloguing and shelving them even more pleasant. When she finished, her worry for James crept in again. She looked at the town clock – six forty. It was newly repaired after the bomb, when it had stuck at ten past one, the moment the bomb struck the nurses' home.

The wind was getting up, the October chill creeping in through her coat as she stepped into the street. The air raid wardens had kindly brought all of their clothes down from the damaged building, so at least they had enough warm jumpers. Most of her original wardrobe had been blown up in London. The thought of Grace's lost baby clothes still brought tears prickling to her eyes, and even more so now she wouldn't be able to put them on the new baby.

A sound registered barely above the roar of the sea, not intermittent with each wave but constant, carried in by the wind. More than one bomber, she thought, suddenly anxious that they weren't British. An old man, his white hair picked up in the falling light, stomped out of the pub in a cloud of cigarette smoke. 'Sorry, maid,' he said, waving at the blue cloud.

'I just heard...' she stammered, pointing up.

'Bristol Blenheim,' he said, reassuringly. 'Light bomber. They use them all along the coast.'

'Oh,' she said, pressing one hand against the thudding in her chest. 'I just worried, for a moment.'

'I know,' he said, squeezing her shoulder briefly. 'That's why they got new Spitfires up on the aerodrome. Nothing's getting through again,' he added grimly. 'My neighbour's daughter was one of them nurses.'

He nodded to her and walked down the road, and she felt reassured. Until she heard something different, a sort of coughing coming from the sky.

People were coming out of their houses, probably concerned they might be German bombers, too. One woman said, 'That don't sound right, does it?'

Lily walked to the middle of the road, looking up. Two dots high above were circling in the blue-black sky, approaching the runway. A thin trail of smoke dragged behind one, and it seemed to be listing over. *Black smoke. Oliver said that means engine.*

She started running, along the High Street which ran right through the middle of the island, out to the aerodrome and the runway. The planes weren't landing – they were going around again, and the spluttering engine was clearly audible even over the sobbing of her breath. The street opened out onto common land, flanked on one side by the sea and with scattered cottages and a farmhouse. She slowed down and caught her breath before registering how many people had followed her. Several young men, half a dozen boys, a few older people all gathering along the high fence – just a lattice of wires with some barbed wire along the top.

They were circling again, the damaged plane lower than the

other one. Lily shut her eyes and prayed. *Be in the other one, James.*

The damaged plane, slow and losing altitude, started the approach to the runway. From the wire, to which she had pressed herself unconsciously, she could see the glow of flames in the starboard engine. The plane lined up, wobbled, the injured wing dipping almost to the ground, and she involuntarily screamed. The plane fell – stalled, she realised – bouncing hard with a metal crack, then up a few feet. Then it landed again, off the tarmac, the wing digging into the grass and the whole plane cartwheeling closer and closer to the fence. Someone caught her around the middle, dragged her back, as the plane screeched to a clumsy stop.

'Fire!' was all she heard, but she couldn't move; she was pulled away as a fire engine arrived on the runway. Two silhouetted figures clambered up and out of the half-open cockpit, only a few feet from the ground, and threw themselves down. Then another, holding his arm awkwardly, was helped down by a fireman and the whole group was pulling back. Armed guards started rounding up the spectators, more than a few dozen now, Lily's feet going from under her.

'James!' she screamed, with her last conscious breath.

Lily woke on a stretcher, being carried through the darkness towards an official-looking building. 'Lie still,' a voice said out of the darkness. *James.*

Relief surged through her. 'I'm fine, I'll be all right.'

Inside the small building was a medical room, with a couch and a young man who introduced himself as the base doctor. He felt her pulse, which was jumping about as she saw James's sooty face, an angry red patch above his eye.

'Look after your real wounded,' she said, staring at James.

He smiled back, not the tight smile he'd had since Grace's final illness, but a big grin. His teeth almost shone in his dirty face.

'We're OK. A bit scorched and Paddy broke his wrist, but honestly we're fine.' He sat at the request of the doctor and allowed him to wash off the wound. 'Ouch.'

'What were you doing in that plane?'

'I told you, I thought I would try out for the Photographic Reconnaissance Unit.'

She couldn't stop staring at him. 'You promised you would be careful,' was all she could say.

'We were careful, I promise you. But we picked up a couple of Focke-Wulf 190 fighter planes. They got a lucky hit on us. But what happened to you, old girl? I couldn't believe it when you fainted, out like a light.'

He took one of her hands and squeezed it. She could smell the burning oil, fuel and rubber on him, and felt sick. 'Maybe it was the shock,' she said, unable to frame the words in front of a stranger. 'I did see the whole thing, and I had just run up from the town.'

He lifted her hand, kissed it, as the doctor applied a dressing to his head.

'You'll live, Mr Granville,' the doctor said. 'Now, you need to go for a proper debrief and examination. I'll stay with your wife, and we'll get you both over to – Morwen, is it?'

James almost had to be dragged away, protesting, but Lily managed a shaky smile and a wave.

'Now,' the doctor said, sitting opposite her. 'Have you had any medical problems in the last few months? Any changes?'

She touched the scar on her forehead. 'Well, our flat was caught up in the bombing.' She took a deep breath. 'And I'm about three months pregnant. In fact I know when I became pregnant, as we've been apart for a while now.'

'Mrs Granville, I say this as a medical man and with no

judgement. Is the child your husband's? I notice you didn't tell him, and I wondered why.'

'Of course it is.' She was stammering in a mixture of shock and outrage. 'We lost a child—' Her words failed her, as they usually did when she mentioned Grace. 'We lost our six-year-old daughter last year, through illness. Things have been a bit strained, with the war and with our house being bombed. Then James started volunteering for these flights, even though he's just as useful in the cartography office.'

'Well, he may have cured himself of the impulse,' the doctor said, looking even younger. 'Tell him. I think he will come to his senses pretty quickly when he knows what he would be missing.' He helped her up. 'No cramps, backache? Dizziness?'

She was able to straighten her rumpled clothes. 'I feel well, just a bit muddy,' she said, looking ruefully down at the side of her skirt and coat.

'I'll let Mr Granville go as soon as possible, and a navy launch will be able to get you back to the island. Would you like to call ahead?'

She shook her head. She was suddenly exhausted. 'No phone. But they're expecting me anyway. Were the other airmen safe?'

'A bit knocked about, and the pilot broke his wrist. But your husband is very pleased with all the film they shot. But I think any romantic illusions about flying face-down, taking pictures while being chased by Jerry planes, are over.'

She managed a shaky laugh as James pushed the door open. 'Ready, Lily? The Royal Navy awaits.' He disappeared again.

She smiled at the doctor and shook his hand. 'Thank you, doctor.'

He squeezed her hand for a moment. 'Remember what I said. Just because we're in the middle of a war doesn't mean our own little stories don't go on.' His mouth turned down.

She walked to the door, hesitated, turned back. 'I'm afraid he doesn't care any more, if he lives or dies. Or even that he can't cope with carrying on without Grace.'

'Remind him that he still has you. You are his future.' He smiled down at her slim belly. 'And your little passenger.'

47

PRESENT DAY, 26 JUNE

'Josh!'

Nicole's scream was involuntary; she ran over to make sure he hadn't hit the boat, but his head surfaced, swimming strongly towards something colourful racing past. A beach inflatable with two children, one crouched down and one trying to stand. The tiny toy boat was rocking from side to side, being blown by the wind and pushed by the tide. Josh didn't swim directly for it, he was clearly swimming to where he hoped it would end up. She was frozen for a few seconds, then stumbled up the steps, half on her hands. She reached for his phone, left on the desk. She punched in the number for the emergency services.

'Hello, what service?'

'Coastguard, lifeboat. Everyone!' She shouted. 'There are two kids, just babies, in a bright pink toy boat, just past Gannet Rock. My friend has just jumped in after them. No!' she screamed as the child lost her balance and disappeared over the side. Josh reached her, just his feet kicking the surface before he yanked her up. 'Send someone, quick,' she said, wiping tears off her face in a hurry. 'Come quick. He's in the water, one of the kids fell in...'

She jammed the phone, still live, into a waterproof pouch. Grabbing a few flares from his emergency bag and the binoculars, she limped down the first few steps. 'Yes, yes, I'm still here!' she shouted to the phone. 'Please, they're being swept away... No, he's got her, she's in the boat, she's sitting up. She looks like she's coughing. His name is Joshua McKay, he's a wildlife warden from Gannet Rock. I'm Nicole Farrell, I'm taking his boat after him.' She carried on down to the jetty. 'No, no, I have to go. It's a blue and white open boat, called...' she checked the transom as she half fell in the boat and loosened the mooring rope, 'it's called *Skua*. The local fishermen and lifeboats will recognise it.'

The woman on the end of the phone was getting quite agitated, making a very good point that more casualties might slow down the rescue, but as Nicole struggled into the old lifejacket, she could already barely see the inflatable. She rang off, and after a few attempts, while the boat was carried into the current on the same course as the toy, she managed to get the outboard motor running. She steered it out into deeper water, and turned to follow the bobbing, garishly coloured float, just visible when it rose on the biggest waves. Which were getting bigger and bigger out of the lee of the islands.

Hopefully, the local rescue services would know exactly where the wind and water were taking Josh and the children. She sped after them, but the boat was heavy in the water – the wind didn't carry it like the inflatable. She didn't feel she was gaining on it, but it was still in sight. The water looked darker, deeper. It would be colder, and she knew Josh had taken his life jacket off because it was in the bottom of the boat.

She tried the phone, called 999 again. They put her through to the coastguard and she gave her location as well as she could. Even the islet was getting smaller and lower in the distance.

'Wave when you see the helicopter,' a man told her. 'And you are all right?'

'I'm OK. I don't know how much fuel I have, though. I'm keeping them in sight.'

'Fair enough. Just keep going, see if you can get a status report from them.'

She rang off, aware the battery was low, and kept chugging forward, marking Josh's position every time a wave lifted up the pink flamingo head. She checked her watch – he'd been in the water fifteen minutes or so, clinging to the toy.

She caught a bit of a breeze and a good current and thought she was gaining on them. Finally she stood, holding firmly onto the tiller for balance. 'Josh. Josh!' She could see two kids huddled in the inflatable, in bright swimsuits. At least they were both out of the cold water. 'Josh!' she screamed again. A dark head lifted from the side of the flamingo and he waved. She could finally risk throttling up to catch them.

'Throw me a rope,' Josh shouted. She looked around. The stern locker had several coils of rope, and she chose what looked like the longest.

'I'm coming closer,' she shouted back, knowing that throwing would be tricky in the wind. Eventually, she snaked a line right over him, and he reached for it. She started pulling it in, but the line went slack. *Is he already too cold?*

She brought the line back in, hand over hand, and this time managed to throw the rope right over the inflatable, making one of the children scream. But they did grab the rope.

Josh seemed to be talking to them, and the larger of the two girls handed it to Josh. Nicole started pulling gently. The toy might weigh next to nothing, but two children and a large man made it hard work and she was worried his cold hands would drop it. It wasn't until Josh looped his arm over the rope that she felt she could safely pull.

Alongside, the flamingo looked worse: half deflated and

with six inches of water in the bottom. Both girls were shaking with cold. She braced her knee on the bench seat and heaved the little one in, sitting her in the bottom of the boat. Then the larger one, who climbed in with her help. The blow-up toy started to drift away and Nicole looked around for Josh. She saw fingers holding on to the edge of the boat.

She looked over and could see he was cold, and something was wrong. 'You need to get in the boat,' she said, fear making her voice squeaky. *Please be OK, Josh, please be OK...*

'I'll climb in the back,' he said, exhausted. 'Switch the motor off.'

It had been idling, but she cut the engine. 'Are you hurt?' She watched him pull himself along the boat with one hand.

'I think I dislocated my shoulder. I clipped the boat when I dived in.'

She grabbed what she could of his T-shirt and hauled him towards the back of the boat. 'How can you get up?'

'Boarding step,' he said, and she could just see a couple of rungs of a ladder under the water, beside the outboard. He was shaking with cold, but otherwise seemed OK. She could also see his shoulders were asymmetrical, one dropped lower. He swung his legs aboard to slump on the bottom of the boat, cradling one arm in the other. She turned her attention to the girls.

They turned out to be six and eight, huddled together for warmth, and didn't feel icy to the touch, just scared and shocked. She fitted one into her life jacket and tied Josh's inflatable one to the other. She pulled off her top and, to their amusement, put it over both children.

He tapped her on the arm. 'Take my hand,' he said, teeth chattering. 'Hold my fingers. Pull my shoulder back in.'

'No! You could end up with nerve damage.'

He waved the hand at her. 'It's best done sooner than later,' he said, through gritted teeth. 'Or my muscles will go into spasm.'

She took his hand, cold and rubbery in hers. 'They're already in spasm,' she warned, bracing herself against the side of the boat.

'Pull me towards you,' he said, and the first time his groan made her loosen her fingers. Both girls cried out, too. Nicole took a moment to reassure them.

'Again,' Josh said, focused on her, his blue-green eyes staring into hers.

This time she heaved until her own shoulders felt the strain, until her leg twisted in its sock and her back hurt. He shouted something, maybe a muffled curse, and slid to lie down.

'Oh, thank you,' he managed to say, his eyes closed.

She called the emergency services again. 'I've got them in the boat,' she said to the operator. 'The inflatable's got away, but it's empty. I have two sisters, Olivia and Pansy, and Joshua McKay, the owner of the boat. He has an injured shoulder.'

She listened to the questions and answered them. No, everyone could move and talk, they were all cold and Josh had had a dislocated shoulder. On instructions, she took a flare, held it over the water and fired into the sky.

The lifeboat turned up a few minutes later. Josh was rammed into a life jacket, over all his objections, and his arm put in a sling. The children were checked over, wrapped in warm blankets and able to talk to their frantic mum and dad on a phone. Nicole opted to stay out of the way as they secured Josh's boat to tow it in.

Over a thousand objections and arguments, Josh refused to seek medical help, get an X-ray or go anywhere other than back to the shack. Nicole watched his quiet, good-humoured arguments. There was no moving him, he was polite but absolutely firm. After taking a stern warning not to throw himself in the water *ever again*, the skipper clapped him on the back, asked to be remembered to Josh's mother, and let them both back on the island. Under Josh's instructions, she tied up the boat. They stood side by side, waving to the crew and the two children, then she started up the set of steps. With a wrenched leg, they seemed like a mountain to climb.

'Come on,' he said, offering her his good arm. 'We can take our time.'

An hour later, Josh was asleep on the makeshift bed. The sun had just crept behind the islet so the heat had faded a bit, and Nicole was wrapped up in a blanket under the veranda in a rickety garden chair that creaked when she moved.

I'm in love.

With a wildlife ranger who counted birds for a living, who had hardly left these isolated rocks in his lifetime, let alone got a formal education. She couldn't imagine where he would fit in her new life, or even her old life. He was a man who liked to be busy, was a part of his community. She rubbed her face against the blanket; it smelled like him, and salt. She pulled her knees up and hugged them as she looked out to sea.

A change in the texture of the water heralded the return of the Risso's dolphins, just breaching enough to breathe, then forward roll back under the water. When one pushed his head out, it looked like his small mouth was smiling at her. She put a hand on her heart; she was so full of emotion and this creature seemed to want to connect, too. She rested her forehead on her knees and waited for the tears. None came. *I have a multitude of riches, what's there to be sad about?* Maybe love, maybe adventure, maybe the career move of a lifetime.

A hand on her shoulder made her jump. 'I broke into the cake tin,' he said, handing her a plate with a slab of carrot cake on. 'I left you the best bit.'

She smiled at him. He had shed the torn and soaked T-shirt and was now draped in a blanket. 'There's a best bit?'

'Of course,' he mumbled through a mouthful of food. 'The corner bits are caramelised. We can swap if you don't want it.'

'Oh, I want it,' she said, nibbling the corner. He was right, it was toffee flavoured and crispy. 'Cake has been a research interest for you?' she said, teasing. His face dropped.

'I know I'm just a ranger,' he said. 'But life isn't always about research and quantifying things and *thinking*.'

He sat on the decking beside her, head down as he ate the cake. She could see the bruise on his shoulder where he had thrown himself in the sea. 'No, it's not all about thinking,' she said, almost to herself. 'It's about feeling and commitment and seeing things through and playing our parts.'

He glanced up at her. There was a crumb on his lip and she couldn't help brushing it off. He put the cake down, kneeled up and kissed her. This time there was the depth of the sea in it, the smell of the brine. She put her cake down and held him, feeling the warmth of his skin.

'We're going to bed after this cake,' he murmured conversationally.

She smiled. 'I know.'

48

For such a diverse group of people, with so much emotional baggage, James, Lily, Bernie, Oliver and Emma had a delightful breakfast. Oliver was more cheerful, and Bernie wasn't too intimidated by James's 'poshness' as she saw it. Emma was listening to everyone, not talking much but comfortable. James was in a better mood than Lily had seen him for a long time, relaxed, talking to Oliver about his experience of coming down in the English Channel. Although Ollie was offering light answers, James was really listening to his stories. Lily passed around some more toast; Emma had sat up nervously late the night before, and had used the time to make bread.

'Well, lovey,' Bernie said, spreading jam rescued from the bombed flat onto the bread. 'When are you going to tell us all your news?'

Emma bounced in her seat a little, her grin wide. 'Can I say? *Please.*'

Lily laughed at her enthusiasm. 'Well, I was going to tell James first, in some romantic way. But this seems like a lovely time. Go on, Em.'

'Lily told me first,' Emma said, almost proud.

'Well, you sort of guessed.'

'Me too,' said Bernie, smiling.

'Well, I didn't guess,' Oliver said. 'What's going on? You're not going away, are you?'

'Lily's having a baby!' Emma announced.

Lily locked eyes with James, who was sitting at the table with his mouth frozen open. 'I'm about three months pregnant. I know the timing isn't brilliant, but it's happened.'

'And they made it here!' Emma crowed, making Bernie cover her face, shoulders shaking with laughter, Ollie go pink and James smile.

'I suppose we did,' he answered Emma. 'So this will be an island baby. At least, partly. Although I have found a house for you to look at, when you feel up to it. It's in St John's Wood, and it has a garden.'

Lily's heart skipped a beat. 'London?'

'I suppose you'll have to go back some time. But you'll always be welcome to visit,' Bernie said, breaking the silence as it stretched out.

Emma looked at Lily, her dark eyes scanning her. 'You look cross.'

'I'm not cross,' Lily managed. 'I'm... sad. Upset. You know I love it here.'

'But I'm selling the hotel,' Emma said. 'I'm selling Chancel Hall; I've been talking to Cousin Bernie.'

'That's right,' Bernie said, nodding. 'I think Emma could look around at the houses on the big island, so she'll have someone to help her. If she needs it. It would be smaller, more manageable, and she'd have a decent amount of savings tucked away for her old age.'

Lily turned to James. 'But you had some lovely plans for the cottage.'

'I am giving it to Lily,' Emma said, topping up her cup.

Everyone turned to Emma, who sipped her tea, wide eyed. 'You're my closest relative, aren't you?'

Lily stared at her, put a hand over her leaping heart. 'Give it to *me*?' She managed a shaky laugh. 'I suppose I am family, along with Bernie, and Cissie and Oliver.'

Emma pointed her teaspoon at James. 'I don't want you to take Lily away.'

He looked back at Lily. 'My job is in London.'

'Couldn't you do it here?' Lily asked quietly. She thought she knew the answer. The rubble of the blown-up house shot back into her mind, her neighbour endlessly calling for her cat. 'I don't want you flying—'

'Oh, don't worry about that,' he said, pushing his plate away. 'That's over. I'll leave it to the young heroes like Oliver, here. I might be able to teach them to take better pictures, though. Developing and examining the films, printing, that sort of thing is pretty substandard. We often lose good pictures to technical issues. And I can make maps anywhere I have good light.' He looked around the table. 'I could help renovate the cottage if that's what you want, Emma.'

'I want Lily to have it.'

He shook his head. 'At least let us buy it off you.'

She shook her head with such confidence even James backed down. 'You can pay me rent, if you like. Then I'll leave it to you in my – what's it called, Bernie?'

'Your will, lovey.'

'And I can leave the rest of the money to Bernie and Ollie.'

Lily stood up, walked around, and to Emma's discomfort, hugged her in her chair. 'That's so kind. But we *will* pay rent, and we'll do the building work. If you must leave it to us,' she said, head resting on Emma's thick hair, 'leave it to the baby.' She let go.

James looked across at Bernie and Oliver. 'Would that be all right with you?'

Ollie looked stunned. 'I suppose I'd like Emma to remember my mother, too, but it's all a long way off. I can see Emma striding down to the harbour, scandalising the old besoms with her trousers, until she's eighty.' He looked at Bernie. 'And I'll eventually get a job, find somewhere of my own to live.'

'Not until you have to, my dear,' said Bernie, clearing away the discarded plates. 'And one day, you'll inherit the flat and the shop, just as Cissie and I always said.'

Lily walked out to the terrace to sit on the wall, knowing James would follow.

He created a warm space to shelter in, sitting close and putting an arm around her. 'Why didn't you tell me?' he murmured into her ear.

'First, I wasn't sure she would stay put, you hear so much about miscarriage. Then we had the bomb, and I definitely didn't know if she would stay. Then, I just wanted to keep her to myself for a little while.' She stared up at him, his face close. 'We weren't really talking...' He kissed her, and his arm tightened around her. 'And you went *flying*.'

'I know, I'm sorry.'

'It's all right. It was about Grace, wasn't it?'

'Yes, and no. I just felt so out of the war, then Oliver was shot down and I felt so useless, sat in a government basement where the highest risk was from food poisoning from the canteen. And you got injured from a bomb...'

'Ollie told me the maps were crucial. Being able to ditch close to the Breton nationalist resistance probably saved his life.'

He looked around. 'This really would be a fabulous place to bring up a child. What are the schools like?'

'I don't care.' She started to laugh. 'She's not even here yet.'

'And *she* might be a boy,' he said, turning to her. 'Will you be very upset if it is?'

She hadn't given it much thought. 'I just want a healthy

baby. But I do feel like it's a girl because – I feel just like I did when I had Grace.'

'But this won't be Grace.' His whole face was drawn down. She kissed him again.

'Of course it won't. And we'll tell him or her all about their clever, funny big sister.'

49

PRESENT DAY, 27 JUNE

Nicole woke early the next morning with the thud of birds landing on the roof. She squinted at her watch, the only thing she was still wearing. Five o'clock. She was cradled in Josh's good arm and squashed up against the wall of the hut. She also needed the bathroom. She managed to clamber over him with one leg and both arms and drag a shift dress from her bag. They had pulled the composting loo outside, and now she had a spectacular view over the water, shielded from Morwen Island by the back of the hut. She hopped back, filled up the kettle and opened all the doors and windows, the early sun now warming the hut.

She put the kettle on as a curious gannet hopped down to the rocky ground in front of the veranda. It put its head on one side, then tilted it the other way.

'He wants his water,' Josh groaned from the bed, putting his arm over his eyes. 'There's a bowl under the desk.'

She was amused – the sea was all around them. 'Should I make him tea? Offer him biscuits?'

'No, don't feed him. I woke up with him sitting on my chest one morning after I gave him a few toast crusts.'

'You don't eat the crusts on your toast?'

He squinted up at her. 'What can I say? My mother always cut them off.' He sat up, stretched, winced, felt his shoulder. 'I can't believe I hit the boat. That could have been my head. I dive over there all the time.'

'You acted on instinct. You didn't look properly.'

He got up and stood naked in the shade. 'Neither did you. Stole my boat, drove out not knowing whether you would have a signal, had any fuel...'

'I packed flares, waterproofed the phone, called 999 and I knew you had enough fuel to get back to the island at least. I rescued you. I probably saved you.'

He put his arms around her from behind as she splashed hot water into mugs. 'Thank you,' he murmured as he nuzzled her neck. 'The lifeboat helped.'

'Go and sit down,' she said. She put his mug down, filled the bowl for the bird, and sat on one of the stools. She could look over Josh's head as he sat in one of the garden chairs. The bird came closer, looking at the water, looking up at Josh.

'Could you hand me my shorts?' he said, grinning back at her. 'I feel a bit vulnerable here with Moody eyeing me up.'

'Not to mention there's a boat leaving Morwen,' she said, shading her eyes.

He sipped his tea as he looked over the records she'd been making of the birds. 'You missed a few.'

'I recognised them, they just moved so fast,' she said. She hopped over to her bag, discarded on the floor, and pulled out the job offer. 'Here. Tell me what you think.'

He took it but didn't open it, just sipped his tea. 'I can't tell you what to do.'

She dragged the other chair next to his. 'I'm asking as a friend. I don't trust my own judgement right now.'

He looked at her. 'Is this about me, or the accident that took your leg?'

Flashes of horror flickered in her mind. The smell of blood, burning, smoke. 'The accident's part of it.'

'I got the impression you find it hard to discuss...'

She shut her eyes, wrapped her arms around herself. 'It's just I relive it every time I talk about it. I know I'm supposed to, my therapist says it's like letting the air out of the balloon each time. But I'm so... *angry*.'

He put a hand on her knee, just above the amputation. 'Tell me anyway. It seems to me you can't make a decision about this job until you do.'

So she did. Not the well-rehearsed story she'd constructed, that she told her therapists and the doctors. But the way it actually came back to her in sensations; the pressure building as she flew forward, saved only by her seatbelt and airbag; the crumpling of the front of the car over her legs; the smell of petrol and then smoke. Waking over and over into different nightmares, hospitals, people moving her, making her cough, breathe, squeeze their hands. Emerging from dreams that made no sense, not being able to remember simple things like people's names.

'I was so full of painkillers and still concussed, nothing made sense.' She bent her head. 'Until I got to the island. I dreamed about Morwen when I was in hospital, standing in Seal Cove, staring over the sea.'

He didn't comment, just eased his shoulder and drank the tea.

She pushed the edge of her dress away from her chest and touched a puckered scar. 'This was a central line they put in. I was ill for months while they tried to keep my foot alive.' She stroked her scarred wrist. 'Here was where they plated my wrist. I was a mess, and I had a big tear on my scalp, a head injury.' Her voice had choked up to a squeak. 'Then they had to take my leg because my foot had died. I was someone different.'

'So that's why you came here? Somewhere you remember feeling alive?'

She leaned back, pushed her sunglasses lower on her nose to look at his profile. 'It took me weeks to work that out.'

He turned to smile, the snaggle-tooth just touching his lip. 'You know it's all just ego. "Oh, I'm not pretty any more, I can't deal with people being sorry for me."' She swiped at him with her free hand, bumping his arm in its sling. 'Ow!'

'Well, I was pretty.'

'You're not pretty now?' he said, staring at her so intensely she could feel herself colouring up. The words hurt, but stung less than she would have expected.

'No.' She half smiled. 'You're not going to suggest I'm beautiful because of all my history, are you? They say that in rehab.'

He moved closer and cupped a hand around her face. 'You have amazing bone structure,' he said, leaning forward to kiss her cheekbone. She shut her eyes, suddenly embarrassed in the way that she hadn't been when she was naked. 'Your mouth is big, generous, great for kissing.' He put the action to the words. 'And your eyes are so changeable. So dark when you're angry or excited or laughing, they look black. But in the day, they are the colour of the darkest part of the sky, just at the end of the day.'

She couldn't speak as he kissed her again, his hand warm against her face. When it fell away, she managed a little laugh.

'So poetic. That must make you popular.'

'I did win an inter-island poetry prize once,' he said, grinning, eyes shut in the sunshine as he leaned back. 'I knew it would come in handy one day.'

'How old were you then?' she asked, not trusting the little smile still curling his lips.

'Nine. But the prize was an Easter egg inside another egg.'

'Definitely worth it.'

He turned to look at her. 'You are an amazing woman. I don't care about the outside shell, and neither should you. I *am* sorry you came into my life just when you're about to leave.'

She couldn't say what she wanted, needed to say. *I'm not*

sure I'm going. 'Let's take it a day at a time, shall we?'

He stood, stretched and passed her a tube of sun cream. 'I've got to start the bird count in a minute. I'd slap some of that on if you're staying out. I can drop you back at the quay afterwards, if you want.'

She took it, nodded her thanks and went back into the shade and pulled her dress off to put underwear on. She realised how relaxed she was, how unbothered by him looking at her – which he was. She heard the wolf whistle. It hadn't occurred to her that the boat might be so close, that they were heading for the islet. She ducked into the corner to put her dress back over her head before she realised they hadn't seen her – they were whistling at Josh in his skimpy shorts.

'Just delivering visitors!' a voice yelled. Nicole stuck her head out of the hut to see a large open boat, piloted by Corinne. There were two overdressed men with her, one carrying a huge camera bag, and a woman who looked like she was on holiday with a large straw hat covering her features.

Corinne pulled up alongside Josh's boat and tied up to it. 'Sorry, gents, you'll have to step across,' she said, easily skipping from one boat to the other and onto the jetty, helping the men ashore. 'Press for you, Josh,' she called up the steps. 'And a visitor for Nicole.' She stepped back onto Josh's boat to hold out a hand to the small woman in the hat, who nimbly crossed from seat to seat and onto shore.

Nicole recognised her when she looked up, grinning involuntarily. '*Hanami?* I can't believe you're here!' She grabbed her stick and started down the steps, holding on to the railing.

'Well, I had a feeling you were going to refuse our offer,' the slight woman in her sixties said, holding out her arms for a hug. 'I think those gentlemen want to talk to your friend about some rescued children?'

Nicole could hear Josh arguing, explaining he was busy doing the bird count. They would just have to get their photograph at his desk, and fit their questions in around his work. She hadn't heard that irritated note in his voice before, and it made her smile.

'There's an old seat along the shore,' she said, leading the way, hopping.

'I see you're managing on one foot,' Hanami said.

'Just recently. It turned out that moving to an island without a flat surface on it worked like intensive physiotherapy.' She sat down and made room for her friend. 'Thank you so much for thinking of me. A year ago it would have been my dream job.'

Hanami sat back, letting the sun bathe her face. She took a deep breath, calmly blew it out, and Nicole could feel her own heartbeat slowing.

'I wish I could do that,' she said. 'Just calm down to order.'

Hanami smiled. 'I learned to on a Buddhist retreat, a few years ago. I recommend it, although the food was a bit minimalist. I packed chocolate so it was all right.' Her perfect pearly teeth gleamed in the sun and she looked at Nicole. 'How are you? Really?'

A few weeks ago, Nicole would have trotted out her rehearsed package to reassure everyone else, and stop any pressure to do anything. 'I'm happy,' she said, surprising herself. 'I feel *happy*, today, anyway.'

'Has that got anything to do with the bronzed hero being interviewed up there?'

Nicole could hear how angry Josh was getting. 'I might need to take over the count for a moment. He's recording birds on the water.'

'I'm sure we could do that for a few minutes.' Hanami stood up and led the way up the steps, stopping a couple of times to admire the view. 'Look at that water.' As she got to the top, she wrinkled her nose. 'Oh, and the smell!'

Nicole offered to take over for Josh, squeezed onto his stool and Hanami pulled up the other one.

'Do either of you know all the species on the islet?' he said, suspiciously.

Hanami pointed at the water. 'Puffins, guillemots and razor-bill, European storm petrel. Ooh, is that a Wilson's Petrel?'

'Just note them down in their columns,' he said, handing the pencil to Nicole. 'Identification guide under the window.'

The two women sat, absorbed in their task, for several minutes. 'So,' Hanami said. 'You want to stay close to your man?'

'I do,' she said, unexpectedly. 'I can't believe I said that.'

'This must have been a very healing place for you. I was reading your bio. You did your first research project here, got your first funded job in marine ecology.'

'I did. I visited as an undergraduate for a field visit, and just fell in love with the islands.'

Hanami pointed out a cormorant, bobbing up by the edge of the water. 'It truly is a romantic place.' She leaned back to look at Josh. 'I can take over if you want to rescue him. I think he's about to push that photographer into the water.'

Nicole laughed as she hopped outside. The two men immediately came over. 'So, you followed Mr McKay to rescue the children.'

'I did. If you want pictures, you're going to have to get them now, because we are very busy. We are actually working.'

'And the boat's leaving in five minutes,' Corinne said, winking at Nicole. 'Tide.'

They snapped a few shots from where Josh had dived, several of the two of them together, and then one of the boat, which did look small and battered tied up to the quay.

'Thank you,' Nicole whispered into Corinne's ear as she ushered the two men back towards the boat. 'Please email me if you have any questions,' she called down. 'Corinne has our details. Goodbye,' she shouted, over their last-minute protests, and turned back to a glowering Josh, standing by Hanami.

'Thank you, I can take over now.'

'Do you mind if I carry on?' Hanami said. 'You can always supervise. This is fascinating, and I don't know all these birds, I'm more of an Arctic specialist. You have a few northern visitors here, it's wonderful to see them so close.'

'Oh, I'm being so rude,' Nicole said, smiling at them both. 'Hanami, Josh.'

They nodded, both distracted by the task. 'I'll make tea, shall I?' she said, amused by their similar expressions of concentration.

As the hour's observation came to an end, Nicole was dozing in the garden chair, in the shade.

'I looked you up,' Hanami said to Josh, and Nicole jerked awake, to see the other two talking. 'You made a fantastic case for the highest level of protection for the Atlantic Isles. Did you know the Brittany Islands recently based an application on yours?'

'I didn't,' he said, closing the ledger. 'But we were refused.'

'You so nearly got it. If you could have employed an experienced legal specialist and an environmental lobbyist, you would have.'

He made a frustrated sound. 'We didn't have the money.'

She smiled at him and glanced over at Nicole. 'But in the future, One World, Blue will be able to offer expert advice to groups like yours. And get funding to police it, pursue fines for people who break the rules and damage the environment. Even provide alternative technology and market advice for fishermen.'

'That's the project you want Nicole to help with?'

She smiled at them both. 'I do.'

'So she'll move back to the city.' His voice was hard. He looked away.

'Not necessarily. I saw you used to run an aquarium in St Brannock's?'

He shook his head, a puzzled smile on his face. 'Your research into my life seems pretty detailed.'

'I was interested in a site to build our research centre. Land on the islands is so limited and expensive, so restricted.'

'What?' He looked over at Nicole. 'Did you know about this?' He sounded angry.

'No idea. Go on, Hanni.'

'Even the history of your building is iconic: two women, informing the public about the sea at a time of increasing interest in nature. What shape is the building in?'

'Honestly? It's falling down. It needs a complete overhaul, which would make it flexible if you wanted work spaces.' Josh looked at Nicole again, and she smiled to reassure him. 'But I don't want to sell it.'

'You wouldn't have to. We could go into business; you could lease it to us.'

He looked down, frowning. 'I'm not used to having partners. But what you are trying to do is amazing. I've looked over your glossy brochure, and I'd love to see the details. But at my heart, I'm just a wildlife warden.'

Hanami pointed over the water. 'Oh, look over there! Nicole!'

She hopped over to lean against the door frame. 'The Risso's, they were here yesterday as well.'

Hanami looked at Josh and spoke clearly. 'I don't believe all the knowledge and wisdom needed to save this planet is in the heads of scientists like me and Nicole. I think it's shared between every ranger, fisherman and child on the beach. We will need all of that knowledge to save the seas.' She put her head on one side, her eyes twinkling. 'Are you in?'

He looked at Nicole as her smile grew, her heart beating harder. 'Are *you*?' he said, his voice low.

'If you are. Maybe we could do something wonderful?'

'Together...' he murmured, as his lips touched hers.

50

APRIL 1942

Of course, the baby was born in a spring storm, while James paced up and down the stairs of Dolphin Cottage. Bernie was pottering around the kitchen, with its new stove and freshly painted walls, occasionally making him eat and drink.

'You should be in the pub,' was her best advice. 'It's not as if you haven't done this before. It's just a baby, you know it'll come when its ready.'

Oliver was on duty at the airbase, having retrained as ground crew. Emma was sitting on the wall in her usual spot outside, waiting as the light faded. 'Go and take this out to Emma,' Bernie said handing him a mug. 'She's as nervous as you.'

Upstairs, Lily was climbing familiar mountains. Her mother sat holding her hand, her voice the only thing she could listen to. 'I'm so glad you came,' she said, between contractions. Elizabeth cooled her forehead with a damp cloth.

'It's a pleasure to be here for another baby,' she said. 'I was here for Grace, I'll be here for Catherine. Or...?'

'We haven't agreed on a name for a boy,' Lily said, struggling again. 'That's awful, isn't it? We don't even have a name.'

For a minute she couldn't talk, was just lifted up by the wave of pressure.

The midwife leaned over her. 'I think we're nearly there, Lily. Can you give me a push?'

Grace's birth had been twelve hours of steady, bearable pain until the work started. This baby was easier, sliding out into the midwife's hands, her mother laughing with joy. 'Oh, Lily, she's beautiful! *Perfect.*'

Lost in relief, Lily's thought was for her first baby. *Grace was perfect, too.* A wave of fear swept over her. *What if I won't love her enough because she's not Grace? What if she gets ill and dies?*

'Here, my darling,' her mother said. 'This is your baby girl, Catherine. Open your eyes.'

And she did.

EPILOGUE

TWO YEARS LATER

Nicole stood in the church, Josh's hand warm in hers. The music started up – for all her modern take on the world, Millie had gone traditional for her wedding. The groom's side of the church was packed, in colourful summer dresses and suits and big hats. Millie had requested no one wear black, grey or navy to her wedding. Even Josh was wearing a tie hand-painted with dolphins, and Nicole was in sea green.

She had to stand on tiptoes – well, on tiptoe, which was one of the things she would never get used to – to see Francesco's face, a look of wonder dawning as he saw Millie. As the whole church rustled and whispered to turn and look at the bride, Nicole kept her eyes on the groom, seeing the tears in his eyes, the wonder in his face. Despite the difficulties of a long-distance relationship, a previous engagement (snapped off when he went home) and both being students for most of their relationship, it had worked. Claire, the mother of the bride, smiled with absolute pride and joy at her baby girl. Finally, Nicole turned to see Millie.

She was wearing something made entirely of lace, drop-waisted like a twenties flapper dress, and it suited her perfectly.

Her auburn ringlets were threaded with flowers, and lightly covered with a veil. Her father was patting her hand on his arm, as if reassuring her, but she seemed completely confident. While Francesco looked like he was going to cry, she was smiling, almost pulling her father forward to get to the front.

'She looks amazing,' Josh whispered in her ear. 'She's really grown up.'

Millie was an apprentice at a famous tea blender. When not travelling to various tea plantations, she was making certain top brands of tea leaves were consistent. When she visited Nicole, she always brought her own favourite blends and ones she was working on. Nicole and Josh had rented a bigger cottage on the very corner of the big island, overlooking the sea and within easy reach of Gannet Rock, although Josh now shared his bird protection duties with his sister-in-law's son and a couple of students. The aquarium building had been rebuilt around the original features like the mosaic. Laboratories and offices were downstairs and a conference room, IT centre and library were upstairs.

Both Josh and Nicole got teary-eyed over the simple, heartfelt vows, Millie and Cesco staring into each other's eyes with their responses.

As they kissed, then turned back to the congregation, a round of spontaneous applause and cheering broke out. As Millie passed Nicole, she leaned forward. 'You next,' she murmured.

Josh put his arm around her as the couple passed, Nicole still laughing. 'Well?' he asked. 'What about it? My mum would love it. She has said she'll let us have Dolphin Cottage if we do.'

'More pressure.'

He looked into her eyes. 'We're work partners, we're living together. What's the difference?'

She moved aside to let people from the end of the pew get by. 'We're fine as we are.'

Jade, from Morwen Island, walked up, still teary. 'Well, that's the most beautiful man in the world locked up. But I'm glad it was Millie.'

'You did an amazing job with her hair, too.' Nicole looked around. A quarter of the church had been filled with friends Millie and Francesco had made in their one season on the island. 'We'll be out in a minute.'

'You'll be needed for photos,' Jade called over her shoulder.

'We will,' Nicole said, her heart bumping in her chest, looking at Josh whose expression was suddenly very serious. 'But this is important, too.'

'What's stopping you jumping for joy and saying, "Yes, Josh, let's get married"? Is it the accident?'

A momentary picture, the little photo in the shack on his desk, flashed into her mind. 'No,' she said, staring up at his irregular, lovely features. 'No, it's not that.'

His expression changed. 'It's Kellie, isn't it?'

'You never talk about her.' The words tumbled out of her. 'I don't feel like I can ask questions, it feels like that part of you is still... hers.'

He took a deep breath. Someone outside shouted her name. 'I don't talk about her but that's not the reason. When Kellie died, I changed. I got through the diagnosis and the treatment and the death, and afterwards I was just different. I became a bit reclusive, I drank too much, people looked after me. My family helped keep me straight.'

'Nicole, we're waiting!' Claire was standing in the church doorway, flushed with excitement.

'I'll be there in a minute,' Nicole said, smiling at Josh. 'I'm just getting proposed to.'

'Well, say "yes, please" and come out and do your duty as aunt of the bride,' Claire said and vanished into the sunshine.

'I'll always love Kellie,' he rumbled. 'At least that part of me that is thirty-something will. But now I love you, and I'm older and wiser and the feelings I have for you – it's like that feeling you get from the sea. It's just so much bigger than me. Do you know what I mean? So, you have nothing to worry about. Nicole, will you marry me?'

She reached up and kissed him. 'Yes please.'

A LETTER FROM REBECCA

Dear Reader,

I'm so glad you found *Dreams of the Cottage by the Sea*. I hope you enjoyed meeting Nicole and following her journey towards finding happiness and love on the island. I loved writing Lily's journey back to life after tragedy and war. If you did, too, you can keep in touch with other island stories by following the link below. Your email will never be shared and you can unsubscribe at any time.

www.bookouture.com/rebecca-alexander

I have spent many years living on islands. I love the feeling that we have to find everything we need within our community, and even now, a trip on a ferry seems like a new story is being written. My imaginary island of Morwen is based on the village where I live, and wonderful islands all around the south-west of England, like Lundy, St George's and St Agnes. The cobbled alleys, narrow streets and tiny cottages all seemed to have their own stories – and histories.

I've loved writing stories based on island living and the connection to our beautiful seas and shores. Sometimes a wonky cottage leaning against its neighbour just sparks new ideas...

If you want to support me and the books, it's always helpful to write a review. This also helps me develop and polish future stories! You can contact me directly via my website or Twitter.

Thank you and happy reading,

Rebecca

www.rebecca-alexander.co.uk

 twitter.com/RebAlexander1

ACKNOWLEDGEMENTS

This book wouldn't be in your hands without a great deal of work and patience from my editor, Jess Whitlum-Cooper. When I agreed to write three books for Bookouture, I was very unsure I could do it, but Jess was full of confidence, then made it possible. Better than that, she's made it a fun process, leaving me to write the story and characters (the enjoyable bit) while she moulds and tidies my lines and pages into a coherent book through editing.

Thank you also to the wonderful team at Bookouture, for continuing the process of tidying the novel and telling the story smoothly. They also produce the lovely covers and understand all the marketing end, which is a mystery to me. I am truly grateful.

Much gratitude goes to my son Carey Bave, my first reader, who knows all my books. He keeps me writing, asks unexpected questions, and advocates for the characters all the way.

As always, much love goes to my patient husband, Russell, who knows just when to drive me to my favourite island, and leave me there to write.

Printed in Great Britain
by Amazon

25023639R00182